CALL TO KILL

BILLY BILLINGHAM

AND CONOR WOODMAN

CALL TO KILL

HODDER &
STOUGHTON

First published in Great Britain in 2021 by Hodder & Stoughton
An Hachette UK company

1

Copyright © Steel Eagle International Ltd and Conor Woodman 2021

The right of Billy Billingham and Conor Woodman to be identified as the
Authors of the Work has been asserted by them in accordance with the
Copyright, Designs and Patents Act 1988.

A CIP catalogue record for this title is available from the British Library

Hardback ISBN 978 1 529 36455 2
Trade Paperback ISBN 978 1 529 36459 0
eBook ISBN 978 1 529 36456 9

Typeset in BEMBO STD by Manipal Technologies Limited

Printed and bound in Great Britain by Clays Ltd, Elcograf S.p.A.

Hodder & Stoughton policy is to use papers that are natural, renewable
and recyclable products and made from wood grown in sustainable
forests. The logging and manufacturing processes are expected to
conform to the environmental regulations of the country of origin.

Hodder & Stoughton Ltd
Carmelite House
50 Victoria Embankment
London EC4Y 0DZ

www.hodder.co.uk

AUTHOR'S NOTE

I'm guilty of screaming at the TV sometimes. Especially if I'm watching a movie or a show about special forces operations which gets the operational details wrong. And it annoys me when writers describe procedures and drills in ways that real soldiers simply do not operate.

I wanted to write a book that tells it like it really is. I've acquired a unique range of experiences during my time in the British Forces, and I hope the many thousands of readers of my autobiography and people who've come to my sold-out shows can attest, I can tell a story that is packed with action and suspense but still gets those important details right.

The career that I've been lucky enough to experience enables me to bring an authenticity to my fiction that I believe readers will truly appreciate. For although Matt Mason is a fictional character, many of the things that he does are things that I've direct experience of myself.

MARK 'BILLY' BILLINGHAM, MBE
Always a little further

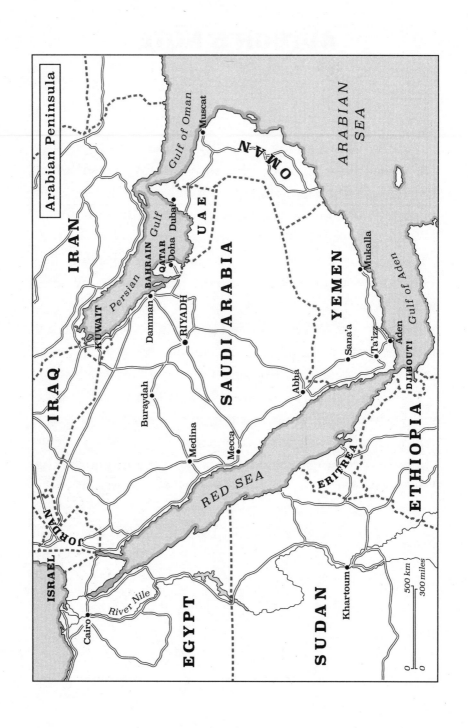

Arabian Peninsula

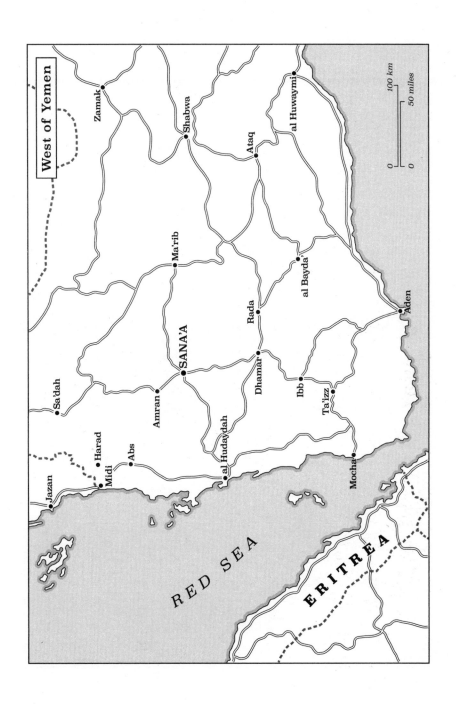

West of Yemen

Zamak

Shabwa

al Huwaymi

Ataq

Ma'rib

al Bayda'

Rada

SANA'A

Dhamar

Sa'dah

Amran

Ibb

Ta'izz

Harad

Abs

al Hudaydah

Jazan

Midi

Mocha

Aden

100 km

50 miles

0

0

RED SEA

ERITREA

PROLOGUE

Eli Drake's driver drove out of the mosque the same way that they had come in: past the guards, past the souk and out on to the highway that circled back to his hotel. While his translator, Karoush, and the driver chatted among themselves in Arabic, Eli sat quietly in the back and reflected on how his meeting with Imam Hari, a seventy-five-year-old revered Shia scholar, had gone. Pretty well, considering their differences. The two grey-bearded clergymen had happily discussed a range of theological issues, and the Imam had listened attentively while Eli explained the purpose of his own organisation, The Christian Apostles, in Arabia. Eli smiled, satisfied with his day's work, as the car passed a group of young men playing football on a dusty patch of ground by the side of the road.

The first thing out of the ordinary that Eli noticed was when two vehicles coming towards them, a minivan and a white Mercedes, veered into the middle of the street and stopped, forcing his driver to slam on the brakes to avoid a collision. Four men leapt out and strode purposefully towards Eli's car. Three of the men were dressed in Western clothes, their beards cut short, each brandishing an automatic rifle. The fourth man was older, his beard longer, wearing traditional robes tucked under a suit jacket and carrying a pistol.

The largest of the men wrenched open the front door and began screaming in Arabic at Karoush, while another came round the far side and pulled the driver out by his hair. Karoush stepped out with his hands raised, begging the men to be calm, while Eli watched, helpless, terrified. What was happening?

The older man with the pistol opened Eli's door, and in heavily accented English instructed him to get out, pointing his gun to make clear it was non-negotiable. No sooner had Eli's feet touched the ground than the last man appeared and roughly grabbed hold of him. Eli thought that he seemed nervous, while the older man was calmer, more confident, shouting what sounded like instructions to the others.

Suddenly Eli's head was shoved down hard on to the bonnet and he felt a sharp pain as the heat of the metal burned his cheek. He saw Karoush and the driver shuffle into his view, noting that their hands had been tied behind their backs. One of the gunmen stood behind them and forced them down on to their knees. Eli wanted to look away but his head was held down too tightly to move. Instinctively, he began to pray, but the words dried up in his throat when he saw the man in charge appear behind Karoush and raise his pistol. Eli watched as a single bullet exploded through the back of Karoush's head, showering Eli's face in blood and pieces of flesh. Eli closed his eyes. He wished that he'd closed them sooner. He heard four more shots. Two and then two more. He was sure of that.

The man wrenched Eli to his feet and shoved him into the back of the Mercedes. Someone covered his head with a cloth bag and the car pulled away, following behind the minivan.

The whole thing had taken less than thirty seconds.

ONE

Sana'a, Yemen

Matt Mason had grown used to that sound. Allahu Akbaaaaaaarrrrr. Even the early morning call didn't grate as much as it had when he'd first encountered it. Instead, now he felt almost becalmed by the rhythm of it. Five times a day, every day, there it was; no matter where he found himself, he heard it. Sometimes it was sung in lyrical tones from a rooftop, others simply screamed out of a poor-quality tannoy, but it was reliable. It gave his days structure. It was as dependable as the bells of Hereford Cathedral.

He thought about religion a lot when he had time to think, which in the Regiment was either a lot or not at all. The Regiment had a way of leaving you to sit around twiddling your thumbs for long periods of time, or taking over your every waking minute until you could hardly remember your own name. After twelve years of it, he knew one thing; he'd seen more terrible shit done in the name of religion than anyone should ever have to think about. Not that he was particularly set on any faith; far from it. In fact, the last time he'd been in a church he'd been a teenager. It was the day he'd married Kerry in the Protestant All Saints Parish Church, to keep her family happy, even if it broke his own mother's Catholic heart. He'd never make that mistake now, he'd never put anyone else before his own flesh and blood.

Now Mason was in Yemen. The reasons for him being there echoed with the reasons he had been sent on every other mission. It wasn't that he didn't care about them, it was that caring wasn't a priority. The Regiment said he needed to be there, so that's where he went. Before Yemen it was Syria, and before that, Libya, Iraq and Afghanistan. It seemed there was no end of shitholes in the Islamic Middle East that the Regiment needed SSgt Matthew Henry Mason to be in.

When he had been a sixteen-year-old cadet, two soldiers from 3 PARA had come to talk to the young lads about Northern Ireland and Catholics and Protestants, and all the politics of it, why it was vital for the British Army to be over there, blah, blah, blah. He'd been bored by it, dozed off for a while until one of the soldiers started talking about a fire-fight at a roadblock in Belfast where his mate had got shot. What struck Mason even then was that he knew if it had been him he wouldn't have got shot, and neither would a lad on his watch. He wouldn't have fucked up like whoever ran that checkpoint must have. He felt it then and he stood by it now. He knew that day that he had to be a soldier, be the best, prove himself, show everyone what he was capable of.

So it was that he was sitting, eighteen years later, in Yemen, in a bare concrete room, with seven other stinking men. The stench of their shit and piss oozed under the door from the latrine outside, filling the air and Mason's nostrils, while he listened to another call to prayer and waited for another order. He lay back on his camp bed, pushing the tatty mosquito net to one side while he lit a cigarette. He picked a loose piece of tobacco from his bottom lip and watched the smoke hang for a moment before it scattered under the draw of the broken ceiling fan spinning above. He chuckled at how pointless that fan was, when already the temperature outside was nearly thirty degrees. He wondered whether this was what he wanted any more or if he'd really ever wanted it in the first place.

What else would he do if he weren't a soldier? He'd never known anything but how to fight and survive. He'd beaten a grown man half to death when he was nine years old, which wasn't the last time he'd been in trouble either. Without a doubt, the army had saved him from an alternative life spent behind bars. Five years in 3 PARA were followed by twelve and counting in the Regiment. The army had given him a career; a status as a special forces soldier, decorated by Her Majesty the Queen no less, for valour and some other bollocks he couldn't remember.

Mason thought about the day at the Palace when the Queen had pinned a medal on his uniform, probably the last time his now straggly dark locks had been cut, long before he'd let his stubble become a permanent fixture on his chin. The medal was now in a wooden box under the bed where his wife was fast asleep back in Hereford. He thought about how she must still be expecting his imminent return, even though last week he'd put in a request to delay his leave. He hoped that prick, Captain Peter Hopkins, would sign it off and keep Mason there for another month. With any luck, he would hear another one hundred and fifty-five calls to prayer before he had to face Kerry and the kids again.

The muezzin fell silent and Mason could hear the men sleeping, snoring and farting next to him again. Outside the glassless window, behind the shutters broken by the recent sandstorms, he was aware that the city was starting to wake. Cars beeping, even before dawn, was another sure sign that you were in an Arabian city.

The squad had been placed in an old police station on the edge of Sana'a, the capital of another country where civil war seemed to quietly rumble on while the rest of the world worried about Trump, Brexit and pandemic paranoia. Officially, the SAS weren't here of course, just like they hadn't been in Syria or Libya, because being in those places would be counter to British government foreign policy and would probably break a million UN conventions, but since when had any of that bothered the Regiment? Mason had spent most of his career in places where he never officially was. His whole professional life was deniable.

Before Mason left Hereford last month, he'd been briefed on the current situation in Yemen; a classic one country, two presidents type sketch. In theory it was an internal conflict, but in reality the Saudis were fighting hard for the old guard, while their sworn enemies in Iran backed a rebel alliance known as the Houthis. Now you had a classic proxy war, two belligerent countries settling their differences in a third, where the place had gone to shit, and famine and cholera were everywhere.

Mason unpicked a small photograph tacked to his wall and looked at the face on it closely, the long grey hair and beard, the piercing blue eyes. Eli Drake, a priest from Norwich, was fifty years old and had been in Yemen since 2018, spreading the word of God. As if this country needed any more of that. Drake had been doing the wrong thing in the wrong place at the wrong time when the Houthis had lifted him. He'd been missing now for three months but new intel put him in Sana'a, at a Houthi-held compound, four miles north. The fly in the ointment was that their source believed Drake's execution was imminent, so London had decided now was the time to go and get him. Even though the fucker left clear instructions before he left Norwich about not wanting blood spilled on his behalf. Mason sighed. He hated civilian rescues; they were always complicated.

He slid Drake's photo into the clear plastic wallet strapped to his arm. In a rescue situation it was paramount that the hostage was immediately recognisable as the guy you didn't want to shoot. Mason had another wallet reserved for the ones he did. Next to Drake's picture were photos of the Houthis and Iranians thought to be behind his capture. The hierarchy of bastards was similar to what he'd encountered in Kabul and Baghdad, a mixture of ex-Al-Qaeda, ISIL mercenaries and former Islamic Revolutionary Guards, many released from Sana'a's prisons as soon as the Houthis took over. Mason looked closely at one picture in particular, a poor-quality, long-range photo of Tango Seven, the mastermind behind Drake's kidnap, an Iranian general called Ruak Shahlai. The Americans had tried to assassinate him numerous times but Shahlai apparently wasn't ready to die. Mason smiled. Respect was due to anyone who could stay alive when the Yanks wanted you dead.

A new smell wafted into the air, fried meat with onions and something spicy. Mason took a full breath, sucking it deep into his lungs; it beat the stink of the latrine. In the bunk next to him, one of the newest lads to the squad, Andy Foster, began to stir. Andy wasn't a bad lad: Scouser, a bit cocky with it, but he had potential if he learned to shut up sometimes. Andy's shifting woke Mad Jack on the other side of him and Mason sat back and sighed again. Here we go, he thought, they'll all be awake now.

He looked down at Andy's kit laid neatly next to his bed. A special forces soldier's weapon is the thing that tells you all you need to know about him. The green army has strict rules about what kit you use, but in the Regiment nobody cares as long as you use it right. The new kid's rifle was already painted with desert cammo. In the army slang of the new boys, it was all 'Gucci this' and 'Ally that'. Andy had his gun pimped with a laser sight and two magazines strapped either side, one upside down so he could reload without pausing to flip. Mason looked along the row of beds and smiled at Mad Jack's weapon in comparison. No scrim, no paint, no laser, no magazines. The old sweat needed none of that shite. He was fast enough to load a magazine in his sleep if he needed to. Jack didn't wear body armour or elbow pads or chest rigs either, preferring, like Mason, to just wear the army green; spare ammo tucked into a simple webbing, trusting his instincts to keep him alive. Jack was the best demolitions or 'dems' specialist Mace had ever met. Give Jack a rifle and something to blow the arse out of and he'd be happy, probably smoke a rollie while he did it.

Mad Jack and Mason had fought alongside each other for most of his years in the Regiment. They were both West Midlands boys, grew up a few miles from each other and knew a lot of the same faces from the pubs of Walsall and West Bromwich. Compared to Mad Jack, Matt Mason was a saint. Jack was a naughty little fat bastard with a dodgy, porn-star moustache and scruffy long hair. If you saw him in Hereford Tesco's carpark, you'd probably give him a quid for a cup of tea before you ever suspected he was Regiment. People often made the mistake of thinking SAS guys must all be six foot four and built like brick shit-houses, but the truth was they came in all shapes and sizes. It was what you had inside that counted. Mason himself had always been the skinniest guy in the squad. As a lad he'd boxed in the flyweights and even now at nearly thirty-six there still wasn't much to him. Not that any of that mattered, because he knew that every man in that room, Jack, Andy Foster, Briggsy, Pom, Jonny Elves, even Craig Bell, every one of them was a machine, capable of the most incredible things, from stripping a Land Rover and putting it back together blindfolded to throwing an injured man over his shoulder and running him out of deep jungle to save his life. These were the finest of men and the best of soldiers anywhere in the world.

Someone let out a fart that sounded like a dying duck. A ripple of laughter followed it around the room.

'You dirty bastard,' someone said.

'Wasn't me,' said Andy. 'It was Hopkins.'

'Too meaty for a Rupert,' said Mason, sad that the delicious smell of fried onions had once again been replaced by a foul stench. He had no love for his superior officer, Captain Peter Hopkins, a typical young Rupert, green and cocksure and a near constant pain in Mason's arse. These young officers were rare in the Regiment but the ones that made it through were pretty much all the same: fancy boys with lots of education but no idea how proper soldiers fought. Nobody learns how to fight at Oxford, and qualifications won't save you when you come face to face with Jihadi Bob and his AK-47. It takes a few years in the Regiment to teach them that.

'Morning gents.' Right on cue, Peter Hopkins' voice was suddenly audible, sucking the life out of what little air there was in the room. 'Task on. Mace, are we ready?'

'Of course we're fucking ready.'

Everyone in the room was already up on their feet. Next to each man's bed was a grab bag filled with grenades, ammunition, food and a radio with spare batteries. Next to that was whatever body armour, helmet, night-vision goggles, gloves or shotgun they chose to roll with. Some of the men had gas grenades or extra hand grenades. Andy Foster was strapping on his elbow pads as Mason tightened the belt of his second pistol, at the same time checking that he had his map and GPS.

'Wheels up in five.' Mason said it calmly, making sure everyone in the room had heard.

He turned back to Peter Hopkins. The straight-backed officer, his mousey hair parted neatly to one side, stood watching them all while visibly twitching. Ruperts usually shat the bed when they knew there was action in the air. Most of them never got a chance to carry a gun or actually kick some doors in. A Rupert might be senior to the staff sergeant on paper, but in reality it was always the staff who ran the task, which was why Mason usually chose not to take them at all. They were best left back in Hereford or liaising with the ambassador in the embassy, doing the Ruperty bullshit educated talk that they all enjoyed. But Hopkins had some potential, so Mason had already decided he could come along on this task.

They were minutes away from engaging with whatever force the Houthis had assigned to guard Eli Drake. Mason's experience suggested they were likely to meet with resistance, so it would be good for Hopkins to get a taste. There'd also be a ton of paperwork to file, which Mason could then pass on to the Rupert.

'You'd better get your kit,' said Mason.

Hopkins snapped to action, running back out to do exactly as the Staff had instructed him. Meanwhile, Mason slung his rifle over his shoulder and scanned to make sure everyone was ready.

'What are those grenades hanging off your body armour, Andy? Get 'em in your pouch now or I'll shove 'em so far up your arse, they'll blow your fucking tongue off.'

'Oh come on, Mace, they look ally there, man.'

'No, they look like you've never been on an op before.' He glanced at his watch before he took a breath and nodded to Jack. 'Dems good, mate?'

'We're all good, Mace.'

'Right, let's fucking do this.'

TWO

London, England

If she was honest, which was rare these days, Erica Atkins preferred London since the coronavirus pandemic had ripped its heart out. The empty space was much more to her taste than the old London with throngs of tourists and drunks packing the narrow streets, cramming the bars and creating lines outside its best eating spots. She more enjoyed the sophisticated side of London, the city where Richard Curtis characters cavorted in high-class restaurants before disappearing off at weekends to go shooting in the country.

She liked all that because it was so different to her own life. Atkins was a tall, wiry South Carolinian with a barely controlled fitness addiction that gave her the body of a professional athlete. She liked to keep her raven-black hair cut short, which combined with what could most generously be described as a 'strong nose', meant people more often described her as handsome than pretty. She grew up near the beach, dressed for most of her childhood in board shorts and slippers, surfing and eating BBQ in God's own country. Her adopted parents had done right by her, taken her in and given her a good life, prioritising her education, pushing her to get a place studying engineering at Stanford. She graduated at the top of her class and turned down offers from Google and Facebook in favour of an eye-wateringly lucrative salary at Southerlin Webber, one of the world's great modern armaments manufacturers. Based out of Arlington, Virginia, Southerlin specialised in aircraft engines, avionics, cyber security, air defence systems and drones.

Now, fourteen years later, Atkins was running her own division in production on the Y-56 – the world's first true drone fighter-jet. It was capable of undertaking surveillance and strike missions without pilots, could be launched from land or water, was completely undetectable by radar and capable of delivering a payload of over ten thousand pounds. The Y-project had been running for over four years now, as the 56's two prototypes, the Y-54 and Y-52, had both been considered but then cancelled by the US Navy. Atkins had put her reputation on the line when she had persuaded the Southerlin board to back her for a third run. She staked her whole future on being able to build on those failures and learn from her mistakes. And she had done just that. She had created the uncreatable – the Y-56. The tab for this gamble was now north of one billion US dollars, but with each Y-56 unit retailing at nearly a hundred million dollars, she was within touching distance of ensuring Southerlin's future for the next decade.

She shrugged the arm of her newly tailored Gormley & Gamble suit, another good reason to come to this town, and checked the time. She was late. Good. She crossed the street and stopped outside of her London club, Home House, checked for new messages on her phone and lit a Treasurer

Slim. Another couple of minutes wouldn't hurt. It might do the asshole some good to have to hang around for her.

When she'd finished her cigarette, she slid inside the heavy black door of the club, noticing immediately that on the other side of the room, Dominic Strous, MP for Totnes, Devon, was sitting at the bar alone. She watched him check his phone four times in the space it took her to check her coat. Probably googling himself, she thought.

Strous was one of Erica's most useful assets in the UK. Three years in the Ministry of Defence as a junior minister had come off the back of a successful stint on the Foreign Affairs Select Committee. The new PM had left him where he was in the recent reshuffle and his networks in the British corridors of power had continued to grow and develop very fruitfully. Southerlin had initially approached him as the company's British factory was by some margin the largest employer in his constituency. Gradually, other 'opportunities' emerged for them to discuss developments that could be to their mutual benefit and increasingly she'd started pushing him for information from higher up the chain.

She observed him again. He looked a little sad hanging around in a bar on his own. God forbid the press would ever get a shot of him in here. But they were safe. She would happily concede that Home House was disgustingly nouveau and full of Russians, but the membership fees did always ensure a reliable degree of discretion.

'Thanks, I can see my friend,' she said to the approaching hostess, loud enough that he would hear her. She followed as the younger woman led her across the club towards the bar, Erica's eyes carefully evaluating her backside, comparing it unfavourably with her own. 'Spins,' she thought to herself, 'but not enough.'

'Dominic, good to see you. How's life in the "entertainment branch of industry"?' she said as she eased into the stool next to Strous and extended one of her exquisitely manicured hands.

Strous forced out a half-smile. 'Funny. Was that Orwell?'

'Close. Zappa.' Atkins turned to catch the barman's eye and pointed to Strous's empty glass, saying loudly in perfect Russian, 'Two more of these, please.'

Atkins laughed at Strous's obvious discomfort. The Brit's eyes darted around the bar. Clearly he did not want to be seen publicly cavorting with a Russian-speaking woman, not least in a London members club. Atkins got a kick out of watching him bristle.

'I'm afraid we may have to keep this on the brief side,' said Strous, flashing his watch. 'I did explain to your assistant—'

'Another IWC man, I see,' Atkins interrupted. She felt rather satisfied that Strous had a much less expensive model than her own.

'Oh . . .' the minister seemed momentarily disarmed by the observation.

'Hey, we're real excited about moving these Y-project lines to the UK and we want to get you much more involved.'

'Oh . . . well, great.' Strous was a sucker for being needed.

'But,' Atkins shrugged nonchalantly, 'we've hit a little bump in the road.'

'That's unfortunate,' Strous said.

'Our mutual friend on the Peninsula has been making . . . how can I say it . . . ambivalent noises about the Y-project.'

'Feeling the pinch from the oil price drops?' Strous suggested.

Atkins sighed at his ignorance. The barman delivered her drink as she retrieved an envelope from her bag. She slid it across the bar to the minister and observed him closely as he looked inside. His face contorted as he took in what it contained; a full set of export documentation, bills of lading, end-user agreements and shipping dockets for a consignment of Southerlin-manufactured small arms and artillery. It was a small order in the grand scheme of things, no more than one hundred million dollars total. The weapons were all produced at the Southerlin factory in Devon and were destined for Saudi Arabia. As Strous scanned the items listed, he began to spot several irregularities. Although everything was on the approved list, the quantities of many items were higher than usual. Someone in Saudi was topping up the routine order and didn't want to draw attention to it.

'What is this?' he asked.

'Our mutual friend wants us to handle this particular shipment a little differently to the usual ones, is all,' she said. 'It's not worth disappointing him at this delicate stage in proceedings. He's the guy who signs the final Y-project order, so we don't want to piss him off now.'

"We"?' he whispered.

Before he could say another word, she laid her hand across his arm. 'Relax, Dom. I'm all over this. I just need you to keep the customer happy right now until we land the Y-project.'

The minister's phone rang and, glancing at his screen, he raised a hand to Erica to say he had to take it. She gestured for him to continue.

While he took his call, Erica looked around the bar. A face she vaguely recognised from the House of Commons, Miranda something or other, who did comms for one of the Foreign Office guys, caught her eye. She returned a polite smile. Atkins liked the atmosphere that her club generated. She enjoyed the low hum of quiet conversation that filled the place; patrons who had a lot to say that was not for public consumption. Like good English Victorian children, they were there to be seen and not heard. Even an innocent drink in the club could have a clandestine air to it, so a clandestine drink felt positively conspiratorial.

A minister meeting with senior management of an arms company was not in and of itself untoward. The problem was that, as he had risen through the ranks of government, Strous had become increasingly resistant to doing what he was asked. Signing off on the paperwork in that file could put an end to his career, but at the same time she knew he needed the Y-project as much as she did. Strous relied on Southerlin's jobs to hold on to his constituency in the next election.

'Fuck,' he said as he hung up the call.

'Problem?' she asked.

'It's amazing how many of the problems I have start in fucking Washington,' he said before he knocked back what was left of his drink. 'Less than an hour from going live on a hostage op and they want to take over.'

'Eli Drake?' she asked. Everyone had seen the news over the last three months since the Christian missionary had disappeared in Yemen. Franky, she'd felt for a while that it was about time the Brits got round to pulling him out. But she was genuinely in the dark as to why the US would want involvement in that.

'You know I can't confirm that,' he said.

'Sure, but what interest does Washington have?' she said, completely ignoring him.

'Oh, come on, Erica.'

She could see he regretted having told her as much as he had. But once the cat was out of the bag, you couldn't put it back.

'Dom, you know anything you say is strictly between us?'

'Yeah, sure,' he said with a sarcasm that only expensively educated Brits can pull off.

The hostess appeared at their shoulder, gesturing towards the empty glasses. 'Can I get you two another?'

'No, just the bill, thanks,' Strous said. He turned to Atkins. 'I really have to go, I'm afraid.' He again scanned the room. This wasn't just career-ending chat, this was public enquiry territory. Not only was he in possession of a dodgy arms order she wanted him to grease through the wheels of pro-curement, but now he was also in danger of sharing classi-fied information on a live military operation with a foreign national. 'I'm on the 19.50 train to Totnes. With any luck, the person in question will be on a flight back to London tonight and you and I can watch the PM take all the credit for it on the *Andrew Marr Show* tomorrow morning.'

Atkins slid back in her stool. This was the part of her job that she cherished. What Strous didn't know yet was that he was going to tell her what she wanted to know. Erica had buried her hook so deep inside him a long time ago that she could just reel him in, but first she wanted to feel that pull on the line. The struggle was the fun part. Politicians loved to talk about how politics is a dirty game, but they didn't know half of what was really going on. The wheels of power turned only because they served to screen the truly powerful from view. Atkins would be in that bracket before too long and then she would send the next generation of Atkins out to do her dirty work, and they would pull the strings of the next generation of Strous. And so it would go. On and on. True power lay in the business of war. War would always make powerful men rich and keep rich men powerful. Now women too. If you wanted a picture of the future, imagine a boot stamping on a human face – forever. Now that was Orwell.

'You know James Drayson, right?' Atkins said it as casually as she could, smiling as the hostess returned with the cheque, which she covered with her Amex Platinum. Of course Strous knew Drayson, he had been his predecessor at the MoD before he left government and became a non-executive director on the Southerlin board. 'Well, James is moving on. Bought the island next to Branson's and now he wants to go live on it. Crazy bastard.'

This was news to Strous. Drayson was a good chap, a loyal member of the party, did three terms in Westminster before moving out the US to work with the Yanks. It was Drayson who'd first suggested to Strous that a meeting with the Southerlin people could help him to secure the factory deal that brought a thousand new jobs to Devon. But what had Drayson's retirement got to do with him?

'With James's position vacant, the board's been looking around for names . . .' Atkins slid the envelope along the bar, closer to Strous. 'It must feel pretty great to own your own island, huh?'

Erica kept her gaze calmly fixed on Dom's face, giving a non-committal shrug when he looked back to her all confused and conflicted. She didn't have any sympathy for him, he knew the game. In the end, all the Dominic Strouses of this world had an eye on was the final pay cheque. What she had offered him was just that, and all she had to do was wait another couple of seconds for him to give it up.

Strous started typing on his phone. When he'd finished, he turned the screen around so that Erica could see the name that he'd written on the screen – 'Shahlai'.

'You know him?' Strous asked.

Erica shook her head.

'Well, you should. Your lot have intel that he's at our target location. We suspected that he might be behind Drake's capture, but nobody thought he'd actually be there. Anyway, Langley are now insisting that he be made top priority. They even want one of their own guys on it.'

Erica mulled over what he'd just said. Of course she knew exactly who General Ruak Shahlai was but she wasn't going to let Strous see that. She knew that the CIA had tried

19

to have the Iranian general assassinated again recently and that he had survived and gone to ground. Shahlai's involvement in the whole sordid Eli Drake kidnap was of no surprise to her, but she was now concerned with what the fallout could be from his kill or capture. Erica's focus was on ensuring that the Saudis followed through on their investment in the Y-project – tech that was designed specifically to keep them safe from people like Ruak Shahlai. Taking out Shahlai wouldn't exactly be good for business.

'Can you delay?' she asked.

'No way,' said Strous. 'This is a live operation, Erica. What possible explanation could I give for that?'

'I guess you better go deal with it then.'

Strous looked like he was going to bust a gut, but Erica gave him her best sympathetic smile. Their original deal was that the minster would share a few choice scraps of intel, introductions, the odd heads-up on strategic commercial decisions maybe in return for Southerlin's continued investment. It had moved on to the next level – expediting irregular shipments and sharing intelligence on live British operations. She was pleased about that.

He held up the envelope containing the Saudi arms order. 'I'll take care of this.'

'Thanks, Dom,' Erica said, and waved as he hurried to the door.

When he was safely out of sight, she took out a second phone from her bag and began to dial.

THREE

Sana'a, Yemen

Matt Mason led his squad outside; all six men ready to complete the task they'd been assigned. The mood was focused. They were now on the clock, but they all knew that working calmly and systematically was the fastest way to get the job done. Out in the yard, the support teams were already loading kit into the front of two trucks, classic jingly wagons, customised to look like a pair of local farmers' lorries. The front cab of each was battered and dented, while the back was stacked high with hay bales piled up to the roof, bits of straw poking out through the bars that lined the sides.

'Outstanding, Jonny,' said Mason, giving Jonny Elves a nod.

Jonny was someone who could step up when you needed him. He was also the best mechanic in the Regiment and a master of disguising a vehicle to make it look shit when it was anything but. Jonny took a certain pride in his work which Mason respected. If Jonny was on the team then you knew that whatever else happened, the wheels would keep on turning.

'Running flats.' Jonny started circling the front vehicle, pointing out its features. 'Engine's humming, Kevlar-lined inside and I even spread a couple of buckets of goat shit in there for you.'

Mason's troop piled inside while he inspected the hay bales, trimmed three inches thick, giving the vehicle a perfect front beneath the layer of protective Kevlar. The men squeezed in along two long benches that ran either side, shoving bags and rifles between their legs. This would do nicely, Mason thought. From the outside, the vehicle looked like any Yemeni hay truck, but on the inside, it was a fully equipped, comms ready, fortified, bulletproof Ops room.

'Support vehicle's kitted out the same and you've got local Toyotas front and back,' Jonny pointed to two old Corollas he'd prepped to run fronting and backing vehicles. They would flank the jingly wagons front and rear, driven by local translators on the payroll, dressed in civilian clothing, clearing the route: their eyes and ears along the road.

Mason checked his watch. The sun was still not quite up as Hopkins appeared with a tall red-headed woman, boyish frame, piercing green eyes scanning the yard, already wearing full body armour. She slid off her helmet and extended a hand towards him. 'Agent Redford, you're Mason?'

Mason ignored the question and turned to Hopkins for an explanation.

'We've got company, Mace,' said Hopkins, looking like he'd shit his pants.

'What?' Mason didn't like the sound of this. 'Why?'

'Sanctioned by Hereford.'

'Why the fuck am I only hearing about this now?'

It was highly irregular for operational details to be changed this late in the day, let alone for the brass to sanction a foreign operative to ride along. Even if she was a spook, there were protocols, and Mason didn't like surprises.

Hopkins shifted uncomfortably from foot to foot. He knew that they were heading for another confrontation because Mason was always a little too quick to the fight and nothing Hopkins could say would calm him down. After a month of working together, the captain was used to getting grief from Mason. So, instead of answering, he looked at the floor. He wasn't going to say another word, not bloody likely, not unless he wanted his ear bitten off.

Realising that he wasn't going to get anywhere with Hopkins, Mason turned his attention to Redford, giving her a cold once-over. He reckoned she must be early thirties. Confident, calm, the accent suggested West Coast. California maybe?

'I've reviewed all the intel,' Redford said. 'Can I make a suggestion?'

'No,' said Mason, stone cold. He didn't have time for this.

Redford chose not to acknowledge his response. 'I thought we could use some securing forces at the rear of the target building. The reconnaissance shows that there's a gate to the outside that appears vulnerable.'

'Support vehicle,' Mason said, shaking his head and pointing her towards the second wagon.

'The captain will take care of you.'

'Staff Sergeant . . .'

'My men have been drilled on the plan. I don't see any reason to jeopardise our task for the sake of a gate.'

Mason looked back at the forlorn Hopkins. He'd brought her into this so he could babysit her while the real soldiers took care of business. Mason didn't like working with spooks. They always thought that they could handle themselves in combat situations, but in his experience, it was better to leave the soldiering to the soldiers. He turned away and took no more notice of either of them, scanning the yard one final time. The job was on. Everything was in order, so he climbed into the truck and pulled the door tight behind him.

The light inside the jingly wagon was red, enough to see by without danger of penetrating the hay or giving you night blindness when you stepped outside. Mason found himself still thinking about Redford. He wondered what she was there for and why he hadn't been told about her before now. He should be focused on the job, making sure the blokes were sorted, but instead his head was full of questions. Did Hereford not trust him? He was leading a task into God-knows-what, so he needed to know the trust was there. Trust that ran both ways. He didn't like surprises, but even more than that he didn't like going into something unless he knew he could rely on every single person going into it with him. Everything was going to be different now, from how he was supposed to act in front of her to what he was allowed to say. It was all going through his head and it was making him angry.

Not to mention that he hated doing things with the Yanks. Mainly because they had such a unique way of doing everything: usually over the top, usually overkill, usually making a mountain out of a molehill but always leaving the

British to clear it up. They hadn't wanted them there in Afghanistan and they had been a nightmare in Iraq too.

He stood up and walked to the front of the vehicle. He peered out through a spy hole that connected the back to the front cab, from where he could see out to the street, still quiet, still dark, yet to come alive with people. Most of the buildings in Sana'a were handsome towers made from red burned-mud brick, with ornate white stone window frames that shone gold in the light of the dawn. A hundred minarets rose into the sky from the city's mosques, blending with the red mountains that surrounded it on all sides. It was prettier than Kabul, that was for sure. Soon the sun would come up and people would start leaving the mosques after morning prayers. But before that, his men would be at work, doing what they'd come here to do.

Like the city outside, there wasn't a sound inside the truck. The banter had fallen away and the men were silent, each thinking about the job in hand, anticipating what was going to happen. Mason sat back down, feeling Mad Jack's larger bulk squeezed in against him. Like Mason, Jack had been in this position a hundred times before. Even the younger lads like Andy had a few successfully completed tasks under their belts. This was bread and butter for his team and indeed, the feeling inside wasn't of nerves but quiet, focused confidence. Once they reached the target, the operation would run like a well-oiled machine; each part had been carefully designed, fabricated and polished to perform its role to perfection. In and out. Just like last time. Just like the time before. Just like the time before that.

Mason's mind flickered back to the CIA woman. Her presence wasn't just a headache, it was a sign this task wasn't as straightforward as he had first thought. Their target was British, so there must be another reason for the Yanks to even be here.

He put her out of his mind again and pulled out his map, quickly locating the target location, tracing the direction of approach with his finger so they could all see.

'We'll pull over two streets from target . . . here. Fan out and wait for the command. Once Jack's breached the compound . . . here . . . we enter here. As planned.'

They all knew the drill, they'd heard it a hundred times, but Mason liked to run it again anyway to give them a focus outside of their heads. A man could have too much time to think about things sometimes.

'Briggsy, Pom, you're with me. Lead in, grab any bastard you see and beat him until he tells us where the target is.'

The two big men nodded. They were used to running point. Steve Briggs was six foot four – the lads joked that if he didn't have such bowed legs, he'd have been seven foot. Blessed with the biggest head you've ever seen on a human being, they called him 'Camelhead'. You'd never send Briggsy on a diplomatic mission, but there's no better man for kicking a door in and dropping every living soul on the other side of it.

His partner in crime was Carl 'Pommy' Cash. The strongman from Portsmouth had the hairiest chest you'd ever seen on a human. He was mad as a fish outside of a battle. But in the heat of the fight, he had a rare calm and a deadeye that meant he could take you out from seven hundred yards with a rifle or just as easily pick up a Javelin and hit you with a rocket from the same distance. Nobody knew how Pommy was still alive, but he'd been the first name on Mason's team sheet ever since they first worked together in Afghanistan.

Mason turned to the two younger men. 'Craig and Andy, behind us, sweeping up. We want any evidence −' Mason handed them black drawstring bags and latex gloves, 'hard-drives, pictures, the whole lot. No prisoners today, just the target, in and out. Understood?'

Craig Bell was a quiet Jock from the Borders, respectful, diligent, but tough as boots. He could have done anything in life, being a smart kid with a gift for learning things fast. He was also fluent in eight languages and easily the best Arabic speaker in the troop. In the Regiment, they were all linguists in one way or another, quite a few of the lads had decent Arabic. Mason had learned near-native Dari during his time in Afghanistan. His Arabic was colloquial albeit ac-cented with the Baghdadi slang he'd picked up in Iraq, but he still relied on Craig and their Yemeni translators driving in the Toyota Corolla up front, Adara and Saladin.

'We have a problem.' Mason instantly recognised Saladin's deep voice over his comms. 'Big crowd, sandbags, men on the roof, looks like maybe a new checkpoint.'

'Redirect. Take another route.' Mason was clear, decisive, no point in risking being stopped when they had options. There were other routes to reach the target.

'Anything?' Mason directed his question to Craig.

Mason always had Craig run communications for the team because as well as his language skills, he was a cool head in a crisis, capable of seeing the angles and making good choices. He trusted the two translators but that didn't mean he wasn't covering his back the whole time. The fronting vehicle was equipped with their own sneaks, a bugging device monitored by Craig, listening the whole time to Adara and Saladin's private conversation.

'Nothing unusual, Mace.' Craig shrugged.

The jingly wagon turned right and Mason reviewed his map of the city again. In his ear, the comms from HQ confirmed the new route. He knew Saladin and Adara had it in hand, but he didn't want to talk to them too much, needed them to look normal, not draw attention to themselves.

A checkpoint on the route need not mean anything sinister. The Houthis were constantly moving checkpoints around the city to keep their own people guessing. They had successfully held the nation's capital now for nearly eight years and they hadn't achieved that without solid organisation. Saudi spies and people loyal to the Houthis' enemy, President Hadi, were everywhere. The intel pointed to Iran being heavily involved in training and arming the Houthis and a few of the Houthi leaders, including the main boss Abdul Malik, had spent a good bit of time in Tehran with the Iranian Republican Guards. These guys might have started out as a bunch of rag-tag tribal rebels but they were now a well-funded and organised fighting force.

'Call sign Bravo One, stand by.' It was HQ on comms. The jingly wagon was now only four minutes from target so Mason knew this would be the final update on intel from the Ops room before all call signs went silent. 'Be advised,

Tango Seven believed to be on target. Kill or capture. Repeat, kill or capture.'

Mason felt the mood in the vehicle stiffen. Shahlai at the target location was potentially a game changer. It meant whatever was going down there this morning was important. It also meant they were likely to have a larger welcoming committee than they'd anticipated, and everyone in that jingly wagon knew it. Mason also realised something else. That's why she was here. Hereford must have known this was on the cards and the Americans probably wanted to make sure they had boots on the ground if Shahlai was taken. All of them must have known and yet they were only telling him now with four minutes to spare? What was going on?

He shook his head. He didn't have time to think about all that now, he had to concentrate on getting his troop in, completing their task to rescue Eli Drake and getting out again. Things were going to get serious pretty fucking soon and there wasn't time to be distracted by whatever crap the fucking Ruperts and Yanks had planned behind his back.

The vehicle pulled in two streets from the target and the troop piled out, shaking out in the shadows along the wall. Mason walked along the line, making sure everyone was ready. He checked his watch again; the helicopters would be in the sky by now. Three in total, two Little Birds and a Puma with another eight blokes on board who could fast rope in to give support if needed. Everything was go, the job was on.

The troop moved in file, double time along the wall of the compound, night-vision goggles on, reaching the point of entry and taking up positions as Mad Jack got to work, laying demolitions shy of the main gate. Their intel had told them the compound opened up on the other side of this exact spot. Pommy and Briggs stood on Jack's left, guns raised, ready to go first through the hole. Mason crouched behind them, then Andy Foster, Craig and Jonny brought up the rear. All comms were silent now, only the sounds of the city could be heard, louder now that morning prayers were over and the mosques were emptying people out into the streets. There was the rising sound of car horns, honking as the traffic built again for a new day.

Further along the road behind them, Mason knew that the support vehicle would be in position, Hopkins with the CIA woman and more lads from the Regiment, ready to give them cover along the road, ready to follow them in as soon as he gave the all-clear. Jack gave Mason the thumbs up and he nodded back.

'Stand by. Stand by.'

BOOM!

The sound of it enveloped everything for a moment, then the dust followed, rising into the air, solid lumps of debris landing all around them. Mason saw Briggs and Pommy disappear into the middle of the cloud, noticing too that the lights were coming on in buildings down the street and the sounds of car alarms were ringing all around him. Somewhere a water pipe must have exploded because water splattered on to the face of his respirator. Suddenly there was the sound of gunfire from the other side of the wall and so, giving Andy and Jack a nod, they all piled into the dust cloud.

FOUR

Sana'a, Yemen

Inside the building, Ibrahim Manar dropped the Playstation controller into the lap of his thawb. The game, PlayerUnknown's Battlegrounds or bubji as they called it in Arabic, carried on playing on the screen without him. It was a game he played online, sometimes with up to a hundred players from all over the world. Young men from Yemen, Saudi Arabia, Iran, even the UAE. Dropped on to a virtual island, they fought to the death; the last man standing wins. The in-game voice chat was a mélange of Arabic dialects, young men promising to murder each other in the most sadistic of ways. Manar took off his headphones and looked up to the ceiling, confused by the small white flakes of plaster falling, dusting him like flour.

Manar liked Sana'a but he resented the boredom of guarding hostages in the safe house. He much preferred being out on the checkpoint, part of the hustle and bustle of the city, creaming a little backsheesh here and there from people whose papers weren't in order. There was no extra money to be made in the safe house though, just long hours of nothing, playing bubji online with kids he would never meet. But whatever just happened was very different. The whole building had shaken with the force of an earthquake, and when Manar looked down at his hand he saw it was trembling. He squeezed it to try to make it stop, but when he looked again it was no different. Whatever was happening was no game and it seemed that his body had worked that out long before his head.

The door to the room flew open and Manar leapt to his feet, immediately recognising General Shahlai, from the Islamic Revolutionary Guard, who had arrived from Qom that morning. Shahlai was as broad as a bull and barely squeezed into the blue suit jacket he wore over his thawb. Manar noted that the jacket barely concealed a Browning HP pistol tucked into Shahlai's belt. The general gabbled into his phone in Farsi, and though Manar couldn't make out what he was saying, he could tell that he was angry with whomever it was he was talking to. Shahlai spoke Arabic perfectly even though, being Iranian, it wasn't his native tongue. Manar, on the other hand, couldn't understand the Farsi that all the Iranians spoke, not here in Sana'a nor the ones online who played bubji. The letters looked the same, but the words looked like they were all mixed up. Even though his father had spoken both languages, his mother had only ever spoken Arabic to him and so he had never learned the tongue of their allies.

Manar stood bolt upright to attention, fearing the man in front of him even more than whatever had caused the explosion outside. He wondered whether he should say something, but before he could think of what to say, he heard the sound of gunfire and felt his hand trembling again. Manar daren't look away from the general, who stood in front of him still listening to his phone but staring back as though he'd forgotten who the boy was. The feeling was excruciating. Manar wanted to run away back to his village with his family, he wanted to be anywhere else but in that room with the man from Qom. For a couple of seconds he thought about places where he might be able to hide until, finally, the general hung up.

'It's the British,' he said, absently toying with the enormous ruby ring on his little finger with the stump of thumb that remained on his left hand. The American drone attack earlier that year, the second that he had survived, had removed nothing but the end of his first digit, and he had developed a habit of playing with the ring, enjoying the phantom sensation that still remained.

'Come.' The general started rearranging the furniture in the room, pushing Manar's chair into the centre and gathering up his rifle from the floor with a handful of ammunition.

Manar watched as Shahlai worked calmly and methodically, completely the opposite of how he felt. The older man seemed assured as he surveyed the room, mentally working through the permutations of what was likely to occur next. He pulled Manar by the shoulder and eased him down on to the seat, laying the rifle in his hands, guiding the boy, showing him exactly where to aim at the door. With Manar in the right position, he crossed the room and unlocked the door, leaving it slightly ajar, already picturing how things would play out.

'They will come in here,' he said, pointing to the open door. 'You wait and when you see them, you shoot. Understand?'

Manar nodded although he wasn't sure of a single thing the general had just said. Instead, the voice in his head kept repeating, 'this is really happening, this is really happening.'

The general put a hand on his shoulder – the older man's strength felt solid and assured against Manar's trembling flesh. 'You are a brave warrior,' Shahlai said. 'The infidel will never capture you alive, insh'allah.'

Manar dutifully manned his new post and watched as Shahlai gathered more ammunition from around the room, stuffing it into a small backpack that he slung over his shoulder. He walked to the window and peeked outside, mumbling again in Farsi under his breath, cursing their luck, one more hour and he would have completed everything. The message from Tehran had been clear: the Houthi name must ring out in the West, even more loudly than Al-Qaeda or Daesh. What happened here today, the execution of the Westerner, the broadcast to the world, would have delivered that message clearly. Then, when the time was right, Tehran would be on hand to broker the peace between the Houthis and the West. Instead, now everything was fucked.

Shahlai looked at the ceremonial sword and the video camera fallen forlornly on to its side, the Houthi flag hanging from the wall and again at the wretched boy. Frankly, the boy was an imbecile but even an imbecile could be a powerful weapon if he was prepared to martyr himself. The movement needed acolytes to achieve its mission, but Shahlai knew this one's chances of survival were non-existent. Tomorrow he would be in Paradise, a martyr, rewarded with riches and virgins as it was written in the Koran: 'They shall recline on jewelled couches . . . with a cup of purest wine . . . And theirs shall be the dark-eyed houris, chaste as hidden pearls.'

He held out his hands, palms up, reading the Arabic words written across the Houthi flag, 'Allah is Great, Death to America, Death to Israel, Curse on the Jews, Victory to Islam.' He placed his right hand over his left, bringing them to his chest and bowing slightly before he turned again to Manar. 'May the hand of the Prophet, peace be upon him, guide your hand,' he said, before he calmly left the room.

Manar realised that he was alone again, holding a gun again, waiting to kill or be killed again, only this time, it wasn't online bubji. This time it was for real.

FIVE

Sana'a, Yemen

Mason ran through the smoke, blind for four or five metres until he was inside the courtyard, looking for cover as the helicopter arrived and began circling above him. Its arrival had been timed to perfection and the blades began dispersing the dust a little, so that Mason could make out a figure on the other side of the compound running for his life out of a back gate. He paused for a second, considering pursuit, but chasing Tangos was not part of the plan, and in any case, he was more concerned about the gunfire pinging around his head.

He was surrounded by multiple enemies, one engaging him from a position on the roof and another two firing from behind a small fortification of rocks and sandbags maybe fifty feet away. From Mason's position, he figured it was more prudent to start with the two closest to him, so he steadied his Diemaco rifle and aimed, dropping the first shooter and then the second with a double tap. He turned his attention back to the rooftop but the shooting from there had already stopped. The sun was coming up, so he was better able to make out the silhouette of the helicopter sniper hanging out of the skids, laser sight attached to his 7.62 chain gun, scoping the compound for more Tangos.

He stood and ran towards the two bodies he'd dropped, keeping down until he reached the wall of sandbags, hopping over and dropping behind them for cover. He looked either side of him to check the two fresh corpses, taken out with pinpoint-accurate headshots. They were the safest way to neutralise a target – you never knew when someone might be wearing a suicide vest.

'All call signs, courtyard clear.' Pommy's voice came over the radio. If he said the area was clear, then you could be bloody sure it was. The hairy bastard had never let Mason down once in ten years.

Mason gave the signal for all three teams to advance on to the main building. Everyone went to work. Mason waited behind Jack as he laid door charges on the main entrance, Andy and Craig scurried down a ladder to a basement window, while Briggs pushed the clacker on a charge that sent the metal side door flying clean off its hinges. Mason heard two more explosions almost in unison. Boom, boom, boom. Three clear points of entry. Alpha, Bravo and Charlie teams were inside just as they had planned.

Mason stuck close to Jack's considerable mass as they ran into the building and Jack launched a flashbang through an interior door, setting off a series of explosions on the other side. Above and below them, he could hear gunfire and then another huge explosion. The support team from the helicopter must be on the roof, making their entry from above.

Jack led them into the room he'd just filled with fire and smoke, guns raised, clearing left and right. Right away Mason noticed the flag hanging on the wall, covered in Arabic text. Next to it lay a sword, a broken video camera, a widescreen TV and a Playstation. The walls were covered in A4 sheets of Arabic script and DVDs sellotaped into plastic wallets.

He saw a young Houthi man lying stunned on the floor, blood already oozing from his nose, soaking into his beard. Jack kicked away the guy's rifle and flipped him over, plastic-cuffing his hands behind his back.

'Clear!' Jack shouted, ready for Mason to give the okay to move through the door to the next room.

But Mason paused and instead moved to the man cuffed on the floor. He scanned his face, mentally running through the pictures he had seen of targets of interest. This was one he recognised, Tango Four, Ibrahim Manar Al-Bajazi, a junior Houthi soldier, no one important. Mason had an idea. He took hold of Manar by the throat and squeezed firmly as he asked, 'Where is the hostage? The Christian?'

Manar spluttered and spat a mouthful of blood on to his chest before he shook his head defiantly. Fucking kid had some balls, Mason thought, right before he hit him hard in the centre of his face, sending his head bouncing off the stone floor. He repeated the question, only this time Manar either thought better of his defiance or just couldn't maintain it any longer. His eyes flicked towards the door on the other side of the room.

'Okay, let's see,' Mason said as he yanked Manar to his feet, lifted him clean up off the ground and held him out in front of his body like a shield. He stopped momentarily, checking that Jack was ready, and then on his signal, the big lad from Walsall launched a boot at the door, busting it open so that Mason could run through, still holding Manar aloft, his feet six inches off the floor.

Mason was standing at the foot of a steep, narrow staircase and Manar lifted his chin to show that it led to the place he was looking for. Still holding the young Houthi man aloft, he ran full speed up the stairs, using Manar's body as a battering ram to break open the door at the top, charging inside behind his human shield.

The room was full of dust, and dark save for a little sunlight that crept in through a small opening in the ceiling, otherwise blocked by rebar. Mason figured the helicopter team must have made a failed entry and moved on, but whatever explosives they'd used had done a lot of damage. He dropped Manar on to the floor and lifted his rifle to scan the room, looking through the gloom for bodies. He saw nothing to his right but as he turned to the left, he saw something in the shadows. Sitting on the floor, looking up at him through the dust was a young, bearded Houthi smiling from ear to ear, pointing an AK-47 rifle right at Mason's head.

For the rest of his life, Matt Mason would remember that smile. He would never shake the memory of the man beaming at him the instant before he fired a volley of 7.62 short rounds, at six hundred rounds per minute, straight at Mason, from six feet away.

But he would get the chance to remember it because every one of those bullets flew harmlessly past him except for the one which cascaded into the laser sight mounted on his Diemaco rifle. That bullet smashed into the Laser Light Module Mk3 at over seven hundred metres per second, showering glass fragments in every direction. One shard glanced off the centre of Mason's forehead, opening up a gash in its path, while a second sunk itself into his left shoulder. Not that Matt Mason noticed, as his adrenal gland had already released half a milligram of adrenaline into his bloodstream, rendering him numb to the pain. Instead, Mason stood frozen, rooted to the spot, still looking down at the man smiling back at him.

Suddenly, from behind, Mason heard a familiar muffled sound, de-dum, de-dum. Almost instantly, the smiling man's head exploded and his body recoiled back with the force of the double headshot, coolly administered by Mad Jack. Mason turned and looked back at the spray of bullet holes that had peppered the wall behind him. At least thirty bullets had somehow missed their intended target.

'That's another one of your nine gone, Mace,' said Jack, kicking away the dead man's rifle.

Mason reckoned he'd used up all his nine lives a long time ago; someone must have given him a bonus one. The evidence was right there on the wall. Seeing as how he was still alive, he thought, he might as well get on with things, so he stepped over the fallen body, raised his rifle again and kicked in the next door, crashing inside, this time making no mistake as he cleared left and right.

The room was darker but Mason could see a figure curled up in the corner lying on the floor, hands bound, chained to a concrete slab. He walked towards it and reached down to remove a cloth bag that had been pulled over the figure's head. Underneath was a heavily bearded man, struggling to see, squinting up at him through the dim light.

'British SAS,' Mason said, crouching to take a closer look at the man's face. 'You're safe, you're safe.'

The man began to weep, shaking with small, weary sobs as Mason put a steadying hand on him, only now noticing the blood running down his own arm. He looked at the photo he'd placed behind the plastic wallet strapped to his uniform. He'd studied that photo many times before and thought he knew the face as well as his own, but when he looked back to the crying man, he realised that something was wrong.

'Who the fuck are you?' he said, 'Cos you ain't Drake.'

SIX

Sana'a, Yemen

Agent Redford resented being made to wait outside of the compound with the support team. Demolition and evacuation were areas she was highly experienced in and she could hold her own with arrogant assholes like Matt Mason any day of the week. If this mission hadn't been beyond her jurisdiction, then she'd have gladly pulled rank on him, but as it was, she bit her tongue and decided to enjoy being there at the discretion of Her Majesty.

Redford had been recruited by the CIA after graduating from Harvard. Her application had stood out due to a rare mix of language skills acquired during her time growing up in the Middle East. The Agency sent her straight to the Directorate of Operations, where she trained as a covert operative at 'The Farm' and placed top of her year. Her first deployment was, by her own request, to Somalia, where, under the cover of being a US diplomat, her primary role was to recruit foreigners willing to sell secrets to the US. After that and a brief but arduous stint in Djibouti, she'd finally landed in Yemen, building an impressive network of agents and informants across the whole region. If the US ever woke up and realised the magnitude of threat that this place posed, then Redford was primed and ready with the intel her country would require.

However, the sad truth was that few people back home knew where Yemen was, let alone how important its politics were to the balance of power in the world. There was no doubt in Redford's mind that a war was brewing in the Muslim world, and when it came, the shockwaves would be felt from the shores of Bar Harbour to Key West. Instead, the country for which she put her life on the line was more interested in fighting with itself, one side of the political divide constantly looking for ways to catch out the other, tripping themselves up, wasting time exposing hypocrisy or untruths about matters of triviality. Her countrymen were so intent on finding the enemy within that they'd entirely overlooked the real enemy; the forces that would destroy them in a heartbeat.

'All call signs, clear.' She recognised Mason's voice coming over the comms in her earpiece, giving them the signal that it was safe to enter. She watched Hopkins check along the line, ensuring that the rest of the support team were ready, and then followed him into the same hole that Mad Jack had made four minutes before. Behind Redford, the sergeant major, medic and a couple of younger British guys followed close, double-timing into the compound and across to the main building, where Briggs was waiting for them.

'Two out here, another on the roof, two more inside, Dave,' Briggs addressed the sergeant major, counting out the dead for him to see.

'Tango Seven?' Redford asked. Shahlai was her only concern.

'Unseen, Ma'am,' Briggs said before he turned and led them in the main door and through the room where they'd found Manar.

Redford took it all in – the flag, the sword, the video camera – figuring that in another hour or so someone would have lost his head on livestream. She saw Andy Roberts bagging up the camera along with some photographs and DVDs taped to the wall. No doubt they contained footage of previous rocket attacks, operations, maybe even executions. These idiots always seemed to want to film themselves, despite the fact that it would provide their enemies with vital intel.

And Redford was their enemy. She despised the threat that maniacs like Shahlai posed to everyone's security in the name of Islam. She'd studied the Koran at Harvard, translating from some of the oldest surviving texts in dialectic Arabic, and produced an interpretation in Aramaic for her master's thesis. She had concluded that many 'insights' made by male scholars were actually linguistic errors, such as the assertion that countless *houris* or virgins were awaiting martyrs in heaven. She contended that the word *hur* was not intended to mean virgins at all, but white grapes. Redford knew that book as well as anyone who claimed to fight in its name and despised those who deliberately misinterpreted it in ways that suited their own ends. She knew that Shahlai was not a holy but an evil man, and she'd made it her life's work thus far to ensure that he was stopped.

As she climbed the stairs, Redford heard shouting from the room above and through her earpiece, Hopkins was already calling the helicopter to the LZ. By the time she reached the top, Ibrahim Manar was on his knees, wrists cuffed behind his back, bruised and bleeding, while Craig Bell pressed him aggressively for locations of boobytraps and the whereabouts of his missing comrades. She scanned the room, wondering only where Shahlai was. There was no sign of him. Her next thought was, 'Where's Mason?'

Redford stepped over the broken glass fragments of Mason's smashed scope and moved into the last room. The party was well and truly over, and the team looked like they were preparing to get the hell out of there. Mason was pressing a makeshift dressing on to what looked like a wound in his shoulder, another trickle of blood running down the side of his face. Hopkins and the sergeant major were standing around him, relaying immediate, need-to-know intel, all the while glancing over towards a skinny, bearded man on the floor. Redford turned her attention to the hostage getting checked over by the medic. Something was missing. She still couldn't see him. Where was he? Where was Shahlai?

Redford crouched down next to the hostage. She took out a photograph of Shahlai and pushed it under the wretched man's nose, forcing him to focus on it. 'Did you see this man? Look closely.'

The man recoiled and tried to cower behind the medic but again Redford forced the photograph on him. She didn't care about his pain right now, this might be the only chance she got. The jungle drums were already beating and in another couple of minutes they would be out of this place and her chance would be gone. If Shahlai had ever been here, in this room, then she wanted to know it.

'Enough.' She heard Mason's voice behind her. 'Take it back to HQ.'

'It's a little late for your help now, don't you think?' Redford could barely conceal the anger in her voice. If he'd listened to her, if he'd put a detail on the back gate like she'd told him to, then they'd have Shahlai in custody now.

'Now, wait a fucking minute,' said Mason, taking another step towards her.

'Wait for what, Staff Sergeant? For him to come back?' Redford fired back, jumping quickly to her feet.

They stood toe to toe, the American spook eyeballing the British soldier, her fury searing right through him. Redford was aware that Hopkins was now standing next to them, trying to pull them apart, saying something about how they should calm down, but she couldn't concentrate enough to hear exactly. She had spent four years tracking Shahlai, this was as close as she'd ever come to apprehending him and she wanted to hear Mason at least admit it to her that he'd fucked up.

The helicopter pilot's voice came over her comms confirming pickup in two minutes, as Hopkins finally forced his body between them and began reminding Mason that he had a team to evacuate before the situation became problematic. Mason snarled at her and turned away, ordering his men to move.

'Roger. Confirmed. Figures two.' She could hear him speaking into his comms, moving quickly back down the stairs. 'All call signs to the LZ, we're done here.'

Redford watched the medic help the hostage to his feet and follow behind Mason and Hopkins, leaving her alone in the room. She used her last seconds to scan for a clue, anything, some physical evidence that Shahlai had been in that room, but of course there were none. She'd studied the Iranian for years and felt that she understood him as well as his best friend. Shahlai was no amateur, he knew the game as well as she did. She could feel his presence but nothing real. She followed the team outside, noting that every single piece of furniture had been turned over, ripped open, broken apart in the search for evidence. These British boys were thorough, she'd give them that.

They left the compound by the rear gate and the RAF Chinook landed in a small carpark two hundred metres to the south. The helicopter's twin engines roared as its sixty-foot rotors spewed dust in every direction. The sergeant major stepped up into its open rear, checking off the teams as they boarded behind him. Bravo team, the support team, Mason's team with Manar and the rescued hostage in tow, followed by Hopkins and Redford. With everyone confirmed on board, the helicopter rose up, nearly two thousand feet per minute, high into the sky above Sana'a. A lone gunner scanned the roofs below with his M60, ready to pick off any hostiles who considered firing a parting shot in their direction.

Redford loosened her body armour and removed her helmet, shaking out her hair and taking a lungful of air, cleaner up there than it was down in the Sana'a dust. She blew it out, trying to let go of her anger with it. She watched the city pass underneath. She knew that Shahlai was down there somewhere, on the streets below, now full of cars and carts, or in the market thick with crowds of people buying food. It infuriated her to listen to the same sounds that he must be able to hear too; horns beeping, children shouting, normal life resuming. She had made the Yemeni people the centre of her universe, even though none of them would ever know hers. The vast majority of them would never even visit a Western country, fewer still the USA. Yet she cared about their freedom, she wanted them to enjoy a quality of life that people in the West took for granted, free of the oppressive control of men like Shahlai.

Redford had to refocus. She told herself that she still had a job to do, even if the Brits had just made it considerably harder than it should have been. She couldn't afford to dwell on what might have happened or what should have happened. She needed to stay on point and play the politics of what happened next. She felt the muscles in her neck relax as she found renewed purpose, formulating a plan, taking control again. She knew herself well enough to know that life was easier when she could understand the task she had to complete.

She looked down the length of the Chinook, deliberately avoiding eye contact with Mason and instead looking for the man they had apprehended. Manar was flanked by

Jack and Andy, cuffed and bagged, sitting upright and still. She would take a run at him the first chance she got. She sank back into her seat, feeling the tension inside of her subsiding. There was nothing more she could have done back there, she had simply prioritised the target she'd been assigned to.

The chopper began its descent on to the secure LZ at the HQ and Redford felt calmer again. She had a potential lead, so the sooner the interrogation began, the sooner she could get on with bringing the Iranian general into US custody. Today had been a setback, nothing more. She was still on top of this and in the end, she would prevail.

SEVEN

Sana'a, Yemen

Racing up the hill on the back of a motorbike, already three miles to the north of the abandoned compound, Ruak Shahlai tapped the shoulder of the driver and waved for him to stop. He climbed down off the bike and took a deep gulp of water as he watched the Chinook helicopter fly southeast. From its bearing, he calculated that it was headed to the west of the Sayyan hills. He pulled a phone from his pocket and called one of his spies who operated near there.

'You see it?' he asked. 'Good. Follow where it lands.' Wherever that chopper landed, the British HQ would be close. He wiped the water from his beard and climbed back on to the bike. Immediately, they sped off again along the old town road as fast as they could.

He knew the narrow streets of Sana'a well, having visited the city many times before. When he was a boy, a young Houthi named Hussein Badreddin al-Houthi, a direct descendent of the Prophet Mohammed, had come with his family to live in Qom. Hussein and Shahlai attended the same Shi'ah seminary school in Qom and became close friends, playing together every day after class by the river, imagining that they were soldiers fighting against the Shah or sharing sticky sohan toffee from the market. Finally, his friend returned to his home in the Houthi tribal lands of Yemen, but they had remained in contact, exchanging letters, maintaining their bond and strengthening their friendship.

When the Shah fell to the Islamic Revolution, seventeen-year-old Shahlai joined the military and was selected for the Revolutionary Guard. He rose quickly through the ranks, leading a division in the Iran–Iraq War, and became the youngest general in the Iranian Army at the age of forty-two. Hussein had been among the first to congratulate him. His Yemeni friend was also furthering his own career, rising up to become a member of parliament for the al-Haqq party, making a name for himself back in Yemen, representing the Houthi people.

But when the Yemeni president Saleh turned against the al-Haqq party, Hussein fled Yemen and returned to Qom. The two friends were united again. Shahlai persuaded his friend to embrace the Shi'ite faith and bring his followers under the teachings of the Supreme Leader, Ayatollah Khamenei. Hussein gradually turned his back on the primitive readings of the Koran favoured by his Zaydi tribesmen and began to accept the true sanctity of Shi'ism represented by the Twelve Imams. In return, Khamenei gave Shahlai his blessing to set up a secret mission in support of Hussein and his plan to return to Yemen and overthrow President Saleh. Just as they had when they were boys playing by the river, the two men set about overthrowing another despotic ruler, only this time in Yemen and not Iran.

As the motorcycle continued to make its way along the road north of the city, Shahlai saw how well the roads of Sana'a had been repaired since the last Saudi bombing campaign. He saw too how the market stalls were again brimming with fresh produce. Sin and ruin had been replaced by order, law and the word of God under the rules of the Sharia. Compared to the bad old days when the city was in the hands of the dysfunctional Saleh and his corrupt Yemeni government, it was night and day.

The only downside of the Houthi success was the return of the Saudi jets, dropping bombs and lighting up the night sky. People in the city had become frightened to turn on their lights after sundown for fear of the Saudi pilots flying above. Shahlai was sickened by the Saudis, who considered everything, even the hospitals, to be targets for their bombs.

The bike continued north, passing the monument where there had once been a funeral home. Two years before, Saudi planes had bombed the city and specifically targeted the funeral of a Houthi official where one thousand men, women and children were gathered to mourn. The first bomb had flattened the building, killing some instantly and sending others running for their lives. The second bomb landed as rescue teams came to the assistance of the wounded. People were set on fire, many burned alive, many of them children, their bodies exploded, their limbs strewn all over the site. Shahlai had seen the destruction with his own eyes.

In total over one hundred and fifty people died that day and another five hundred were wounded. Soon after the attack, diggers clearing the site looking for more survivors discovered in the wreckage a bomb shard bearing the identification number of an American company: Southerlin Webber.

Finally, the bike stopped and Shahlai got off, waving to the driver before he tore off back down the hill. He took another gulp of water and watched an old woman carefully reviewing the produce at a fruit stall, meticulously investigating the oranges on display, ensuring that what she could afford was as fresh and ripe as possible. He idly wondered whether she had lost sons or a husband in the fighting for Yemeni freedom. He praised the women who had married a mujahid, it was an honour for any woman to have lost a husband in battle just as Umm Salama, the wife of the Prophet, was previously married to Abu Salama who had died as a shaheed. Shahlai spat on the ground and cursed the American devils who had made the bombs that killed women and children and the Saudi dogs who dropped them. He vowed that one day soon, he would ensure that they reaped what they sowed.

Officially, his work in Yemen was done without his own government's knowledge. Tehran's line was clear – Iran must always be able to reject foreign claims that it was supporting the Houthi rebellion and stress the need to preserve Yemen's integrity. However, the truth was that Iran regarded Yemen as part of its front line, standing side by side with the Houthis just as they did with their brothers in Gaza and Lebanon. Iran must defend the Houthis just as they had the

Palestinians because their new leader, Hussein's brother, had followed the same path as the Imam Khamenei and Iran's Shi'ite revolution.

Across the street from the stall was the gate to the Houthi military compound. As Shahlai approached, it swung open and he passed into the courtyard beyond the walls. Thinking about the dead made him think of his friend. He still felt the pain that had cut through him when he heard the news of his assassination, the anger that had coursed through his veins. He remembered the solemn vow he had made to Hussein's younger brother, Abdul Malik, that he would fight by his side until vengeance was done and the lands of Yemen, from Thamud to Al Hudaydah, were under the control of the Houthi people and the true Shi'ite faith. He rushed past the anti-aircraft guns that were trained on the sky above and knocked at the door to the building inside. It swung open and standing behind it he saw Faisal Ahadi, a junior Revolutionary Guard officer, and his most loyal aide. He stepped inside as Faisal bolted the door behind him.

'Fucking British,' Shahlai said as the young officer followed him inside.

'Praise Allah that we found out with enough time to warn you, General,' said Faisal.

'Your source?' Shahlai asked, rushing down the hall towards the rear of the building.

'Chatter online,' Faisal explained. 'We picked it up when they brought in the CIA.'

Shahlai paused to consider this intel. 'We must share this with Tehran.'

'Everything is ready, General,' said Faisal, trying to remain calm for the good of his boss and their mission.

Shahlai gave Faisal a respectful tilt of the head to acknowledge the young soldier's good work. He'd had his doubts about the boy when he had first come to his attention, but since he had brought him to work with him in Yemen, he had proven himself to be an asset, not least because of his skills with computers. He'd done an impressive job to set up the unit with what appeared to Shahlai's old eyes as state-of-the-art equipment.

The communications room that Faisal had assembled was indeed extremely well equipped. A single bank of LED screens lined one wall, showing the output from over fifty cameras placed strategically around the city. In the centre of the room, a bank of computer monitors glowed, illuminating the faces of a dozen young men analysing the intel that was being continually fed to them from the Ministry of Intelligence in Tehran. They had spared no expense on the Yemen operation, investing heavily in intelligence gathering. From this HQ in the north of Sana'a, Shahlai could keep a close eye on everything that was going on in the country.

Faisal motioned to his boss that a screen had been set up for him. He entered the password as the general sat down.

'It's a secure, encrypted line via satellite to Tehran and Al Hudaydah,' he said, stepping back to allow Shahlai access to the terminal.

Shahlai was relieved to see the two faces that appeared on the screen in front of him. The first was Abdul al-Houthi, the leader of the movement and brother of his friend Hussein, patching in from the Al Hudaydah port to the west of the country. The second was Mahmoud Sadra, a hard-line cleric and minister of intelligence in the Iranian government. Having both anticipated that the hostage execution video would be posted on the internet that morning, they looked eager to be brought up to speed on the latest developments.

The interruption by the British had been an unexpected inconvenience but not catastrophic. Shahlai's initial assessment was that a live online execution would send the world a message and put the Houthi's rightful claim to power in Yemen on the international stage. Now, even though he felt a vengeful sense of resentment at the intrusion they had suffered, he reassured himself that there was a certain balance to executing the British man instead. He was relieved that he had ordered the British priest to be moved, otherwise they would have lost two valuable hostages that morning.

'Brothers,' he began, 'today we were sent a test.'

'Americans?' Abdul Malik was angry. He should have been front page news around the world and the Houthi name should have been ringing out on CNN and the BBC.

'British SAS and CIA,' Shahlai corrected him.

'And the priest?' Mahmoud Sadra was a man of few words but had the ear of the Supreme Leader. Shahlai would never accept that Sadra was his superior but he was cautious enough of the cleric's influence in Tehran to keep him onside.

'I relocated him this morning, brother.'

'So we move on to the second option,' said Sadra, more as instruction than suggestion.

'Agreed.' Abdul wasn't going to argue with Tehran, and in any case, executing the British priest had always been his favoured option.

'If I may make one suggestion, brothers?' Shahlai could barely contain the glint in his eye. 'The British knew of our intentions today. We should assume that they will know again.'

'We can delay no longer!' Abdul pounded the table with his fist. It was a frustration to Shahlai that the younger brother lacked his elder sibling's guile.

'Of course, brother,' Shahlai bowed his head in deference. Despite his feelings, Shahlai knew Abdul was the rightful chosen one to lead the Yemeni people. He deserved respect. 'I only ask that you allow me to prepare for every eventuality.'

Sadra nodded. He realised what Shahlai was driving at. There were spies at work but sometimes a spy could be put to good use. 'Very well,' he said. 'Continue, General Shahlai. We will talk when it is done, insh'allah.'

Both screens went dark. Shahlai knew what he had to do but there was little time to prepare everything. The British would be working hard to find Eli Drake's new location.

EIGHT

Sana'a, Yemen

Kilo opened his mouth just wide enough to show off his forty-two razor-sharp teeth, saliva drooling out of his mouth, a deep, guttural snarl rising up from the back of his throat, finally exploding in a demented roar. He lurched forward, violently pulling against his chain, craning his neck almost out of its socket and snapping down hard with his jaws in his best efforts to sink them into the flesh of Ibrahim Manar's face.

Manar recoiled in abject fear, wrenching against the plasticuffs that bound his wrists and ankles, contorting his naked and bruised body in vain and failing miserably to put any more distance between himself and the terrifying Belgian Shepherd.

Matt Mason watched it all from a screen in the Operations room. He had to hand it to the big Jock from Human Intelligence and his devil dog. The Scot was the nastiest bastard Mason had ever encountered; never once saw him hesitate to push a man to absolute breaking point in his search for the truth. Mason had hated every second of the interrogation phase of SAS Selection and he almost pitied the poor fucker who was now going through it all for real. Almost.

Craig Bell had already done a great first stage shock-of-capture interview back at the compound, but still all the Arab lad had confirmed was his name, rank and some small details on where he came from. Crucially, he was keeping tight-lipped about members of his network and the where-abouts of Eli Drake. Mason was going to get that information from him though, along with where his boss, General Ruak Shahlai, had disappeared to.

Hopkins came into the room looking like he'd just squeezed out a painful turd. 'Well that went down like a cup of cold sick,' he said, slumping into the seat next to Mason.

The CIA woman had been pushing for access to Manar's interrogation, which was not only totally against protocol, but also at odds with Mason's personal feelings about her. She was a live wire and right now he didn't trust her. He certainly didn't want her anywhere near his hostage, at least not until he'd finished working him. He'd sent Hopkins to give her the bad news.

'She'll have him in good time,' Mason said, grimacing as he watched Kilo take another snap at Manar, this time al-most taking the boy's bollocks off.

The protocols gave them only two hours with a hostage from the second the helicopter touched down until they had to hand him over to the Yanks for processing. 'Right,' Mason said, standing up and taking a last gulp of shitty Yemeni tea. 'Showtime!'

Despite the searing heat inside of the portakabin, Manar's body was trembling all over. Dogs were the most despicable animal in Islam, other than swine, so the humiliation he felt was nearly as great as the fear that the filthy beast was going to bite him. However, he also knew that both paled into insignificance with what his comrades would do to him on the outside if he ever talked to the infidels.

Everybody knew how betrayal ended under the rule of Abdul Malik, how the Houthi leader publicly punished those who betrayed him in ways that would make being eaten by a dog feel like a merciful death. Betrayal under the Houthi code was apostasy, punishable by flogging and death, and Manar had witnessed it first-hand. Many times he had stood among the crowds in Tahrir Square, cheering and shouting abuse while the guilty were whipped until the skin on their backs was torn apart like mincemeat. The people jeered while the accused pleaded for mercy and crowed when they were laid face down and shot through the back of the head. Many had filmed the brutality on their phones while the bloodied corpses were strung up from a crane for all to see, left for the vultures to pick at for days thereafter. He did not want that for his fate, much less for his mother and sister to ever be in the crowd watching it; much better to die a martyr than an apostate.

The door opened and he saw a pair of size-ten boots step inside. He recognised the British man's voice acknowledging the dog handler. It was the man who had brutally used him as a human shield to smash in the door of the compound. Manar felt a sense of dread, he'd endured the dog attack but he knew that he would have to strengthen his resolve in the face of what was coming next. He reminded himself that he had Allah on his side and the word of the Prophet, peace be upon him, in his heart. He would smash any kuffar who sought to beat him and his people.

Mason lifted his boot and slammed it into Manar's chest, knocking the wind out of him and sending him crashing down on to his knees. He grabbed the boy's head by the hair and thrust it towards Kilo, only pulling it back again at the last second before the dog took off his nose. The animal was now incandescent, barking at full throttle, desperately trying to free himself from his chain to rip Manar apart. Mason lifted Manar up on to the lone plastic chair in the room and took a good look at the Houthi lad. From the look in his eyes, Mason could tell that he was rattled but not entirely broken. The kid had something left in him. That was fine. He could work with that.

'Where is Eli Drake?' he asked in English, holding a photo of the Christian priest in front of Manar's eyes, letting Saladin, the huge Yemeni translator, convert his question into Arabic. He'd chosen to use Saladin for this part of questioning for a couple of reasons. First, the bloke was massive, a source of intimidation all to himself, and second, he'd placed Adara and another female translator in the next-door portakabin with clear instructions to wait for his signal.

Saladin translated the question into Sanaani Arabic, creating an opportunity for the boy to catch his breath and answer in his own tongue. Mason had to assume that Manar spoke no English, even though, from experience, he knew that most of them usually did.

'We will conquer you, break your crosses, and enslave your women,' Manar said with a barbed defiance that surprised even himself. He'd learned these words from a video he'd seen on YouTube and liked to say them to his opponents on bubji. It felt so much more satisfying to say them to the British man face to face.

Mason punched him so hard that he fell off the chair again and the dog launched another attack, but Manar, emboldened by his own defiance, felt less scared than he had done before. If anything, he felt numb. He smiled as he realised that he had moved to a higher state where pain and fear were beginning to fade away. Mason recognised it too. It was time for Plan B.

Mason took out his phone and said in clear Arabic, 'Strip the women.'

Suddenly, from somewhere outside the walls of the portakabin, the room was filled with the muffled sound of women screaming. The words were indistinguishable but the fear and distress in their cries were unmistakable. Whoever was making that noise was having a fucking awful time.

'You recognise them?' Mason asked the boy.

Manar was momentarily confused by the British man now addressing him in his own tongue but he was also desperately trying to make out what the cries from outside were. They were Sana'a women for sure, make no mistake, but their screams were too distraught, too hysterical for him to understand exactly what they were pleading for.

Mason crouched down close to him. 'That's your mother and your sister.' He nodded with a devilish smile as he said it, satisfied by the visible distress that was now showing on the boy's face. 'The infidel next door, my soldier, is stripping them naked, just like you. Next, he will set the dog on them too. Is that what you want?'

The truth was that the screams from next door were being made by Adara and the other female Yemeni translator, but Manar couldn't possibly know that. There was no way the British SAS would ever abduct and torture innocent civilians, no matter how guilty their relatives were. The British Army held themselves to a higher standard than the terrorists they fought. Manar's mother and sister were safe and sound in their own home on the other side of the city. But Manar didn't know that. All he knew was that the screams from the next room grew even louder and in them he began to hear familiar voices. He started to hear the cries as those of his mother and his sister, pleading for mercy, wailing for release.

Manar felt a rage rise up in him. This British bastard had taken his mother and his sister and now they were suffering the most shameful thing a Yemeni woman could ever endure. He couldn't bear to think of them naked, standing before a man, an infidel man no less. It was no wonder they were screaming. The shame would be more than his mother could take.

'No. No,' Manar implored Mason. 'Stop. They have done nothing.'

'Where is Eli Drake?' Mason repeated.

'They moved him. Please stop,' he said, now speaking English. Mason could see the change in his eyes. Manar's look of defiance had melted away to weakness and Mason wasted no time in exploiting it.

'They? Shahlai?'

Again the screaming raised up a notch until it was all that Manar could hear. His poor sister, sixteen years old, still a virgin, being ruined by those British pigs. He could stand it no more.

'Yes. Shahlai moved him to Al Hudaydah, a house behind the Al Aswady mosque. I will show you everything. Or kill me. But please make your man stop hurting my family.'

NINE

Sana'a, Yemen

Scooter Williams sat in the briefing room, nibbling on the sandwich that he'd been given and eyeing the cup of milky tea next to it with suspicion. After he'd cleaned himself up, the medic had told him to eat and drink slowly on account of the risk his stomach could explode. It had been nearly three weeks since he'd last eaten something that could be described as a meal. The subsistence rations of beans and rice that his captors had given him had caused his stomach to shrink to the size of an orange.

Two months before he'd been captured, he'd realised that the news cycle was finally moving on from the global pandemic and falling into the more familiar pattern of following the next US presidential election. That was one circus ride he didn't want to get back on, so instead he'd made a best guess as to where the heat would land on the new administration, whichever side won. Past experience suggested that rogue Arab states left to their own devices became breeding grounds for extremists; Iraq, Syria and Libya were prime examples. He figured Yemen would likely be next. That was when he started to develop an interest in the Houthi story.

He began by making contact with an Arab kid he'd seen posting some arty photos on Instagram with the hashtag #Sana'a. The kid's posts were written in pretty decent English and a little flattery got you a long way with bored youngsters in Third World countries desperate for a little validation. The kid had invited him to join a chat room where his friends hung out, discussing video games, English soccer teams and the usual small-talk bullshit that you'd expect from teens.

At first, when he'd asked if they'd seen many Westerners around Sana'a town, they'd laughed but they'd been interested when he said that he wanted to come and see the city for himself. One of the kids suggested that he could introduce him to an uncle who lived in Dubai and often came back and forth to Sana'a on business. When he'd followed up on the lead, the uncle checked out and had offered him a deal – he'd help Williams get to Sana'a for two thousand dollars. After a bit of creative pitching to his editor, where he may or may not have promised an exclusive interview with Abdul Malik al-Houthi himself, he eventually got the green light to go. The only problem was that he hadn't yet been in contact with the Houthi leader. He figured that he'd work that part out when he had boots on the ground.

Scooter Williams landed in Dubai a week after making contact, to meet a man he still knew only as Hassan and who claimed to have a shipment of cement due to leave Mirbat in Oman three days later, bound for Sana'a. Hassan's plan was that his driver would smuggle Williams over the border in the cab of the cement truck and drive him there.

He flew from Dubai to Mirbat the following evening and, following the itinerary set by Hassan, rendezvoused with the lorry driver and crossed the Yemeni border.

The roads across Yemen were better than he'd expected, long empty tracks of desert allowed them to make good time and they easily passed through the few government-run check-points they came across in the east of the country by hiding Williams in the storage compartment under the driver's bed. He'd started getting used to the routine of hiding and being pulled over until finally, fifty miles east of Sana'a, on the road outside of Ma'rib, they were pulled over by a group of Houthi rebels, who'd discovered him immediately. They dragged him from the lorry, bagged him and threw him into the trunk of an SUV. Everything had basically gone to pieces from there.

The door to the briefing room opened and Williams was disappointed to see the red-haired woman from the compound again. This time she was carrying a file.

'I told everything I know to the British guy already,' he sighed.

'I'm Agent Redford with the CIA,' she said, sitting down across from him. She glanced at the debrief notes Hopkins had made, already marked with inconsistencies and omissions she had spotted.

'Do we have to do this now? I've kinda had a rough few days.'

'Buddy, you were fifteen minutes from being decapitated live on YouTube. A team of brave men put their lives on the line to rescue you. One of whom took a bullet today. So yes, you need to do this now.' He bristled at her tone, but the stone-cold bitch just ignored him, returning her attention to the file. 'You say you felt the guys that ambushed you knew you were coming?'

'Yeah, it was a total set-up for sure.' For a guy who had just wandered into a war zone on the say-so of a kid he met on Instagram, Williams still conveyed the air of a cocksure, privileged white boy who thought he was the smartest guy in the room.

'Was this man one of them?' She slid Shahlai's picture across the table. The same picture she'd shown him when he'd been handcuffed to a bed and crying like a baby.

'No,' he said. 'He arrived today.'

'Are you sure? What else can you remember about him? Distinguishing marks or features? Anything you might have heard?'

'Like I said, I already—'

'This is important.' Redford's tone went up a notch. She was starting to really piss him off. What he didn't realise was that if he didn't start playing ball soon then things were going to get really ugly.

During her interrogation training, Redford had been given access to Al-Qaeda and ISIS prisoners at so-called 'black sites'. She'd been taught how to extract information from resistant individuals using torture, physical and psychological, if it was required. She wasn't in the mood to fool around and the way she looked at Williams was deliberate. It said, 'I'll waterboard your ass if I need to.'

'He was missing a thumb.' Williams took another bite of his sandwich. Fucking tuna. He hated tuna. He put it down again. 'That weird enough for you?'

Shahlai's missing digit from the US drone attack last year was not public knowledge nor had it appeared in any media. The fact that he knew about it was the proof Redford needed to hear that Williams must have seen the Iranian with his own eyes.

'Where did you see that?'

'In the room. He got a warning call right before you guys showed up and he sort of held the phone funny.' Williams mimed the action of holding a phone with four fingers. He was struggling to recall more details. This was hurting his brain. Was this what they meant by PTSD? He made a note to pitch his editor a piece about PTSD in hostages. First person. Put himself at the heart of the story. Maybe he could still come out of this a hero.

'What do you mean, "warning call"?'

'That's what it felt like. He answered his cell, then a minute later the shooting started and everyone in there started to freak. Except him. He was just gone. Out of there. Like he already knew.'

Immediately, the briefing room door opened, and Peter Hopkins appeared. 'We need to have a word,' he said, holding the door open for Redford to pass by him into the main Ops room.

While Redford and Hopkins talked in hushed voices, Scooter Williams watched through the doorway. He may have been unable to make out what they were saying, but he was taking a keen interest in everything that he could see happening on the screens behind them.

TEN

Army HQ, Marlborough Lines, Hampshire

Major General Ronald Llewelyn Giles Blandford put down the phone to Dominic Strous MP after what had been one of the most humiliating dressings down that the eighteenth Baron of Berkeley had ever received during forty years of service to Queen and country. The snivelling little turd from the MoD had shown the temerity to not only hold him personally responsible for the failed hostage capture in Yemen, but to add insult to injury suggested that his position as Director Special Forces, as well as his long-promised retirement job as Gold Stick-in-Waiting to Her Majesty, were now somehow in jeopardy. The quid pro quo of it all was that if he didn't provide the head of the Iranian general Shahlai on a silver platter by the following morning, then the government might take the view that both Regiment and Monarch would be better served under the protection of someone else.

The general stood up from behind his desk, placed his hands behind his back and paced the room, a drill that had served him well over the years when he had needed to think. Despite pushing sixty, he was still very trim, his hair greased back in the traditional military short back and sides, although perhaps a slight hint of grey was showing at the edges. He puffed out his ruddy cheeks as he fixed on what he had to do next.

Ordinarily, Blandford would have picked the phone straight back up and called on the old school tie to go around to Strous and show the little bed-wetter just how the world actually worked. But the sad truth of the matter was that since the new PM had taken over, senior cabinet was made up of a rag-tag bunch of girls and grammar-school boys. Nothing could be done there. He sighed again at the bleak future the country faced under this nouveau status quo before he called his secretary and requested that she got whoever was running the Yemen op on a secure line immediately.

It was time for Blandford to go on the war-path, especially since he had personally ensured that the intel on Shahlai that Strous had passed on had worked its way down the chain of command into the hands of the Sana'a OC. What should have been a routine kill or capture task had somehow gone south enough to let the Iranian escape. What made everything worse was that they hadn't even come back with the right bloody hostage. Maybe with the British pastor in hand, Blandford could have appeased Strous and bought himself some time, but when they reported back with an American of all things, that option had been kicked firmly into touch.

The light on his phone began blinking. He pushed the intercom to hear his secretary confirm that Captain Peter

Hopkins was on the line in Yemen. Hopkins? He scanned his memory banks but came up blank. He didn't know him. He sat down in front of his screen and began the call.

Hopkins appeared, standing in front of the main monitor in the Ops room. This was the first time that he'd spoken to The Director and he wasn't happy with the circumstances in which it was happening. Also on the call were the OC in Hereford and the British Military Attaché in Aden. Hopkins knew he was about to publicly bear the brunt for the failed task even though the truth was nothing he could have said or done would have made any difference to the outcome. When you had a man like Matt Mason as your staff sergeant then you were very much along for the ride.

He looked momentarily distracted. Perhaps it was the sight of a manicured English lawn he could see behind the general, which made him realise just how much he missed England, missed the green of the place, even the rain that made it that way. Perhaps he was just surprised that the general, a notorious ball-breaker, seemed so relaxed.

'Peter,' Blandford began, 'sounds like you've had one or two operational snags out there.'

'Yes, sir.' Hopkins had rehearsed exactly how he was going to play the situation. State the facts, avoid analysis, allow his boss to work it out for himself. Nobody in the Regiment liked a whinger, but if he presented the facts the right way then it would be obvious that he hadn't been to blame for the outcome of the rescue. He just had to tell it in such a way as to make clear that while he felt responsible, he had in fact not been responsible. Mason was the one who had led the task and it was Mason's plan that they had followed. If someone had to eat shit for all this, then it should really be him. But before Peter Hopkins said another word, the door of the Ops room swung open and in walked Matt Mason.

Mason walked directly to Hopkins' side and peered at the faces on the screen. 'Ronnie,' he said with an airy familiarity.

'Bloody hell,' said the general. 'Matt Maddog Mason. I didn't know you were out there, Mace. What the devil is going on?'

Hopkins' face fell. Of course Mason and Blandford knew each other. They were practically the two longest serving men in the Regiment. Different career paths, but they'd probably served together in Iraq. Hopkins gave Mason a resigned look, preparing for the worst, accepting of whatever flack was now coming his way.

'All on me, Ronnie,' Mason said. 'It was my call not to reinforce all exits. I hold my hand up. This is on me. I'll fix it.'

'For heaven's sake, Mace. I'm getting it deep in the arse from London over this.'

'Ronnie, we have new intel with a possible location and confirmation that Drake was alive as recently as this morning.'

'Well that's something, I suppose.'

'I propose we waste no time. But we can't go noisy on this one, Ronnie.'

'Why's that?'

Mason sucked the air in through his teeth. 'It's right in the UN ceasefire zone in Al Hudaydah. It's got to be hush.'

'Oh Goddammit.' The general knew immediately how that would play with the MoD. Walking into an internationally agreed humanitarian ceasefire zone risked creating a major international incident. But in the circumstances, there wasn't much else he could do.

'Fine. Go. And Mace?'

'Yes, Ron?'

'Don't fuck up again. There's a good chap.'

ELEVEN

Red Sea, West of Al Hudaydah

Mason pulled up the zip of his SSOV polypropylene suit. The temperature inside of the C–130 had dropped from 35°C at sea level to a chilly -25°C at their current altitude of 25,000 feet, and the Saudi Army fatigues that he was wearing underneath were inadequate protection from that kind of cold. The last thing he wanted was to get frostbite. He'd already lost a toe to it back in Afghanistan.

He attached the hose of his oxygen mask and checked that his comms were clear while looking around the plane, nodding to the other boys. He chuckled at the state of Andy Roberts' face, lost in concentration, trying to appear cool in front of the lads. Most of the Regiment boys were recruited from the Paras but the Scouser had come up from the Engineers and he still shat his pants on the technical jumps.

They had dispensed with any kit that could betray their true identity. For this mission they would be carrying the Steyr AUG A3s that the Saudis preferred over the M16. The rest of their kit was mostly British or American, but it was the stuff they sold on and not the newest, first-generation issue that they kept for themselves. Even the food they were carrying was Saudi. It was crucial that anything that could potentially get left behind would look like it was from a Saudi covert special op and not British.

The huge engine of the C-130 growled, the pitch dropping deeper as the pilot slowed its speed, settling into a pace of 130 knots. Any faster than that and the pressure would be too great for their bodies to bear. Mason took it as his cue to take several deep breaths from his oxygen, flushing any remaining nitrogen out of his bloodstream.

The metal door at the rear of the aircraft lowered and he stuck his head outside. He could see the stars in a dark cloudless sky; these were perfect jumping conditions. He stepped steadily towards the edge of the ramp and tumbled forward into the darkness without stopping to think about the process for a second. He'd done thousands of jumps in the Paras before he'd joined the Regiment; jumping was in his DNA and he felt a quiet peace when he was falling that he rarely found at ground level.

He righted his body again and assumed a comfortable horizontal position, arms out in front, head tipped back, so that he could look to his left and right, seeing four green lights that let him know the rest of the lads had fallen into place without incident. For the next two minutes, his mind drifted to Hereford and he thought about his kids tucked up in bed. He especially missed his eldest, Joanna, who was beginning her exams next week. If she did all right, then she'd hopefully get a place at naval college. The girl loved boats; she could end up in the Marines, in which case, he chuckled to himself, he'd have to disown her. His youngest, Sam, was a good kid too. A gentle boy, one year younger than his sister to the day, Sam was one of those lucky kids who seemed to breeze through life. He'd be all right, whatever he did. Mason felt a sadness that in no time at all they'd both be out in the world, living their own lives, making their own choices, and then he and Kerry would be what exactly? Friends? Companions growing old together? That just didn't seem likely.

The men spaced out as they reached terminal velocity and the ground raced towards them at 120 mph, looming large until they reached an altitude of 3,000 feet where they deployed their SOV-3 parachutes. The combination of late deployment, rapid downward speed, minimal forward airspeed and the fact they were carrying only small amounts of metal meant they would be invisible to radar in the area. It also reduced the time that the parachute would be visible to anyone on the ground. HALO – high altitude, low opening – was the gold standard of stealthy insertion.

They glided to the LZ and splashed silently into the dark waters of the Red Sea, which felt to Mason like a warm bath. He checked the stats on his watch, noting that the air was still 25°C even at 8 p.m. He listened keenly in the darkness, trying to make out the surrounding sounds over the noise of the other men pulling in their chutes and swimming towards him.

Across the water, Mason heard the sound of a deep throaty engine and smelled Diesel fumes before an old junk appeared before them, emerging from the night. The seventy-foot fishing vessel pulled up alongside and a fat Arab man, his face creased like a packet of crisps, his eyes shining bright, dangled over the edge holding a long pole with a hook on one end, ready to scoop them out.

On board the vessel, they collected the jumping equipment and handed it over to a young deck-hand who took it away for disposal. The fat man reappeared and led them down below, into the guts of the boat where he opened a door leading to a small storage room that stank so strongly of fish that Briggs actually wretched. The fat man pointed to the corner of the room, instructing the British soldiers to move fast and huddle tightly together, while he and his young assistant covered them with old, heavy ropes and fishing nets.

'We will reach Al Hudaydah in seven hours,' was all he said before he shut the door, plunging the room into total darkness.

'Anyone fancy a game of I-spy?' said Andy.

Mason chuckled as he closed his eyes. He prided himself on being able to sleep anywhere. It was a good skill to have. When you were on a task, getting sleep was often a luxury, so to have seven hours uninterrupted in a dark, warm place, albeit one that stank like Birmingham Fish Market, was too good a chance to pass up. He settled in and slept for what felt like the first time in days.

He awoke to the sound of the boat's engine slowing and he heard the door to the room creak open. The silhouette of the fat man appeared, pulling away the ropes and old fish nets again.

'Come!' he said. 'I do not want to wait here.'

The fat man climbed the stairs back to the deck, followed closely by six British soldiers dressed as Saudi soldiers. The sky above them was lighter now, the moon having risen late. There were only three hours before dawn and Mason knew he had to lead his men to a place of safety before the sun appeared. Their chances of discovery increased exponentially in the daylight. The fat man took the rope that tethered the vessel to the port wall from the deck-hand. He wasn't going to tie it up. He didn't intend on staying there that long.

'Thanks for the lift,' Mason said as he stepped off on to the shore.

'Don't thank me, British,' the fat man called out, already pushing the boat off with his foot. 'I do not do this for you. I do this for your money.'

Mason gave him a wry smile before he checked his GPS. They were exactly where they should be, three kilometres north of the city of Al Hudaydah, the largest port in Yemen. The city had seen the worst of the fighting in 2018 and taken heavy civilian casualties from the Saudi bombing raids. After a couple of failed attempts, the UN had finally got everyone to agree a ceasefire on the proviso that the troops withdrew and the port was allowed to resume as a gateway for humanitarian aid. But according to Mason's intel, the Houthis were flagrantly breaking that arrangement by stashing Eli Drake in a fortified compound within the ceasefire zone.

By Mason's calculation, they had just enough time to cover the ground necessary to get to a safe spot close by the Houthi compound, where they could sit out the day-light and run obs on the location. They would launch the raid when it got dark again later that evening. All being well, they could use the evening prayer as a cover to get in, find Drake and get out again. With Drake safely returned, pouring his heart out in front of the TV cameras, the world wouldn't care about the specifics of where he had been held beyond 'somewhere in Yemen'. It wasn't like the Houthis were going to own up to it.

The squad moved slowly through the empty streets, tak-ing extra precautions at every corner, observing, waiting, listening, smelling, ensuring that they considered all angles and outcomes before they moved on. It was painful work but vital that nobody saw them. Every footprint was rubbed out behind them, every time one of them kneeled or sat, the imprint they left behind had to be covered again. They touched nothing that didn't absolutely have to be touched, moving like ghosts through the darkness.

And Hudaydah was pretty much a ghost town at 3 a.m. The only sign of life was the constant sound of dogs. One dog would kick it off and within minutes it seemed like every other dog in the city was barking too. They'd calm down for a split second until another dog snapped and kicked it all off again. Mason had often wondered what was the point of a guard dog that never stopped barking.

At least the state the city was in made things easier for them. The bombing had created ruins from many of the buildings and they used them for cover, hiding in among the rubble, using blown-out windows as look-out points.

Mason was surprised that so much of the destruction included civilian homes. One building looked as though it had once been a hospital. The Saudis evidently hadn't spared the sick during their relentless assault on Al Hudaydah.

By 5 a.m. they were within sight of the Houthi compound to where Ibrahim Manar had told them Eli Drake had been moved. The satellite imagery had suggested they could use a blown-out house eighty metres north for cover and hide out there until the day had passed. It gave them twenty-five minutes to cover two hundred metres before the local muezzin started limbering up for another morning call and the streets came back to life for the day.

Mason took out his map, silently directing everyone where they were supposed to go. He and Andy would move along the far side of the street, staying close to the shadows in front of the buildings, while Briggs, Craig and Jack moved along the opposite side in staggered file. They would pass the compound where Drake was being held and enter the bombed-out house, opposite the mosque. Once safely inside, they could find a hiding place where they could lay low and wait out the day. With everyone agreed on what they had to do, Mason gave the sign for them to move.

Andy ran point, scampering along the road that led to the compound, crouched low, ducking under the windows, keeping his body close to the walls. The only light on the street came from the moon overhead but with the shadow cast by the roofs, even Mason could barely make out his shape. The kid from Liverpool was so light of foot that you'd have more chance of hearing a mouse. It was impressive. Mason could see Andy's potential and he made a note to discuss sniper training with him once they returned to Hereford.

When they reached the building immediately before the compound, Mason afforded himself a second to do a quick scout on the location. Tonight, after dark, they would scale the perimeter and extract Drake from the building inside without making a sound. The wall was only eight feet high, just as Manar had described, so Mason was relieved that he had made the call to dispense with climbing gear.

Andy turned to face him, catching just enough moonlight that Mason could see him raise a finger to his lips. He saw Andy's eyes widen, warning him that something was off, but before Mason could react, the lad from Liverpool vanished around the corner into the blackness. Mason crouched low, making himself small, pushing his body hard against the wall. He quietly removed the 9mm Saudi service pistol from its holster, silencer already fitted, clicked off the safety and stopped breathing.

He had been in similar situations a hundred times before, but it still excited him to do it again. He didn't feel fear exactly, never really had. When he'd been a kid and proved himself to be handy in the boxing ring, his uncle saw an opportunity to take him down the gypsy camp outside Bloxwich, where the young boys would fight bare knuckle on the back of a flatbed truck while the men placed bets on them. He might have learned how to box in the ring, but Mason had learned how to fight from the gypsies. They taught him that there wasn't room for fear in any fight you wanted to win.

Mason smelled the cigarette smoke before he heard the steps. The Houthi soldier came walking around the corner, AK-47 hanging limply by his side, cigarette perched on the edge of his bottom lip, for sure thinking about anything other than his own imminent death. He stopped rock still, frozen while his brain struggled to acknowledge that the shadow he saw in front of him could be human. He let the cigarette fall from his lips and fumbled for his rifle, but before his hand had even halfway reached the firearm, Andy Roberts appeared behind him, weapon drawn and placed inches from his skull. Andy pulled the trigger and double-tapped two into the kid's brain, the silencer ensuring that the only sound was that of the two bullet cases hitting the floor a split second after the cigarette. The body jolted and fell forward, right into Mason's outstretched arms. Mace and Andy froze, holding their breath while they scanned up and down the street. Happy that nobody had heard anything, Mace collected the two spent cases from the dust and they carried the latest casualty of Yemen's war across the road into the bombed-out ruins of the house opposite.

TWELVE

Sana'a Old Town, Yemen

A group of old men nattered among themselves, chewing khat and discussing politics, barely noticing the woman who hurriedly made her way past them along the tight winding streets of Sana'a's old town. The dark ochre-coloured mountains that surrounded Sana'a would have blended seamlessly with the town's red-brick towers were it not for their ash-white geometric decorations that shone brightly in the late afternoon sun.

The woman pulled her abaya close around her, keeping her head bowed, careful not to make eye contact with anyone that she passed. In the last couple of years, the Houthi leaders had clamped down harder and harder on women in particular. Their campaign resolutely targeted anything that might lower the barriers between men and women, and they had mercilessly applied pressure wherever they could to stifle joy, laughter and entertainment.

She cast an eye around each corner, looking for the Houthi soldiers who routinely beat women in the street for flouting the rules. Wearing a belt around your abaya would

earn a woman forty lashes. The charge? Creating a silhouette that might distract a man. Women were banned too
from attending cafes and restaurants for fear that they might
frequent with men. All Sana'a's fashion stores and beauty
salons had been forced to close down too; female grooming
was now deemed redundant under the new regime.

But the greatest fear the woman had was that she might
encounter a group of other women who were feared
throughout the town. The Zainabiyat were a paramilitary
women's organisation set up for the express purpose of
policing other women. Their battalion were instantly recognisable, shrouded in black, their faces hidden, their AK-
47s draped across their chests. The Zainabiyat had been
trained by the Iranians to patrol the streets of Sana'a and to
be the eyes and ears of the new Houthi regime. On their
say-so a woman could be taken without charge to Dar
Al Hilal, the new women's prison converted from an old
school on Taiz Street. Many school teachers, activists and
even rebellious teenagers had gone to Dar Al Hilal and
never returned.

When the woman reached the market, she pulled a
light cloth bag from inside of her robe and made her
way along the stalls towards the northeast corner of the
square, browsing the produce on offer and occasionally
buying fresh citrus fruits – oranges, lemons and limes –
with coins drawn from an old leather purse. She kept her
conversations to a minimum, not because she feared her
accent would draw attention to herself (she spoke the
Sana'a dialect like a native) but rather because her green

eyes were too often a talking point among the Yemenis. Where did you get those eyes? Your eyes are very pretty. Are you perhaps descended from the tribes of Zabid? These were questions she heard often. Green eyes were not unheard of in Yemen. Hundreds of years ago white slave girls were popular and had been traded on the human markets of Aden, adding their light-coloured eyes to the gene pool. But still they attracted casual attention and that was definitely not what Agent Redford wanted to do.

She took up a position next to a trader whose oranges were neatly laid out on a sheet on the ground. A crowd of women were gathered around, and Redford did her best to blend in among them. Her eyes were trained on a doorway down a street that led east from the square. The sun had shifted to the west on its path to dusk which gave her the perfect light by which to see.

After around ten minutes, the door opened and Redford saw her target. She moved away from the other women and followed him across the square. His huge size made him easy to spot in the crowd, but years of training prevented her from breaking protocol. She stayed close but not too close to be noticed, following in his wake all the way to the southern edge of the square where he sat down at a low plastic table outside a cafe next to the mosque and ordered a coffee. His enormous size made the small table look ridiculous. Like an adult sitting at a child's tea set. Happy that her target had stopped moving, Redford took up a position out of his line of sight and began rummaging in her bag like an ordinary housewife who was checking she had everything on her shopping list. Only occasionally did she glance up to make sure that Mohammed Saladin was still there.

She had run a full background check on him overnight, liaising with her opposite number in British MI6, who had initially recruited him as a translator. They'd turned up nothing special. Saladin was a regular kind of guy. No kids. Not married. Lived alone with his mother and father in the townhouse she'd just watched him come out of. The Brits had recruited him out of Sana'a University where he'd done well and caught the eye of a professor who was no friend of the Houthi regime.

The truth was that nobody ever fully trusted the translators that they recruited. Saladin, like all translators, was being watched constantly by the Brits and his phone was bugged and tracked. Redford would admit that translators got a rough deal. They were expected to live right in the firing line, within the community that they were secretly betraying, all for two hundred dollars a week and the promise of a UK passport one day. For what? So they could drive an Uber through the rainy streets of London for the rest of their lives? Redford almost pitied the poor guy. Or at least she would have, if she hadn't suspected him of double-crossing them on the Drake raid.

'Move!' She felt a sudden stabbing pain in her lower back and turned around sharply to see two Zainabiyat women standing over her. One of the women poked her again with the end of her rifle, motioning for Redford to keep walking. Redford instinctively felt for the Glock that was holstered underneath her abaya, but she controlled the urge to pull it out. It was enough to know that she had it, even if she didn't need to use it.

'I am not yet finished with my shopping, sister,' she said, and flashed the contents of her shopping bag filled with fruit. 'I must buy some bread.'

'You are finished, now move!' the woman barked, lifting the rifle again to show that it wasn't a topic for discussion.

Redford glanced towards the cafe to check that Saladin had not taken an interest in what was happening. But as she looked, she saw that he had now been joined at the table by another man whose back was to Redford, preventing her from making a positive ID. She'd been trained time and again not to draw attention to herself in a situation like this, not to resist, not to take risks, but she needed to see his face.

She tried to step to the side but again the Zainabiyat woman shoved her with the butt of her rifle. Another group of women who were shopping together noticed the commotion and one shouted out to her, 'Foolish woman. Do you want them to send you to the jail?'

Redford hesitated, standing her ground, breaking more protocols. 'Please sister . . .' she implored, but the Zainabiyat woman was now looking angry.

More women began to gather around, eager to see what the source of the drama was, keen to get involved and offer their opinions. Women in Sana'a did not defy the Zainabiyat ever. To do so was to ask for trouble, and Sana'a's female population had fallen into a collective acceptance of this uncomfortable reality because to do otherwise was to invite disappointment and bitterness to your door. It was too much for most people to even think about without feeling the urge to tear out their own hair, so seeing it happen to another woman was not something anyone enjoyed.

'Go home!' a woman shouted before she gave Redford a shove.

Again the American CIA agent bowed her head. This was becoming distinctly uncomfortable. She touched her service weapon again for comfort.

'Is she deaf?' another woman screamed.

'Throw her in the jail,' came another cry.

The crowd around her grew thicker and the Zainabiyat women struggled to hold them at bay. Redford could see that she was getting swamped from all sides, yet she still craned her neck to look towards the cafe where Saladin sat with the unidentified stranger.

One of the Zainabiyat women lifted her rifle and held it across her chest, using the butt to push the crowd back. The other took a rough hold of Redford's arm, pulling her closer as a stone thrown from the back of the throng clattered into the top of Redford's head, knocking her off balance. She fell to the ground, instinctively reaching for her Glock. The situation had got out of hand and she realised that there wasn't a way to talk herself out of it any more.

She mentally ran through her options. Pulling her firearm could get messy very fast, but allowing the militia women to take her in would create a diplomatic headache that she didn't need. Just then she spotted the cloth shopping bag on the floor next to her. She reached and grabbed it, deliberately tipping it over, sending its contents spilling across the dusty floor. Oranges, lemons and limes scuttled over the dirt, rolling among the sandalled feet of the women around her. Suddenly, she heard a change of tone in their screams as the mood morphed from one of anger to excitement.

She stood up again quickly, aware that the shrouded assailants who would have happily lynched her only moments before were now bent double desperately scrabbling to grab what they could of the free bounty she'd offered. Even the Zainabiyat women seemed to have lost interest in her, wading into the crowd, more concerned with restoring order to the chaos. It was starting to get dark and all women were supposed to be indoors by curfew.

Redford stepped back quietly, creeping away from the mêlée, careful not to draw attention to herself. Seizing her opportunity, she sank anonymously into the crowd and dropped her head. Just another faceless woman in a sea of veils. She pulled her robes around her and made her way out of the group, stopping for just a moment to sneak one final look at the cafe.

She saw that Saladin was on his feet again, his coffee finished, the bill paid. He and the other patron had finished their business and were walking to the street. Saladin bowed his head to say farewell and walked away while the other man turned back towards her. He took in the scene in front of him and frowned, clearly disapproving of the sight of thirty women scrabbling around on their hands and knees minutes before curfew. But Redford was no longer interested in them, instead her eyes were trained on his face. It was the face of the man she knew well. Mohammed Saladin had been having coffee with Faisal Ahadi, an Islamic Revolutionary Guard, a de facto senior member of the Houthi regime and, crucially, Ruak Shahlai's right-hand man.

Redford began to run. If Saladin was passing intel to Shahlai then Mason and his team were in danger. Saladin would have known everything about the new mission to rescue Drake from Al Hudaydah. She needed to get back to the British house fast to warn them because it was already getting dark.

THIRTEEN

Al Hudaydah, Yemen

The corpse was putrefying so quickly that the stench was in danger of giving away their position. The forty-degree heat had rapidly increased the decomposition process so that the purge fluid was leaking out of the lungs. The dark ooze was seeping from the nose and mouth, attracting a swarm of flies jostling with each other for a taste. By tomorrow morning it would be covered in maggots. The heat had catalysed the enzymes inside the body too, so that every few minutes the guts let out a blood-curdling fart that hung in the air with a stink that nobody should ever have to experience. Fuck knows what the guy had eaten before Andy dropped him, but by the smell of it, it wouldn't have done him any good.

Mason's team had spent twelve long hours hiding out in the rubble of the bombed-out two-storey house directly opposite where Eli Drake was being held. Nervous hours spent taking turns on watch, observing the comings and goings inside the compound. They had formulated a decent pattern of life for the men who were guarding the enclosure, noting the timings of their patrols, where the dogs

were and what time they were fed, when the guards prepared food and what time they ate. By the time the sun
began to lower in the sky, Mason was confident that there
were only two guards posted at the main gate to the north
of the main house, one of whom strictly observed prayer.
They had seen nobody else enter or leave, but he guessed
one or two guards might also be stationed inside to keep
an eye on Drake. Now they waited for the call for evening
prayer, when the mosque would be full, the streets empty
and they would have the perfect cover to strike.

Mason's primary fear was that Manar's capture could
provoke a reaction from General Shahlai. The young man's
weakness in the interrogation room would have been entirely predictable to Shahlai. The Iranian general was experienced enough to know which of his men could sustain
pressure and which would crack. Manar had rolled over so
easily that Mace suspected Shahlai would be keen to get on
with Drake's execution as soon as possible.

The one advantage that Mason had this time was that he
knew the layout of the compound and exactly where his
target was being held. He'd decided that the southeastern
corner between the perimeter wall and the mosque offered
them the most secure access. Once they were over the wall,
the house would shield them from the guards on the front
gate, and if they could find a point of access to the house
from the rear then they could grab Drake with minimum
engagement and extract him to safety.

Should anything go wrong or the situation escalate, they
had stationed three helicopters, two Lynxes and a Puma, at

the UN base four miles away. Hereford had fed the UN some bogus excuse about securing a diplomatic visit. They'd swallowed it and granted temporary landing clearance. Not that Mason envisioned needing support. This should be a straight in-and-out job and they would be back at the port with Drake within the hour to RV with the extraction team. Insh'allah.

'Allahu Akbaaaar . . .' The tannoy rang out across the town the second the sun hit the horizon.

There it was again. Mason watched the street below swell with people, rushing to the mosque for evening prayer. The muezzin's words may have been a call to prayer for the faithful, but for the second time in two days, they represented a call to arms for him and his squad. He didn't have to say anything to the guys, they were already packing up their kit, ready to go.

'See ya later, sweetheart,' Andy Roberts whispered, and blew a kiss at the bloated body.

'More your league than the ones you usually go for,' said Pommy.

They moved silently downstairs and through what had been the front door of the house before a Saudi jet plane had taken out its front wall. The street that had been bustling with people only a few minutes before was now eerily silent. Only the donkeys tied up outside of the mosque saw the six shadows scurry over the road and around to the back of the compound. One by one they disappeared up and over the perimeter wall.

Briggs and Pommy, as usual, were first over, immediately scuttling along the rear wall towards their position on the southwestern corner of the house. Briggs paused halfway, noticing a small letterbox window on the ground floor that had been left ajar. He waved to Mason, who nodded to acknowledge that he had seen it. That would be their way in. Mason gave Briggs a thumbs up and he followed after Pommy to the corner of the house, crouching low, weapons drawn, ready to engage anything that may come at them from the west side of the building.

Jack and Craig took matching positions on the opposite corner allowing them to give cover along the east side. Peeking around the corner, Mason could see a single guard at the front gate watching videos on his phone. He figured the second guard must be praying. They had picked the optimal time. He and Andy crept along the south wall until they reached the open window. Mason dropped on to one knee and boosted the younger man up so he could reach the underside of the frame. With Mason taking his weight, the Liverpudlian moved delicately, silently, slowly lifting the windowpane so he could slide his head inside.

'Fuck,' was all he said.

Mason felt the force of the blast like he was being hit by a car. There was no noise at first, simply the feeling of the wall breaking apart, pieces of it smashing him across the face and thumping him in the guts. The sound came afterwards. It was the sound of the air sucking back in towards the house, roaring through his bones like a thunderclap. He tried to hold himself in position, but his body was no competition for the weight of it. As he flew to the ground, rubble cascaded down on top of him and his last conscious thought was that he could taste burnt metal and flesh.

Steve Briggs was the first to react. The blast had also thrown him to the ground, but he quickly picked himself back up and ran along the wall towards the blast site. His ears were ringing, and the sky had taken on a strange purple glow that made him suspect that he'd sustained a concussion. He tried to take in the extent of the damage but the whole back of the house was now missing, replaced by a pile of bricks and a cloud of dust. What he could see, sticking out from the debris, was a human arm. From the thumb, he could see that it was a left arm, detached at the shoulder, inanimate, no longer alive, no longer of use. Still, Briggs' gut told him to pick it up. The Saudi uniform it was wrapped in meant that it had to belong to either Andy or Mace; either way, they were going to need immediate medical assistance. But before Briggs could move, the sound of gunfire stopped him. He looked back to Pommy returning fire along the western wall where a group of Houthis had piled in through the front gate to the compound. They'd been set up. The house had been booby-trapped and the explosion had been the sign for them to attack. He ran back to the corner, slotted in behind Pom, lifted his rifle and began to return fire.

On the opposite corner of the building, Jack was firing rapidly, dropping Houthis left and right. Behind him, Craig Bell remained calm, setting up the radio to call for support. He had reached the same conclusion as Pommy, that they had fallen into a trap and now they had no choice but to withdraw. He got on the radio, screaming over the gunfire all around him.

'All call signs. Priority One. Hot extraction. Now. At Decon Alpha Landing Site. Over.'

Once he had confirmation that the helicopters were deployed, Craig put down the radio and sprinted along the wall of the house. He found what was left of Andy Roberts among the debris. His left arm was missing and his torso was riddled with shrapnel holes. Craig crouched to his knees and lowered his head sideways until his cheek was directly over Andy's mouth, listening for signs of life. He felt a faint breath on his cheek. Andy was alive. The hard bastard was alive.

He saw Briggs climbing over the rubble towards him.

'Where's the others?' he asked.

Before Briggs could answer, there was another loud explosion, and moments later Pommy appeared.

'Go!' he yelled.

Together they lifted Andy and carried him back to where Jack was holding off the remaining Houthis. They lay Andy on the ground and took up positions from which they could return fire at the advancing Houthi soldiers. Meanwhile, Craig got back on the radio.

'All call signs. Man down. Repeat man down. Confirm Landing Site Decon Alpha at grid 3QRF26971873.'

He had barely finished speaking when they heard the sound of helicopters overhead. The two Lynxes were circling around the perimeter. The Houthis had stationed shooters on the rooftops opposite the compound, which the gunners on each side of the choppers began blasting out from their positions. Rebels with their AK-47s were no match for the .50-cal heavy machine guns.

'He's gone into arrest,' Craig called to the others. He worked fast, loosening Andy's body armour, pushing his fingers between his pale lips to clear his airway before he began to blow into his mouth.

'Cover!' bellowed Briggs, throwing himself to the ground as a grenade exploded yards away from them, showering them in yet more rubble and dust.

The gunfire got more intense. There were grossly out-numbered, way too many Houthis for them to hold off any longer. The more they took out, the more that seemed to appear through the gates. The Houthis had decided to throw everything at achieving victory in Hudaydah.

Craig scrambled back to Andy and climbed on top of him, pumping down on to his chest. A rock, thrown from the other side of the wall, struck him in the shoulder and knocked him off balance. Another larger rock followed soon after it and then another. More and more rocks started to rain down on them from behind the wall. People piling out of the mosque and realising what was going on had decided to join the fight, helping in whatever way they could. Cries of 'Death to America, death to the infidels' grew louder and louder.

'This is fucked,' Jack said under his breath before he launched two grenades at where the Houthis had taken up new positions. 'Where's that fucking chopper?'

Suddenly a bullet whistled past his ear. From its trajectory, he realised that it must have been fired from above them, and as he lifted his head, he saw that a shooter had climbed up on to the roof above. The shooter took another pot shot which struck the unconscious Andy in the leg. Pommy took aim and dropped him instantly, dodging to his side to avoid the body as it fell.

Satisfied that the immediate threat had been neutralised, the Lynxes moved aside and the larger Puma advanced on to the landing zone, lowering down until it was directly on top of them. There was no way it was going to land in the middle of a firefight, but there was just enough room between the house and the perimeter wall for it to hover a few feet from the ground.

Jack and Craig launched a blanket of fire in the direction of the Houthis, giving enough cover to Briggs and Pom for them to lift Andy on to the Puma. The medic on board began ripping off the remainder of his clothes to get access to his chest. As he prepared the defibrillator, the two men climbed on and took their turn to cover the position while Jack and Craig climbed on board.

'All on, all on,' Craig shouted over the roar of the blades, seeing that the medic was already shocking Andy, trying desperately to resuscitate him, while Briggs applied a field dressing to the gunshot wound in his leg.

The chopper lifted rapidly into the air, climbing to a height where it would be safe from enemy fire. As it did, an RPG screamed past the open door. The men threw themselves backwards more out of instinct than logic. If the grenade had made contact with its target then they'd have been vaporised.

'Get out of here!' the medic screamed over his comms.

The pilot banked the chopper as the two more powerful Lynxes took up positions again on either flank, the gunners blasting with everything they could muster in all directions. Seconds later they were clear of the imminent danger, out of range of any more RPGs and heading for the safety of the UN base.

The men looked at each other, speechless, shellshocked, covered head to toe in dust and smoke. Even the unflappable Pommy looked a little traumatised. Jack took a cigarette from his pocket and put it into his mouth. As the most experienced of the group, he was the first to regain his composure. But before he could light his fag, he could tell that something was very wrong. He looked around the chopper, unable to believe his eyes, his face a picture of denial and confusion as his brain struggled to accommodate the terrible reality that had hit him.

'Where the fuck is Mace?' he screamed.

Everyone looked around the helicopter for the man who was evidently not there. They looked at each other and then they looked deep into themselves. Every one of them knew in that instant that they had fucked up in the worst possible way. They had made the error that no soldier in any regiment of any army ever wants to make. Their worst nightmare had come true. They had left a man behind and there was nothing they could do about it.

FOURTEEN

The Savoy Hotel, London

Erica Atkins emerged from the ensuite bathroom at the Savoy. Her usual suite, the suite she always requested when she was in town, was the one with floor-to-ceiling views looking west along the Thames to the Houses of Parliament and east to the City. She liked to stay in a hotel that gave you a sense of where you were, and much preferred the Savoy's mix of Edwardian and Art Deco styles to the old-fashioned, stuffy grandeur of the Ritz.

She rubbed her wet hair with a towel as she reached for the remote control and turned up the volume on the television. For the last twenty-four hours now, Al Jazeera had been showing rolling coverage of the British fiasco in Al Hudaydah, and it was showing no sign of letting up. The story had been picked up on all news agencies, but so far the Brits had been officially denying it. Meanwhile, the Russians and Chinese were making the most of the British discomfort, openly furious and indignant at their flagrant disregard for a UN ceasefire. Even the French were revelling in their old foe's troubles, tabling an emergency meeting of the UN Security Council to discuss whether to publicly censure the UK government. The anchors in the Al Jazeera studio were speculating on whether a minister or two might even face the sack.

Erica hadn't anticipated that the British would screw up so royally. Poor Dominic Strous. He had seemed so confident before that General Ruak Shahlai would be in custody or dead by now. Neither of which would have been Erica's preferred option. The old general's antics in Yemen over the last couple of years had kept the Saudis on their toes, which in turn was good for business. The fallout from his death would be too unpredictable. On one hand, it could force the Iranians to retaliate, but on the other, it could hand the new Democratic administration in Washington leverage to bring Tehran to peace talks. Peace was the last thing she wanted. No, it was safer all round to have Shahlai still out there, at least for now.

As Erica sat down on the bed, a figure stirred next to her. With the remote, she slapped the sole of a bare foot that protruded from under the duvet.

'Okay hot stuff,' she said. 'Time for you to go now.'

She returned her focus to the TV, flicking channels until she settled on a familiar face. Sky News was lining up none other than Dominic Strous to answer questions in the studio. She felt a distinct sense of satisfaction at how uncomfortable he looked in contrast to his usually unshakable confidence.

'This should be good,' she said, more to herself than to the young man getting out of bed next to her.

'What was that?' the figure next to her asked with a distinct Australian twang to his accent. He was exactly her type. Six two, mid-twenties, strapping chest and shoulders, washboard abs and massive arms. Had he said he was a rugby player?

'Don't worry, sweetie,' she said, looking back to the screen, 'it's on the side there.'

Without looking, she pointed to the dresser where two white envelopes lay neatly side by side.

'And . . .' she paused, clicking her fingers together over and over as if trying to remember something that she'd forgotten more than once before.

'Simon, Erica, S-I-M-O-N.' The voice came from the ensuite bathroom and belonged to another huge, sculpted Adonis, even more chiselled than the one still getting out of bed. Simon swaggered into the bedroom, wrapped only in a bath towel, smiling with a mouthful of flawless teeth.

'Your envelope is there too, Simon.'

Simon dropped his towel and Erica allowed herself one last admiring look. It had been a fun night. She was rarely disappointed by the service on offer when she was in London. The agency that she liked to use had a steady stream of hard-bodied young men who knew how to fuck. There was really no point in wasting time on a half-soaked tourist you might pick up in the bar. Odds on, he'd have nothing more than a ham-fisted fumble and a semi-hard cock for you. Instead, for the price of a bottle of vintage Krug, you could have two willing and able professionals, who packed up and cleared out the second you were done with them.

'The PM has spoken with Secretary-General Guterres this morning.' Strous was flannelling like a true pro, keeping the

journalist at bay with the kind of assuredness that only comes
from a two-hundred-thousand-dollar education. 'I'm confident that we will find a solution that all parties can sign up to
and then we can get on with what's really important: the vital
humanitarian work that is so desperately needed by the people of Yemen. That is absolutely the right thing to do, and,
I'll remind you, something this government had been proud to
have been at the forefront of since we spearheaded the ceasefire agreement two years ago.'

Erica smiled at Dominic's concealed discomfort. Doing it
for the poor people of Yemen? Who was going to buy that?
She was losing what little respect she had left for this guy.

There was a knock at the door and Simon opened it to
reveal a waiter pushing a trolley laden with breakfast. Erica
waved at him to unload it on the table in front of her – half
a grapefruit, egg-white omelette and black coffee. When he
handed her the cheque, she signed it and added a generous
tip while barely acknowledging her two companions shuffling out of the door. She gave the waiter a wink, quietly
revelling in his confusion as it slowly dawned on him what
he had just witnessed. He turned his trolley around and left
just as Erica's phone rang.

'Gray,' she said breezily. 'Don't you sleep? It must be 3
a.m. in DC.'

Graham Kaplan was the chief executive officer and chairman of the Southerlin board of directors. Ten years ago, he'd
come over to Southerlin after leaving a senior executive
role at General Electric and then worked his way up the
company through the Missions Systems sector. Graham sat

on the board of directors of several other Fortune 500 companies in all sectors of the economy and his contact book
in Washington was impressive. He was also the person who
would fire Erica's ass if the Y-project stumbled.

'Fox News is covering this shit-show,' he said.

That really was news. Fox hadn't shown much interest
in the Middle East since the last drawdown of troops from
Iraq. Yemen wasn't on the American public's radar at all.
Still, it wouldn't hurt to have the so-called hawks in Washington reminded that their ally was still engaged in the war
on terror, while they argued about whether the ex-presi-
dent had cheated on his taxes or not.

'It's all win-win, Gray,' she said as she absentmindedly
moved the omelette around on her plate with the end of
her fork. 'Anything that undermines the ceasefire arrangement plays nicely into our hands.'

'Just so long as it doesn't come back on us, Erica. The
Chinese are waiting in the wings to capitalise on a wrong
move.' Erica knew that Graham was a tight-ass paid to worry about things, but she'd come to live with it over the
years. She knew that, for now, played right, Graham was a
valuable ally. Until, that is, she was ready to take his job.

Graham was right about the Chinese too. They were desperate to get another slice of the Saudi defence budget. Last
year they'd made inroads into the market with the sale of
thirty CH-4 drones, which had annoyed Erica greatly. This
current situation could potentially be a chance for them to
get another slice of that action were it not for the fact that
the mistakes made in the hostage rescue had all been British

ones. As long as the Brits were taking the heat, there was no room for the Chinese to point the blame at US companies.

The main thing was for Erica to be ready. When Shahlai and the Houthis made their next move, she would be there, ready to help the Saudis protect themselves. Southerlin would capitalise on the Saudi demand for more hardware. She was so close to getting them to sign up to the new Y-project contract that she could almost taste the ink on the cheque. And the best part was that none of it would have happened without her.

'This story isn't over for the Brits yet, Gray,' she said cryptically.

'Oh yeah? How much worse does it get?'

'Plenty,' she said, happy that she had Graham's attention and that she could use her secrets to buy kudos with the chairman of the board. 'They're doing their best to deny they were there right now. But that's gonna get a lot harder when the Houthis prove otherwise.'

'They leave something behind?'

'Someone.'

'Oh.' Graham was catching up. 'Fuck.' He sounded genuinely shocked and genuinely impressed.

'Yeah. Get some sleep, Gray. This is gonna run and when it breaks, the ceasefire is toast.'

She hung up and put down the fork, her omelette still untouched. She took another swig of coffee before she resumed drying her hair. The British could be ruthless when they wanted to be, she admired them for that. But to abandon a soldier behind enemy lines was a risky strategy. Especially given what she knew about Matt Mason's current whereabouts.

FIFTEEN

Al Hudaydah, Yemen

The second that Matt Mason regained consciousness, his whole body wretched at an odour so foul that he could taste it in his mouth. His neck spasmed, instinctively trying to turn away from the source, only to find that he couldn't move in any direction. He blinked hard trying to make out where he was, but he could see nothing, not so much as a shadow or a prick of light. A cold panic rose up in his chest as he remembered back to the blast at the Houthi compound and he reasoned that he must have been blinded by it. His heart began to pound as his mind ran through all the things that he would never see again: his children, the sky, the Herefordshire countryside. He fought to control his breathing, forcing himself to fill his lungs with the foul air and hold his breath for a moment. When he released it again, it came out as nothing more than a sad and desperate sigh.

'Ah, he's awake.'

If Mason had felt disorientated before, then the sound of an English voice in the darkness made him feel downright lost. Was he in hospital? He touched his body and realised that he was naked and that the reason he couldn't move was that there were several other naked bodies pressed up against him on all sides. He registered that the smell burning his nose was unmistakably human excrement. No, this wasn't any hospital. Could he be dreaming then? Was this a nightmare from which he could just wake up? He shook his head and squeezed his eyelids together as hard as he could, but when he opened them again he could still see nothing.

He was afraid to speak. Without the security of knowing where he was or who he was with, to speak was to give away something for nothing. It was better to remain silent if you wanted to stay alive, and for the time being, that was Mason's number one priority.

'Hello?' The same voice came again.

This time he heard an innocence in the voice that reassured him somehow. He decided to take a chance. 'Hello?' he replied.

'English?' This time the reply had more of a note of shock about it.

'Yes,' he said. 'Where am I? Why can't I see?'

'Do not be afraid, none of us in this place can see. Only by the light of Jesus Christ.' Mason felt a hand touch him on the knee. 'My name is Eli.'

'Oh fuck,' Mason sighed. Eli Drake. The very same man that he had been assigned to rescue was now his new cellmate.

Over the days that followed, Mason began to take stock of the place in which he was being detained. He had to hand it to the Houthis, this was one of the worst places he had ever encountered.

The men referred to the pitch black cell as the 'pressure cooker'. It was a room in a basement measuring ten feet by six that held twelve men, including Matt Mason and Eli Drake, completely enclosed with no natural light, no artificial light, no running water and no toilet. The cell had not so much as a nail hole to let in fresh air and the temperature was well over 40°C. The sun outside could rise and set but the men inside of the pressure cooker would never know it.

The first task Mason set himself was to work his fingers along every inch of the pressure cooker's walls, feeling for a way in or out, any vulnerability, anything that he could use. But he found nothing. The room had no vents, no windows, no drains. The door was the only way in and out and it opened inwards, giving him little chance of forcing it.

Eli explained to him that one corner of the room was designated 'the toilet' but it was simply the place where the men deposited their effluence into plastic bags. Eli said that the guards came irregularly, sometimes to take away the waste, sometimes to deposit food, sometimes to drag a man away or to deliver a new one.

'We know that those who leave us do not go home,' said Eli gravely, 'but we pray that they go to a better place.'

It was surprising to Mason that Eli seemed so accepting of his situation. It was as though he had merely extended the work of his mission to the new congregation of the pressure cooker. Eli knew very little Arabic, barely enough to make himself understood, but he was relishing the challenge that he believed God had set him.

Mason began to assess the men in the cell, wondering which of them could be relied on in a fight. He thought that maybe if he could put together enough able-bodied guys, they could be organised to launch a counterstrike to overcome the guards.

The youngest of his cellmates was Akili, whose fingernails had been removed by his captors before they had crucified him. Akili explained to Mason that he was accused of stealing from the warehouse at the port where he worked. He swore that he was innocent, but the guards had interrogated him for hours while he hung upside down from a cross. He said that they had made him explain every detail of his working day, over and over, until he had lost the strength to speak another word. That was when he was thrown inside the pressure cooker. Akili guided Mason's hands through the darkness to show him where the metal nails still stuck out from his legs and feet. They were so swollen that Mason realised the man had little chance of survival without emergency amputation.

Another of his cellmates, Assad, told Mason how he too had been hung upside down and repeatedly electrocuted. 'They accused me of pledging allegiance to ISIS and took away my boat,' he said. 'I am a poor fisherman, what do I know of ISIS?' Assad's voice was barely a whisper in the dark. 'They kept me hanging from a rope tied to my legs. The soldiers beat me with a whip and shocked me with a wire. When I asked for food, they brought me water filled with salt.'

'Yes, best not drink the water because they sometimes put salt in it,' said Eli. 'I've been so thirsty a couple of times, I've had to drink my own urine.'

Mason realised that there wasn't a single man in there that he could rely on to fight. They were all simple men, fishermen from the port town of Midi, which the Houthis had lost to the Saudis in recent fighting. He put aside the notion of leading an escape and decided instead to focus simply on staying alive. The boys back at HQ would be looking for him by now and before too long they would find the pressure cooker. He began to spit on the floor and piss away from where the other men pissed so as to create DNA evidence that he had been there.

Meanwhile Eli prayed constantly, conducting prayer sessions in English and sermonising in pidgin Arabic. The other men were too weak to object even though they quietly cursed and mocked him under their breath. The Christian continued undeterred, even though Mason was pretty sure he got the general gist of what the men were saying about him.

Between sermons, Mason listened intently for sounds from behind the door, clues that the guards may be approaching. But the time passed without interruption. In the pressure cooker, darkness prevailed, and a day seemed as if it were a year. There was no way to tell how long he had been inside the room and soon he fell into the same pattern as the other men. When a man needed a dump, they would shuffle their bodies around until he was in the toilet corner. The longer you could hold it in, the longer you got to stay in the opposite corner, where the stench felt a little less acidic.

Finally, the guards did come and the door to the pressure cooker opened. The room was flooded with light from two high-voltage halogen flashlights, enough to blind the men inside. Mason knew to look away, and for the first time he could make out the faces of his co-captives: twelve filthy, bearded, thin men cowering away from the light together like rats in a trap. When his eyes had adjusted, Mason turned back to look towards the door, gradually making out the shape of a large man standing in silhouette.

'As-salaamu Alaikum, brother,' Mason said, keeping his head bowed and his eyes to the floor. He had decided that in the absence of any chance to escape it was important to prioritise survival, which meant avoiding conflict.

The big man bore down on him and smacked him with a club. Before Mason could react, two more men appeared and began to beat him back with the handles of their rifles.

'I am your ruler, jailer, executioner,' the big man laughed. 'Not your brother.'

The guards reached into the pressure cooker and grabbed hold of Mason roughly. They dragged him from the room by his ankles and one of the men pulled a blindfold over his eyes, while the others tied his hands and feet together with an old length of rope. They did the same with Drake, while the big man slammed the door shut again, casting the poor wretches inside back into pitch darkness.

The men who were left behind let out sighs of relief as they adjusted their positions, enjoying the silence and the extra inches of space that the Christians' removal had created.

SIXTEEN

Sana'a, Yemen

Peter Hopkins waited nervously for the secure line in the Ops room to ring. He'd been cursing his decision to remain at the base rather than go on the raid ever since the team had returned with one man in a critical condition and another MIA. Morale was rock bottom in the camp, every single one of them blamed themselves for the things that had gone wrong, and the men who had been directly involved were chomping at the bit to return to Al Hudaydah to search for Mason, be he alive or dead.

Hopkins had wanted to be a special forces soldier since he was a thirteen-year-old cadet at the minor public school he'd attended in Shropshire. The aspect he'd always enjoyed most was the camaraderie, the feeling of being part of something bigger than yourself, although he'd also proven himself to be a decent shot with a .22 rifle. His housemaster had commented that 'they'd finally found something that he was good at'. He got a place at Exeter University, which was fully funded by the army in return for a five-year commission, and after graduating with a rather ordinary

2.2 degree, he'd passed out of Sandhurst. Two operational tours in Afghanistan had set him up to apply for SAS selection through the officer route, which, if he was completely honest, he'd only passed by the skin of his teeth, down to sheer bloody-mindedness rather than natural talent. Hopkins was all too aware that he was a posh boy from a privileged background compared to most of the lads, but he believed that he had qualities that could make him an asset to the team, not least his undivided loyalty.

The screen lit up and Hopkins hit 'Answer' before the end of the first ring. Immediately General Blandford's face appeared. Hopkins scanned for other senior members of command but saw nobody else was joining them on the call.

'I wanted to talk to you privately, Peter,' Blanford said, to the young officer's surprise.

'Not at all, sir.' Hopkins found himself standing to attention despite there being no requirement to do so. 'The men are standing by sir, we just need a "Go" from Hereford and we're ready.'

'I bet you are, Peter. No doubt.'

Hopkins tried to read the older man. Blandford seemed as if he was choosing his words rather carefully, mulling over exactly how best to express himself. The younger officer's assessment was not wrong. Internally Blandford was ill at ease with what he was about to say.

'I'll say this to you man to man, Peter. The situation we've created over there is now rather delicate. Politically, I have no room to manoeuvre and our orders are coming straight from Number 10. I've been to Andover with this, even put in a private call to the PM, but it's a three-line whip and we're going have to play ball.'

Hopkins absorbed the words he was hearing, trying to find the message in between the doubletalk, wilfully not wanting to hear what his CO was trying to tell him. In the end, he had to ask straight out.

'We're not going back for Mason, sir?'

'No, Peter. In any case, our assessment is that Mace is incredibly unlikely to be alive.'

'But sir, it doesn't—'

'I understand what you and your men are feeling—'

'Sir.' Hopkins was barely containing his emotion.

'But this is a direct order. Our interests are not served by pouring oil on this fire in pursuit of what is unfortunately a dead end.'

'A fallen soldier, sir.'

'I've lost men before, Peter. I understand how hard it is. But you have a bright career ahead of you. This is part and parcel of leadership, I'm afraid.'

Hopkins looked away as though something else in the room required his attention. Blandford saw and took the opportunity.

'Right, Captain Hopkins. As you were,' he said, before signing off. Hopkins' screen went dark again.

The captain turned immediately on his heel and crashed out of the Ops room, barrelling down the hallway to the room where the men were stationed. He flung open the door to find Jack, Pommy, Briggs, Craig and Jonny Elves sitting wide-eyed on the edges of their beds, bags already packed, ammo loaded and ready to go.

'Are we go?' said Jack, already getting to his feet.

Peter Hopkins looked at the faces of the men in the room, every single one of them waiting for him to give them the order they wanted to hear, the order that would allow them to stop sitting on their backsides feeling guilty and actually get out and begin making amends for the cock-up they'd all been a part of. Every single one of those men would have stood in front of a bullet for Matt Mason. They all owed their lives to him several times over. Now it was time for that loyalty to be paid back. Fuck Blandford, fuck the army, fuck the politicians who sat behind their desks in London and made decisions about the lives of men who would die for their country.

Peter Hopkins took the only decision that he could. He turned to Jonny Elves and calmly gave him the order.

'Tell the RAF to get the Chinook ready, Jonny.' Jonny didn't need to be told twice, he leapt to his feet and sprinted out of the room to ready the chopper. 'The rest of you, follow me.'

'Fuck yes!' screamed Pommy. He and Briggs gave each other a high five.

'Come on boys,' said Hopkins. 'Let's go and get Mace. Bring the bastard home.'

The five men grabbed their bags, rifles and spare ammo and piled out. They followed Captain Hopkins along the corridor and out through the back door to where the helicopters were positioned. By now, Jonny would have the rotors on the Chinook turning and in three minutes they would be airborne, doing what the army should have done all along.

Hopkins kicked open the back door and they emerged into the blinding desert light. As his eyes adjusted, Peter Hopkins saw that something was wrong. The blades of the helicopters were not turning, a lone member of the ground staff was performing some routine maintenance on one of the Chinooks and Jonny was standing alone in the landing zone, arms stretched out wide. The helicopters were stationary, the pilots were nowhere to be seen.

Hopkins looked back to his men. Their faces were a picture of confusion and bewilderment.

'What the fuck?' said Jack.

Hopkins stormed over to the RAF ground staff engineer who was working on the chopper.

'Why isn't this bird ready to fly?' he screamed.

The engineer's face creased up in blank confusion, but before he could say a word, Peter Hopkins pulled his weapon and pointed it in his face.

'Pete, what's going on?' said Craig, but Hopkins wasn't listening.

'Start it up,' Hopkins ordered, 'or I will fucking shoot you.'

Jack and Craig looked at each other, the reality of the situation kicking in. The Rupert had lost it. The penny dropped for them all at once: the order to go after Mace had not been given. Now Hopkins was in danger of getting them all arrested.

'Pete.' Jack moved towards the officer, his weapon lowered, his hand outstretched.

'Not now, Jack.' Hopkins stood his ground, his gun still pointed at the RAF technician.

'Pete.' Jack stood in front of the gun, taking hold of it and lowering the barrel. 'It's over, Pete.'

'The fucking spineless bastards.' Hopkins couldn't contain the tears. Jack took the gun from him and put a consoling hand on the younger man's shoulder. He had often written off Ruperts as posh boys who were more concerned with furthering their own careers than simply getting the job done. But Hopkins was all right. He would have disobeyed his orders, put himself on the line to save Mason, and that went a long way to win Jack's respect. But if they were going to save Mason, then they needed the whole team and all the support that the army could give them. A cowboy rescue would only get them all killed.

'Come on,' said Jack, leading Hopkins back to the building. 'Mace will be all right. He's the toughest bastard I ever met. If anyone can get himself out of a situation, it's him.'

SEVENTEEN

US Embassy, Aden, Yemen

When she saw the word 'Sodalicious!' flash up on her phone for what felt like the hundredth time, Redford put it down and knocked back the last mouthful of her fourth cup of coffee. She hadn't slept since she'd heard the news that Matt Mason was MIA. Instead, she'd sat at her desk in the US Embassy in Aden playing Candy Crush and waiting for Langley to call. When she'd called in the new intel about Saladin, her superiors had wanted her to bring the translator in for questioning, but Redford had convinced them to hold off and even managed to get them to authorise a trace on Saladin's phone.

In the previous ten years, the CIA had overtaken the NSA in the field of tech-based surveillance. The Centre for Cyber Intelligence (CCI) team at Langley had developed thousands of lines of code, building trojans, viruses and other strategic malware that could be used to penetrate backdoor vulnerabilities in the operating systems of pretty much every commercially available device, so that iPhones, Androids, even the smart TVs and speakers in your living room could be turned on and off from Virginia and converted into covert listening devices without the user's knowledge. While the world was sleepwalking into a system of self-surveillance, the CIA had effectively created its own shadow NSA, with all the power but none of the accountability.

Since Redford's call, the in-house hackers had worked around the clock to set up a wider surveillance operation on Saladin, so that they were now running 24/7 surveillance on all his calls and using the inbuilt microphone on his phone to monitor his real-life conversations. While Redford waited, three CCI analysts were working shifts in Langley, waiting for him to make his next move. She was sure that, sooner or later, the Yemeni translator would make contact with Faisal. With luck, Matt Mason's name would crop up in relation to Shahlai's location.

She poured herself a caffeine refill and wondered whether the British soldier whom she had met a week before was alive or dead. The British decision not to look for him seemed to her to be a gross strategic error, but she also felt that it could be exploited to her advantage. If Mason was alive, then she felt sure that Shahlai would be preparing to make the most of his new asset. If she knew Shahlai, and she did, then Saladin and Matt Mason could be key to helping her answer the questions of how, when and where he was going to strike next.

Redford browsed the file that she had put together on the Yemeni translator. To her, the potential of Saladin was huge. Once an agent knows that a target has been spying, she has leverage over him. There was no point getting upset about it. If you were spying on them, then chances were they were spying on you too – it was just part of the game. So Redford always liked to ask herself how she could turn a vulnerability into an asset. Saladin was passing intel to Shahlai, which meant that there was an opportunity for her to use him to take control, to reverse that flow of information, to manipulate the manipulator. Saladin was a gift that had fallen into her lap; now the challenge was how to use it to her greatest advantage.

Her screen lit up with a message from Langley that Saladin's device was live. She placed her headphones over her ears and listened to the sound of the phone ringing. She glanced at the display, noting that the translator was receiving an incoming call from within Yemen.

'Huh,' she heard Saladin answer in the customary way.

'Can you hear me?' came the usual reply. Cell phone reception was notoriously bad in Yemen and most callers preferred to check that they had a decent connection before wasting their breath on something that wouldn't be heard.

'Yes, I hear you,' Saladin replied.

Redford pressed the headphones closer to her ears, listening for clues as to who the caller might be or where he was calling from. They were speaking in Arabic, but the caller had used poor grammar when he'd asked his question. And in fact, when she thought about it, he had a very confused accent. He was rolling his 'h's rather than dragging them from the back of the throat the way natural Semitic speakers did. She could swear there was a hint of British in it. It had to be Faisal Ahadi.

'The manager has a new customer,' Faisal said, being careful with his words.

'He is alive?' asked Saladin.

'The manager is moving him to the gas station.'

'When?'

'Not now,' Faisal said, and hung up the call.

Redford sat back and thought about what she had just heard. She was pretty certain that the 'new customer' had to be a reference to Mason. So Mason was alive? That was good news. But her assumption had been wrong about Saladin. He wasn't passing information to Faisal, if anything it sounded like the other way around. And if the 'manager' was Shahlai, then it was coming from the top. The obvious question was where was the 'gas station', but the bigger one was why was Faisal telling Saladin all this?

Suddenly, the light on her screen blinked again. This time Saladin was making an outgoing call, but the number he was calling was not showing. Whoever it was had a line that was encrypted well enough to hold off the CCI hack.

She opened a second line direct to one of the CCI guys at Langley.

'You seeing this?' she asked.

'Yup.' She recognised the voice on the other end of the line as Agent Shotton, a twenty-five-year-old hotshot from Texas, recruited from MIT. 'The number he's calling has some pretty good encryption software. Whoever it is has some serious tech behind them.'

'Can you break it?' Redford checked the screen, the call was still live.

'Hold up,' Shotton said. Redford could hear the sound of her fingers tapping frantically on the keys. 'You ain't gonna like this.'

'What?'

'It's US-registered and it's got military-grade encryption. Gonna need more time.'

'Where in the US?'

'Fuck.' Shotton went quiet for a moment. 'No, it's overseas.'

'Where?'

'One second, let me try something.'

Redford began to pack up her things. Wherever that phone was, she was going to find it.

Shotton came back on the call. 'London. I'm running a more accurate trace but . . .' Shotton's tapping became almost deafening. 'Okay. So, the Savoy Hotel?'

'Can you access the hotel log?'

'Sure.' Agent Shotton easily hacked into the Savoy's system, passing unobserved through the back door from where she could scan the database for guests.

'It's a suite. Booked by Southerlin Webber out of Arlington,' Shotton sounded pleased with herself.

Redford wrote down the details. 'Keep working it. I want a route in if he calls it again.'

'I'll do what I can. We got ears on it 24/7 so as soon as he goes live, you'll know. You gonna be there?'

'No.' Redford was already up on her feet. 'I'll be in London.'

EIGHTEEN

Al Hudaydah, Yemen

Faisal Ahadi squatted over the long-drop toilet and swatted away a fly before he lifted his head and checked again that he was alone. Satisfied that nobody else was there, he quickly scrolled through his phone, opened the settings menu and ran a full restore-factory-settings reboot. It was the fastest way to erase all the device's data as well as remove its software – software that he had just used to speak with Saladin in Sana'a. He was confident that nobody would ever be able to trace his number back to the call, but still he never wanted to have to explain why he was running the latest end-to-end encryption tech on his phone. When it was rebooted, restored to new, Faisal pulled up his pants, pocketed the device and left the latrine.

Faisal was Iranian by birth but was educated for most of his life in the UK. It was in the West Midlands where he experienced first-hand the low-level everyday racist intolerance of the British people. He heard white men shout 'Go back to where you came from!' out of cars that passed him in the street, and the older boys at school often called him 'Paki', not caring that he came from Iran. As a result, the young Faisal never quite felt as though he fit in, and so instead he withdrew to focus on his studies. He kept his head down, worked hard and achieved good grades. He received a place to study computer engineering at Imperial College, London, and went on to win a generous industry scholarship to support him there. His parents had been so proud, even more so when he achieved a first-class degree and then an MSc in Cyber Security.

But he had astonished them when, at twenty-two and newly graduated, he announced that he'd decided to return to Iran to do his two years national military service, as all Iranian-born males over the age of eighteen are required by law to do. As a student, he'd been able to defer that responsibility, but once he graduated, the letter arrived from Tehran demanding that he return to the land of his birth and do his duty. Of course, nobody in his family had ever expected Faisal to go. He had already been offered a lucrative job in the US with the company who had sponsored his degree. But when the young man insisted, they realised that his mind was made up. His mother wept for a week. His father offered to put up ten thousand dollars to bribe him out of the obligation. But in the end, Faisal convinced them that, as an Iranian man, who wanted to one day travel freely in the country of his birth and maybe even return with a wife, he really had no choice. Reluctantly they conceded, and Faisal's father bought his son a one-way ticket to Tehran.

Life in the old country was initially a shock to the young man from England. As a resident of the West, Faisal had learned that society served selfish endeavour and celebrated wanton excess, but in his motherland, he saw how Iran offered an alternative. He applied the same devotion to his military duties as he had done to his studies and he began to practice his faith more assiduously. He prayed five times a day, something which he had never done in Coventry or London. Slowly, he had felt happy in Iran with the choice he had made.

Twelve months into his conscription, he surprised everyone again when, with the encouragement of his sergeant major, he volunteered to apply for the Islamic Revolutionary Guards. He passed the gruelling selection process with ease and went on to become a new recruit in Iran's elite fighting force. That was when he came to the attention of VAJA, Iran's Ministry of Intelligence and Security.

Operating secretly from within Iran, VAJA was responsible for gathering and analysing intelligence both inside and outside of the country. A sort of FBI, NSA and CIA all rolled into one. It reported directly to the minister of intelligence, who reported solely to the prime minister. VAJA also took the lead role in organising and conducting terrorist operations, espionage and assassinations around the world, working closely with the Islamic Revolutionary Guard on operational matters.

So when VAJA were informed that a talented young graduate from London had also finished top of his class in selection, they became very interested. Which is to say, very suspicious. Three days later, Faisal was lifted from his barracks by two VAJA agents and taken in for questioning.

Within Iran, VAJA operate several prisons independent of government scrutiny, where it is said the most violent and brutal acts of torture ever carried out happen routinely. Suspected enemies of the state, such as religious heretics, outspoken journalists, political dissidents, and in Faisal's case, potential spies, are all welcome.

For fourteen days and nights, the young man from Coventry was subjected to relentless questioning by interrogators who engaged in a regimen of barbaric mental torture techniques. They kept him sleep deprived, starved and freezing cold. They forced him to repeat over and over the details of his background, family history and scholastic record. They questioned his Islamic faith as well as his motivations for returning to Iran. Again and again, Faisal repeated his story to the letter, remaining consistent and level, not once raising his voice or losing his temper. Eventually, satisfied that the cross-examination was complete, the agents took him back to barracks.

No report on Faisal Ahadi was ever filed with the Ministry of Intelligence, but one of the VAJA agents who had conducted the investigation did put in a telephone call to assure his commanding officer that Faisal had been thoroughly screened as per his request. The CO thanked the agent for his good work and reiterated that the matter should remain between them. The commanding officer's name was General Ruak Shahlai.

A month later, when he had fully recovered from his ordeal, Faisal was once again pulled from barracks. Only this time, he was told he was not being sent to a VAJA prison but instead being assigned to join a special detail led by General Shahlai. Faisal was told to pack his belongings because the following day he would be flying to Yemen.

A year later, the same Faisal Ahadi walked out of a toilet in Yemen, pulling up the zipper of his uniform, knowing that he had become the closest thing that General Ruak Shahlai had to a confidant. The man whom he had, to be frank, feared for a long time, not least for his uncommon cruelty and brutality, had taken to using him as his sounding board as well as trusting him to run his communications with Tehran. Faisal knew everything about the general, including the fact that a single word from him could end Faisal's life in a heartbeat. He knew that because his life depended on knowing it, because conversations like the one that he had just had in the latrine, for example, would be enough to have him tortured and executed.

What the agents of VAJA had never discovered was that Faisal Ahadi was indeed a spy. Not in a James Bond sense. He had never parachuted out of a jet or slept with a Russian double agent. He didn't work for a government or even a branch of the secret services. No, Faisal Ahadi worked for the same company who had sponsored him to study at university. Since he had first written to thank them for their support and their kind job offer, but also to reluctantly inform them of his decision to return to Iran, they had been nothing but supportive. They had written back, assuring him that his position would remain open for as long as he needed it. They even paid his salary into his UK bank account every month and all they had asked for in return was that he 'stay in touch'. Unfortunately for Faisal Ahadi, that was where his problems began.

Initially, 'staying in touch' had meant replying to an occasional text message. He was assigned a 'boss', a woman who sent him everyday questions about his well-being and how he was settling in. At first, it was nice to have someone to talk to about how his training was proceeding, how the army were treating him or how he was feeling. He'd enjoyed having someone knowledgeable to speak to about what equipment he was being trained on or where he was being stationed. In return, she explained to him that the company were happy with his progress, how important it was that he was getting real-life experience in the field, which would all be useful to him later in his career. Everything seemed so innocent that he hadn't even questioned it. As a cyber security graduate, of course he knew the importance of encrypting those messages and conversations. But then he encrypted the messages he sent to everyone.

Things changed when he was taken in by VAJA. The agents had been fixated on Faisal's motives for being in Iran, suspicious of his links to the West. It was only then that Faisal had realised two things. First, that his correspondence with the company could land him in serious trouble. Second, that the agents in VAJA didn't seem to know anything about it. So he'd buried the conversations with the company deep down inside of himself and vowed to leave them there. He told the truth about everything else, about how he was committed to being a good soldier and serving the country of his birth. That was all true. He had been stupid to answer all those text messages, but the most important thing now was that nobody ever found out about them.

After his release, he knew he had to shut down all lines of contact with the company and he told his boss that he had made a new life for himself in Iran, that he wasn't even sure if he would ever return to the West. But she had refused to leave him alone. After she found out about his posting to Yemen, she doubled the salary going into his account and even included a bonus. Then she put more pressure on him to keep communication open and said that she 'worried what would happen' if anyone found out about what he'd been doing. The way she'd said it, it had sounded like a threat. She suggested that in future he should communicate with her via encrypted calls to a man in Sana'a 'just to be safe'. She wouldn't take no for an answer. That was when Faisal Ahadi realised that he had become a spy.

He settled into a pattern of passing on information when he could, relaying everything via Saladin, always setting up the tech to make sure he didn't get caught. Having been so happy with his new life in Iran, he had slowly become anxious and exhausted by the constant duplicity. He slept badly, worrying constantly about what would happen if he got caught. He regretted ever having accepted a scholarship from a Western company and for being so stupid, so blind to how his actions betrayed both himself and his country. Most of all, he feared the man whom he was betraying the most, Ruak Shahlai, ever finding out.

That man now strode purposefully into the room, his piercing brown eyes burning a hole into Faisal's heart. Every time Ruak Shahlai entered any room, Faisal asked himself the same questions. Was this the day when he would be found out? Had VAJA finally cracked the encryption and intercepted his calls? Would Shahlai see through his deceit? He braced himself for the answers as the general began to speak.

'It's time to move the prisoners,' he said. 'The way we discussed.'

Fighting to hide his relief for what seemed like the thousandth time, Faisal nodded his compliance and simply said, 'Yes, General.'

NINETEEN

Somewhere north of Al Hudaydah, Yemen

Squeezed together in the boot of a car, Matt Mason and Eli Drake bounced along next to each other, their bodies wedged in tightly, both still bound, both still very naked. Every bump, every pothole in the road, threw them off balance so that time and again they landed painfully with a thud. When the vehicle finally slowed a little, Mason fumbled around in the space, desperately looking for something sharp enough to cut through the old rope that tied his hands behind his back. He found what felt like the edge of the spare-tyre well and started rubbing his hands furiously back and forth until the rope frayed enough for him to pull it apart. With his hands free, he pulled off the bag that covered his head and explored the space for clues. He had a pretty good knowledge of the internal architecture of most cars, having spent hours and hours listening to Jonny Elves over the years, and so from what he could tell, he was pretty sure they were in the back of a Toyota Corolla.

Since they had been moving, he had been keeping a mental account of every turn they'd made and had slowly put together a map of the route they'd taken. He reckoned that they were still less than a hundred miles from where they had started, which, if he was right, was a holding cell just north of Al Hudaydah. He had also noticed a sudden drop in temperature, which he judged to mean two things: first, the sun had gone down, and second, they were driving north. Putting everything together, his guess was they were halfway to the Saudi border, most likely on the way to Sa'dah, the Houthi tribal stronghold in the north.

Eli Drake had been lying next to him, silently lost in prayer ever since they'd been taken out of the pressure cooker. The preacher had been composing and reciting a bespoke list of intercessions to his god, praying for the souls of each and every single man whom he had met during his incarceration. Mason was happy to let him be, figuring that if connecting with his faith helped Eli to remain mentally strong, then it would help him to stay alive. And that was still Mason's number one priority. But when Mason heard Eli mention his name and begin to pray for him, he decided that enough was enough.

'Will you please shut up,' he said. It was the first thing Mason had said to Eli since they'd left the pressure cooker.

'I'll save your prayer for later, Sergeant Mason,' said Eli.

'Save your breath,' Mason replied as he worked on freeing the rope that bound Eli's hands.

'I'd rather save your soul,' laughed Eli.

'Save me?' asked Mason in disbelief. 'I came here to save you, you bastard.'

'And how is that working out, would you say?' Eli replied.

Mason untied the rope around Eli's legs. 'I'm getting there,' he said.

Mason slid his fingers along the edge of the boot, feeling for the release lever, but when he couldn't find one he concluded that the car must be an older model than he'd assumed. The release must still be controlled from inside the car and, as Mason figured it was a Corolla, then that meant it must also be operated from the driver's side.

'Move,' he said, pushing Eli as hard as he could into the corner of the space. He was focused on one thing, zeroed in on getting them out of that boot. There was no time for niceties.

Eli grunted his dissatisfaction as Mason began to rip up the carpet underneath them, tearing away the cardboard panelling and feeling inside the side of the space below.

'Got it,' he whispered. He could feel the release cable running from the front of the car to the back. He reached out and found Eli's hand, guiding it in the darkness to the lip of the boot. 'Put your hands here,' he said, showing Eli exactly where to hold. 'Get a good grip here. Got it?'

'Yes, I have it,' Eli said. 'What are we doing?'

'Just hold tight and don't let go.'

Mason crawled back over to the release cable, manoeuvring his body around so that he faced the back of the car. His shoulder still hurt like hell from the shrapnel wound he'd suffered days before and his body felt weak from a lack of food and water, but he put it all out of his mind as he braced his legs and wrapped both of his hands round the cable. When he was sure he had a firm hold, he yanked it hard. Behind him, he heard the latch pop.

'Don't fucking let go!' he repeated, half whispering, half shouting.

Eli held on until Mason moved back and eased his hands gradually out of the way. Mason slowly released the pressure, allowing the boot to inch open ever so slightly, inviting a thin sliver of moonlight to enter through the crack. The two men peeked out and saw that they were driving along a highway through the desert. Mason let out a sigh of relief, happy to see that they were not being followed.

His heart was pounding like a jackhammer, but one of Mason's talents had always been the ability to think clearly when faced with a crisis. It was as though his brain slowed everything down the more pressure it was put under. He lived for moments like this. He calmly ran through his options. He had to assume that the vehicle was not scheduled to stop until it reached its destination, most likely a secured compound near Sa'dah. If he waited until then to attempt an escape, it would be too late. There would likely be several more men, heavily armed, and probably enclosed behind walls. The better idea by far was to find an opportunity before that when he could make a run for it.

The vehicle slowed a little and Mason stopped breathing, fearing for a moment that the driver had spotted something in the rear-view mirror, but when the car didn't stop, he breathed a sigh of relief. Again he peeked out through the crack, only this time he could see the dim glow of artificial light in the sky. It was still some way off, but it was an indication that they were approaching civilisation.

He thought through the geography of the area. Prior to leaving Hereford, he'd had to memorise an enormous volume of information, not only about the combatants in the region but also its history, culture and geography. He pulled up a mental picture of the Yemen map and by visualising the roads in detail, he estimated that if they were less than a hundred miles north of Al Hudaydah, then they would soon be passing through the town of Abs. The driver would then have a choice to make; either to continue north on the road that passed along the Saudi border or take a right on a longer but safer route east through the desert to Sa'dah. If Mason were driving, he knew he would sacrifice the extra fifty miles for a route that minimised further interference. If Sa'dah was the destination, then without doubt the car would take a right turn at Abs. The moment that happened would be his chance to escape.

'Okay, Eli,' he whispered. 'We're gonna hit a town in a couple of minutes. That's when we go. There'll still be crowds hanging around after prayers, so we run straight for them. They won't shoot if there's people around us. Do you understand?'

The preacher was silent for a moment, carefully selecting his words. 'Sergeant, we are both soldiers, but your army is not my army. Your path is not my path.'

Mason sighed and bit his tongue, controlling the urge to punch the ungrateful old man in the mouth. But he knew there was no way he could force Eli to run if he didn't want to. He also reasoned that his own chances of survival, and therefore Eli's, were infinitely better if he went alone and returned for him with proper support.

'Okay,' he said. 'You stay alive, Eli, but I will come back for you, you fucker.'

'Insh'allah, Sergeant.'

The sound of the town, vehicles honking their horns and the faint hum of human life, grew louder. The car slowed again and Mason felt another vehicle pass them on the road in the opposite direction. He was sure they were approaching the centre of Abs.

When he felt the vehicle's speed go below 20 mph, he peeked out through the boot again, seeing that they had reached the busy main street. Abs looked like a pretty typical one-street town. They passed a petrol station, a mosque, supermarkets on either side and then as they got nearer to the centre, a handful of stalls selling kebabs and bread. He could see that the buildings all around were heavily damaged by the fallout from Saudi bombings. Few places in the region had escaped the suffering of the war and by the look of it, Abs was no exception.

The car reached the turn in the road and slowed to a crawl. The driver began honking at passers-by who veered into the street, carrying food from market stalls, returning home to eat and sleep. Just as Mason had hoped, the crowds from the mosque had hung around, enjoying the relative cool of the early evening and the much-needed respite from the brutal heat of the day.

When they finally stopped for a moment in the traffic, Mason knew it was time to seize his chance. This was it; it was now or never. 'Stay alive,' he reminded his co-hostage before he released the boot all the way and leapt from the car.

The people of Abs had never seen anything like it in their lives. A naked white man had appeared from nowhere and was running at full speed towards them. Husbands instinctively grabbed hold of their wives and daughters, desperately fumbling to shield their eyes from the most shameful sight. Teenagers pointed and laughed nervously, one even picked up a stone and flung it harmlessly wide of the soldier as he disappeared into the throng and weaved his way towards the light from a supermarket beyond them.

Mason was sprinting as fast as he could, while scanning the street, aware that what he needed most was to find a weapon. He needn't have worried because the weapon found him. Standing outside a gated house on the main road, he saw a heavily set security guard turning towards him and lifting his rifle. Mason sidestepped and switched the line of his run, bounding at the big man, trying to get to him before he could take aim. The guard felt the full force of Mason's naked body as he launched himself headlong at his barrel chest. The two men tumbled to the ground. The bigger man was focused on getting control of his gun while the more experienced soldier, knowing that a gun was no use to a dead man, began to punch him repeatedly in the face.

Over the commotion, Mason heard the rapid sound of gunfire and realised that his captors had caught up with him. Bullets sprayed across the wall above his head, sending showers of paint and plaster everywhere. Mason had a moment of clarity. He didn't want to go out like this, not shot down naked in the street like an animal. He stopped punching and flipped himself over the guard's shoulders, wrapping his arms around the man's throat and using him to shield from the gunfire. As Mason squeezed out his last breath of life, the guard took two rounds to the leg and chest. He didn't know it, but his final act had been to save Mason's life.

The door behind them opened and a young girl appeared, curious as to what the all the noise coming from outside was. Mason took his chance and dragged the dead guard backwards through the door, shouting to the young girl to get inside. He slammed the door shut and wedged the bulky corpse up against it, figuring that the deadweight would slow down anyone trying to chase him.

He took a moment to take in where he was. He was stood inside a small two-storey house with a wide marble-floored hallway. He caught sight of his own reflection in a mirror hanging on the wall, the first time he'd seen himself in over a week. The gash on his forehead was beginning to scar, he'd lost so much weight that he could see his ribs and he was also covered in the dead guard's blood and guts. He looked an absolute state.

His attention was diverted by the shape of two figures approaching the front door. They'd caught up with him and he knew it wouldn't take them that long to move the dead guy and get inside. He had to keep running. He pulled at the guard's rifle, but it was wedged tight between the big man's body and the door. He tugged as hard as he could, but he couldn't get it out, and when the butt of his pursuer's rifle smashed through the glass, he knew he had to give it up. Mason turned and ran up the stairs, taking them two at a time, and then turned to the back of the house where he found a bedroom with a window overlooking the street below. Without hesitating he leapt out and landed squarely on top of a fruit stall below, sending oranges and dates flying in all directions. The stall owner screamed curses at him, but Mason didn't hear them, he was already running again.

Fifty yards down the street, Mason saw a young Houthi man who seemed oblivious to all the commotion and was wheeling his motorbike back towards the main road. What caught Mason's eye was the AK-47 draped over his shoulder and that he was carrying a full shopping bag in his free hand, all of which combined to give him little chance to avoid what was coming his way.

Mason's uppercut landed squarely on the young man's jaw, springing his head backwards and rendering him instantly unconscious. Man, shopping and motorcycle seemed to race for the floor, followed by Mason diving on top of him and wrenching the firearm from over his shoulder. He held it aloft and fired a couple of shots back in the direction of the window. He didn't want to waste ammo, just create enough doubt to slow his pursuers down. He knew that, at best, the magazine contained thirty rounds.

The sound of gunfire sent the crowd into an even greater frenzy. Women screamed and began to run for cover, men shouted at each other and children began to cry, all of which bought Mason valuable seconds. Under the cover of the mêlée, he looked back at the house. He couldn't see his captors, but he knew that they were there.

He turned the bike to face away from the road, and, pausing only to steal the young man's flip-flops, he leapt on and raced off down the side alley that ran along the back of the supermarket. He heard more shots at the same time but was relieved to see them fly far over his head. The bike engine screamed, echoing off the walls either side of the narrow path as he burned out of sight and out of reach of the men who chased behind him. Seconds later, he was past the edge of the town and heading into the desert.

He switched off the headlights and slowed his speed. He already had a good head start. As long as he didn't end up falling into a wadi, then he'd be safe. He had escaped, but he wasn't home and dry yet. He was alone in the desert, naked and exposed, but he had a weapon and he had a motorbike.

TWENTY

Army HQ, Marlborough Lines, Hampshire

After nine hours aboard a DC-10, Captain Peter Hopkins would really rather have taken a shower and put on a clean uniform before presenting himself to The Director, but in the circumstances, that was a luxury that he was not being afforded. General Ronnie Blandford had left strict orders that the young officer was to be brought directly before him straight from the air base at Brize Norton. Accordingly, he had been piled into the back of a Land Rover and driven the fifty miles through the North Wessex Downs and down the A34 directly to the army HQ to discover his fate.

Hopkins had been a loyal and diligent solider for his entire army career. He had kept his nose clean, followed orders to the letter and more than once put his life on the line for his country. He relished the responsibility of command and took a pride in playing his role, acutely aware that he was merely a cog in the wider machinery of the military. He knew his place and proudly performed his part without question. That is how he had succeeded thus far and that is also why being in the position he found himself was so unnatural.

He wondered what had pushed him to disobey an order for the first time since he was at school. He decided that he had done it in the pursuit of what he believed was a greater good: to save the life of another soldier. *Nemo resideo*, or 'leave no man behind', was a vital principle of soldiering. The internal conflict that he had felt about Matt Mason back in Yemen had been profound, and as he bumped along in the back of the Landy, passing through the security checkpoint and up the driveway to the HQ, he still questioned why he felt so little remorse. He asked himself whether he would he have done the same again. And the answer was a resounding 'yes'. You could bet his father's farm on it.

At the entrance to the barracks, the vehicle stopped and an attaché escorted Hopkins to the front door. Inside, he made his way to General Blandford's office, where the DSF's secretary waved him straight in. Hopkins straightened his jacket, put his shoulders back and walked confidently into the room to a blast of abuse.

'Insu-fucking-bordination!' screamed Blandford, already up on his feet, before Hopkins had even closed the door behind him. 'Don't sit down. What in heaven's name were you playing at?'

'Sir.' Hopkins composed himself and spoke up loud and clear. 'With all due respect—'

'No,' interrupted the general. 'There is no respect. You displayed that very clearly when you disrespected my direct orders.'

'Sir.'

Blandford sounded like he was in no mood to take back-chat from a young man who had been responsible for making a bad situation worse. He'd already taken an earful from the MoD as well as the Foreign Office for the failure of the Al Hudaydah raid. So far, the aborted mission that Hopkins had been planning had been contained within the military and he wanted to keep it that way.

'You single-handedly decided you would jeopardise a fifteen-million-pound helicopter, not to mention four of my best men, in the name of a gung-ho raid into the heart of a UN-mandated ceasefire zone, off the back of a cocked-up deniable op? Have you lost your fucking mind, Captain?'

'*Nemo resideo*, sir.'

'What?' The general tilted his head to one side as though he hadn't heard right.

The captain repeated himself. '*Nemo resideo*, sir.'

'Oh, don't you fucking dare or *paedicabo ego vos et irrumabo*. You understand that one, son? It means I will fuck you up.'

Blandford's face was now inches from Hopkins'. His cheeks were red and there was spittle on his chin. He'd killed more men than he ever cared to remember and one more in his office now wouldn't even touch the sides.

'Sir, I apologise if I have embarrassed the Regiment in any way, that was not my intention.'

Blandford was breathing heavily in Hopkins' face, scanning his soldier's eyes for a hint of bullshit. He was interrupted by the ping of the office intercom and returned to his desk to pick up the receiver.

'Send him in,' he said.

The door opened and Hopkins was surprised to see Dominic Strous enter. He had seen the defence minister on the news and recognised him immediately.

'Captain Hopkins. May I call you Peter?' he said, extending a hand.

'Sir,' Hopkins replied.

'Excellent. Dominic Strous.'

Hopkins considered what the MoD had to do with his situation. There really was no reason he could think of for why they should be involved in what was frankly a minor operational military matter. The MoD would be briefed only at the very highest level, but nobody there should have been across Hopkins' infringement in Yemen.

'I've heard all about what happened in Yemen, Peter,' the minister said cryptically.

'Sir.' Hopkins sounded contrite.

'I'd say you're at a bit of a crossroads, Captain,' Strous said, exaggerating a grimace.

'Sir?' Hopkins wasn't sure where the minster was leading him.

'You have a choice between a career in the Regiment following in the footsteps of your illustrious DSF over there. Or . . .' He let the idea hang for a moment. 'You explain to a court martial why you threatened an RAF engineer with your firearm.'

Hopkins considered what Strous was saying. He seemed to be offering him a way out of the punishment that he'd assumed was inevitable. The whole way back from Yemen, he'd been imagining a life outside of the army, some of it possibly spent behind bars. Now he was being given a chance to return?

'I've spoken with the brass at RAF, Peter, and they could still be persuaded to overlook the whole matter,' the general said. 'Encouraged to see the importance of keeping it in house so to speak.'

'Could be persuaded, sir?' He looked at Strous for clarification.

Strous smiled as though he seemed pleased that Hopkins had asked the question.

'We'd like you back in Yemen to take care of things for us, Peter,' Strous said. 'What is vital is that Mason doesn't become a weapon for our enemies to use against us.'

Hopkins looked puzzled; that was the exact reason that he'd fought for Mason to be rescued.

'For Mason's sake,' Strous continued. 'And I say this with the utmost sympathy, you understand? I hope he's already dead. Because if not, then, well . . . you've seen the videos.'

Hopkins tried to keep the image of Mace kneeling in front of the black flag of Islam while some out-of-his-head jihadi sharpened his sword behind him.

'Our priority is to ensure that doesn't happen,' Blandford chipped in.

Strous perched on the edge of Blandford's desk and lowered his voice to a more conspiratorial tone. 'The Americans are working up a lead that could give us Shahlai's location before the day is out. Once we have confirmation, we'll open the door for the Saudi jets to lay waste to it once and for all.'

'Sir, but what—' Hopkins implored.

'Think of Mace's children, Peter. You think they want to see their dad decapitated by some filthy terrorist on You-Tube? You think the country wants to see that?' Strous said.

'No, sir.' Hopkins couldn't disagree.

'We'll need you on the ground to verify that the task has been completed and that the risk has been neutralised,' said Strous.

'That Mace is dead?'

'Indeed, Captain.' Strous nodded to Blandford who returned the gesture. Both men seemed happy that Hopkins had understood what was required.

'Good. Okay, that will be all, Captain.' Blandford waved him away with a cursory shake of his hand.

Peter Hopkins saluted and left the same way that he'd come in, shutting the door behind him. He stood alone in the corridor to gather his thoughts, not knowing what to feel. On one hand there was a sense of relief that he was no longer facing disciplinary action or the shame of a dishonourable end to his military career. But instead, what he felt was worse, because he was being sent to certify that the best solider he'd ever met, Sergeant Matt Mason, was dead. Hopkins shook his head and sighed. If Mace wasn't already dead, then he had to perform a miracle in the next few hours, or he most certainly would be.

TWENTY-ONE

London, England

Erica Atkins checked the reflection in the full-length gilded mirror inside the Agent Provocateur store in London's Mayfair and liked everything she saw. She liked the luxuriously decorated, black-lacquered interior, with its large vintage chandeliers and expensive furniture, but mainly, she liked the way she looked.

Erica's body was her life's work. She controlled what she ate, exercised daily, and nipped and tucked as necessary to ensure that she looked the way she did. Discipline allowed her to enjoy the finer things in life to the full because she understood that life was not about denying yourself but rather about putting enough in the bank to ensure you were always in credit. Her body was no different to her checking account. The more you put in, the more you could take out. Right at that moment, she felt she looked like the physical equivalent of a billionaire.

She had woken at 6 a.m. to squeeze in a two-hour workout in the Savoy gym before she'd hit the city for a mani-pedi and some last-minute shopping on her way to Heathrow Airport. The idea to splash out on some outrageous underwear to wear to her meeting the following evening in Riyadh had come to her while she'd been reading an article in British Vogue that said Saudi women spent more on expensive lingerie than any other nation. It tickled her to think that she could wear something racy underneath all that oppression.

The London boutique sold the full range of AP's collection, including several items which were sadly lacking from their sister store on Madison Avenue. Erica devoured the racks, stopping to examine a two-thousand-dollar gold body-chain. She ran her fingers down the beaded tassels imagining how they would feel on her body, and indicated to the shop assistant that she add it to her basket.

Minutes later, loaded up with shopping bags, Erica stepped on to Grosvenor Street and looked for a cab. She still had three hours before her flight, which she planned to spend catching up on admin in the first-class lounge at Heathrow over a glass of champagne. She figured she might as well enjoy it while she still could; the Saudis were so terribly uptight about alcohol.

Erica had pulled all the strings to get a meeting that evening with Prince Fahd, the Saudi defence minister and key to the country's multibillion-dollar defence budget. She had a plan to carefully push the prince to see the threat Iran and their Houthi puppets posed to his country's prized oil refineries. She wouldn't share explicit intel with him, but she could drop enough hints to steer him in the right direction. She was confident that, in the end, he would pay for the defences she knew he needed. What better solution was there to their problem than Southerlin's own Y-56 pilotless drone technology?

As she reached the kerbside, Erica took in the crisp, cool air. The skies above London were azure blue despite the temperature having crept barely above forty Fahrenheit. Days like these reminded her of the first time her father had taken her to Europe. Before that trip, she'd always assumed that sunshine and heat went hand in hand. Erica spotted a taxi on the other side of the street, but as she went to hail it, a large Audi pulled up alongside her. A tall, thick-set man in a grey suit stepped out of the passenger door and walked alongside her, placing one hand firmly in the small of Erica's back while his other hand eased the shopping bags from her grip. Before Erica could object, the rear passenger door opened and a figure sitting on the back seat called out a clear instruction.

'Erica, get in.'

Erica pulled the door behind her and the car sped off down Grosvenor Street, passing the old monolithic US Embassy building before it turned smoothly into Park Lane. The whole while she assessed her situation. The two huge units in the front of the car were too big to be Brits. They simply didn't make them that size. They also wore matching bespoke covert tactical earpieces, which suggested, on balance, that they were probably Americans. The woman sitting next to her definitely wasn't military though, she had a much more intelligence-services vibe about her.

'What could the CIA possibly want with me?' she asked finally with a mocking puppy-dog innocence.

Erica turned to study the woman sitting next to her in more detail, analysing her while she waited for a reply. She had to admit to being a tad jealous of her long red hair. It was fabulous. But still the woman said nothing, she just opened an unmarked manila folder and handed Erica a photograph that she instantly recognised as Mohammed Saladin.

Erica's face remained as still as a Vegas poker player. She had already concluded that this pantomime was nothing more than a fishing exercise, because if the CIA had any proof, then she'd already be in cuffs.

'Am I supposed to know who this is?' she asked, barely looking at the image.

'Sections 2339A and 2339B of the US Patriot Act specifically provide for whoever provides material support or resources, knowing or intending that they be used in preparation for terrorist activities,' the woman replied.

'Fascinating,' Erica said, handing back the photo.

'It carries a prison term of fifteen years. Unless it results in the death of a person, in which case, it's life.'

Erica wasn't going to be rattled easily. The CIA could posture all they liked. The fact was that she had one of the most expensive legal teams in corporate America to back her up, and anyway, with the kind of tech she was using, there was no way Langley had proof that she'd been up to anything illegal.

'As a proud patriot myself, Agent Redford – can I call you . . .' Erica left it hanging for Redford to fill in the blank, but the agent stared back at her. Erica smiled at the show of indignation before she continued. 'I'm glad to hear you're serving our nation to the letter of its laws.'

Redford's lack of amusement only added to Erica's. She watched the CIA woman turn away and look out of the window at the blue London sky passing by as the car sped over the Westway in the direction of Heathrow Airport. She knew how government agents despised hearing their fellow countrymen from the business world use the word 'patriot'. As though they had a monopoly on patriotism. No, people like Redford envied people like Erica because Erica profited from the business of keeping America safe while Redford risked her life for a government salary.

'You and I are on the same side, you know?' Erica said. 'May I?' She took a menthol Ambassador from a silver cigarette case and lit it without waiting for an answer.

'Let's cut the bullshit,' Redford said and opened the window. 'I know you took a call from Mohammed Saladin at 18:00 hours last night.'

Erica took a long drag from her cigarette. The CIA were impressing her. Their timing of her call last night was pretty accurate but, crucially, the fact they didn't seem to know any details beyond that meant she would assume they hadn't been able to listen in. In all likelihood they didn't know anything solid. She exhaled a cloud of smoke and relaxed a little. She wasn't in any danger, so she decided she might as well enjoy herself.

'You know, Agent Redford, the time when America fought its battles alone is long gone.'

'And whose fault is that?' Redford replied coldly.

Erica considered the concept of 'fault' for a moment. She actually felt a sense of pity for people who still harked back to when America's place in the world had been some source of pride. She felt sorry for the ones who talked about the 'good old days' when the world respected America for the security it brought. Every US administration since World War Two had systematically trounced the good name of America in the name of profit. Yet despite all the bitterness and resentment they had caused, it hadn't impacted one jot on the success of the American arms business. Southerlin was all the evidence you needed that soft power didn't count for much and that only business brought security.

'My job is simple, Agent. Make sure that America can defend itself from its enemies.'

'By collaborating with them?'

'Safety is expensive. Without investment from rich states like the House of Saud, we couldn't afford to research and develop the products that we make. The same products that Americans rely upon. We need them to develop the weapons that our country needs.'

'And a hundred thousand dead Yemeni children are what? Collateral damage?'

'Would you rather they were dead American children?'

Redford looked incensed. Erica would have bet a million dollars right then that she would have put a bullet in her skull if only the British had allowed her to carry her gun. Their quaint laws were probably keeping her alive.

'The law-abiding citizens of the US do not pay their taxes for you to protect other people's children.' Erica lowered her window and flicked her cigarette butt out. 'The Saudis have their agenda, the Iranians have theirs, and it's not our place to tell either of them how to conduct their affairs.'

'All I want is Shahlai,' Redford said.

'Ruak Shahlai?'

'Ruak Shahlai is the single biggest threat to security in Saudi Arabia right now. Aren't you supposed to care about keeping your customer safe at least?'

'My customers buy weapons from me to keep themselves safe from Ruak Shahlai, Agent. I kinda need him, you know? America kinda needs him.'

The car pulled into the parking area outside British Airways first class at Heathrow Terminal 5. Erica was impressed that they already knew what flight she was on. She smiled at Redford, noting how the agent had a steel about her, something that she admired. But as long as Agent Redford continued to miss the bigger picture, there was nothing she could do to help her.

'Thanks for the ride, Agent Redford,' she said, opening her door. 'Let's stay in touch.'

Erica stepped out of the car and collected her bags from the same gorilla who'd helped her into the car. In another time and place, she'd have taken his number and they'd have had some fun. Instead she flashed him a smile and walked confidently to the terminal. She could feel Redford's eyes burning a hole in her as she smoothed down her suit and strode through the automatic doors. Erica Atkins knew that she was a grade-A bitch, but for the time being, she was America's grade-A bitch and that meant she was a bigger asset to her country than the CI fucking A.

TWENTY-TWO

East of Abs, Yemen

Matt Mason woke from what was no more than a doze and realised that he was already shivering from the bitter cold. The night before, he had managed to cover a little under ten miles on the motorcycle that he had stolen in the town of Abs, carefully picking his way east deeper into the desert until he felt that he was safely away from his pursuers. But when the cold had begun to bite harder than he could bear, he had been forced to stop and look for shelter.

Temperatures in the Yemeni western highlands were more pleasant than in other Arab countries due to the high elevation. But while that made life more comfortable during the day, the plateaus of the upland desert stood at well over 2,000 metres, meaning that once the sun had gone down, the temperature could fall to single figures. Much of Yemen's eastern deserts received no rain for years on end, rendering them utterly devoid of flora or fauna, but the western highlands did draw just enough rainfall to create vegetation for goat herding. It was not, however, sufficient to build a shelter. Instead, Mason had searched until he found a small cave, and by wedging his body under an overhang of rocks, he had been able to preserve just enough heat to keep himself alive.

On waking, Mason took stock of his condition. His limbs felt stiff and painful from the cold and the wound in his shoulder was throbbing, a warning sign that infection was setting in. His breathing was sluggish and shallow yet his pulse was racing, signs of how the cold was pushing his body to the brink of shut down. He knew that he had to move, he had to get warm, and crucially he had to find water. He left the bike under the cover of the cave and set off on foot in search of a wadi; rainfall still collected in these low river valleys in the summer. He limped slowly down from the cave, pushing himself to move through the pain, slowly feeling the exercise forcing the blood back into his muscles, warming his arms and legs. He emerged into a shallow ravine that disappeared under the cover of the flat-top mountains that surrounded him on all sides and for a moment was reminded of the time he'd taken his family to the Grand Canyon, a rare vacation, several years before. After around three hundred metres, the ravine opened up into a wider shelf which overlooked a watering hole of turquoise green water. Mason sighed with relief, holding up his face to catch the first rays of morning sun that peeked through a gap in the fifty-metre-high sandstone cliffs that rose up around him.

Mason was thirsty, as thirsty as a man who hadn't drunk water in over twenty-four hours can be, but he forced himself not to drink too much of the cool water. Water made you feel hungry and food was not something he was likely to find any time soon. Additionally, the water was unlikely to be reliable. Cholera was everywhere in Yemen and the last thing he needed was a bout of the shits. He crouched down, still naked, by the edge of the watering hole and used his hands to spoon just enough water into his mouth to keep the thirst at bay. When he was done, he found a spot along the cliff where the sun's rays had warmed the ground. He was careful to keep his skin out of the direct light, but he rested for a few minutes while his body soaked up the heat from within the rocks.

The sun was still low enough that Mason figured he could travel for another three hours that morning before the heat of the day became too much. As long as he kept the sun to his right, and continued travelling north, then he reckoned he could move another fifteen miles closer to the border. If he rested during the afternoon and sat out the hottest part of the day, then he could resume again nearer to sunset, and with any luck he could cover the last ten miles to the border that night.

He looked around for something he could use to collect water to take with him but saw that his options were scarce. There was precious little vegetation for him to use. He resigned himself to travelling without it, hoping that if this wadi was full, there was a chance that he could find more along the route. He was just about to turn back towards the ravine and return to the cave when he saw a goat.

The goat stood frozen on the rocks over his head and stared down at him until, finally, it let out a bleat that echoed all around the watering hole. Mason backed away behind the rocks, keeping his body low and hidden in the cover of the shade. Goats in Yemen did not travel alone. The beast was a sign that human life was not far away and so he needed to move fast. He had to get to higher ground where he could get a view of the watering hole. Any minute now, more goats would arrive to take their fill of the cool water and Mason had to be able to see who was tending to them. One man would be fine; with the element of surprise on his side, he could easily take him out. But if there were two or three, then things would be trickier. He found a foothold in the rocks behind him and climbed up through a crack above. In a few minutes he was on top of the cliff, from where he had a full three-sixty view of the area below.

A parade of goats was already bellowing and bleating its way down into a gorge that ran all the way to the water. Standing at the rear of the line was a solitary figure carrying a staff. Mason tried to size it up. He figured from the height that the herder was young, no older than fourteen or fifteen maybe, but his face was obscured by the traditional black flowing robes that draped him from head to toe and the large white pointy hat, similar to a witch's hat, that Yemeni herders often wore to keep the hot sun off their heads. The main thing was that the boy seemed to be alone and oblivious to Mason's presence.

He decided to wait for the right moment, continuing to watch from his hiding place until the last of the goats had disappeared into the gorge and the herder had followed behind, banging his stick, encouraging the flock into the water. Seizing his chance, Mason leapt from behind the rocks and scampered silently, keeping out of sight, all the way to the entrance to the gorge. He peeked inside and saw that the back of the herder was turned, so dropping down behind him in one move, he stepped up behind the boy, wrapped his arm tightly around his neck and used his superior bodyweight to lever him to the floor.

As the hat went flying, Mason shifted his naked body around and got on top of his captive, raising a fist to administer a cautionary blow. It was then that Mason realised he had made a glaring error. When he looked down he saw that the herder was not a teenage shepherd as he had assumed but rather a teenage shepherdess. A young Yemeni girl looked back up at him in abject fear and confusion. Until that moment in her life, she had never seen a white man, nor indeed, for that matter, had she ever seen a naked man. Confronted with both, simultaneously sitting on top of her chest and preparing to punch her, she duly fainted.

Mason looked at the unconscious girl and sighed. A new problem for him to deal with. He couldn't let her go because she would return to the village and give him away. No matter what reassurances she would offer him that she wouldn't, there was no way he could trust her. The easiest option, and the option that he knew many others in his situation would take, was to kill her. But when he looked at the girl's face, he knew that killing her wasn't something he wanted to live with. He had made it this far in his career without ever killing a non-combatant and he wasn't going to start now. He figured he could tie her up and leave her, but if the girl's family came to look for her in the next two or three hours, that didn't give him enough time to make it safely to the border. There was only one thing to do – he had to take her with him.

First, a few adjustments would have to be made. With all due respect for the girl's modesty, Mason felt she needed to share her clothes. He tore off the hem of her dress and ripped it into two pieces, which he tied back together as a thong, deciding that his own modesty was probably more important than hers in the circumstances. He removed her hat, and by squashing it enough, managed to reshape it to fit his own head in the style of an old cowboy hat. Happy his head and cock were covered, he searched the girl thoroughly, discovering an old Nokia phone (with no reception), a goatskin water bottle (from which he took a sip) and a cloth bag that contained nothing but a few coloured stones. He pocketed the phone, returned the bottle and the bag to her pocket and then splashed the girl's face with a handful of water.

She snapped back awake, momentarily focusing on Mason in his bizarre outfit before she vomited on to the rocky floor. She wiped her mouth and tried to move away but Mason grabbed a rough hold of her. He looked straight at her and shook his head.

'Do what I say or you will die. Do you understand?' he said.

The girl nodded. Mason needn't have worried because not only was she terrified of him, but she was even more terrified of what her father and brothers would do to her if they discovered that she was alone with a man. The punishment that would follow such a crime was far worse than anything Mason could throw at her.

Mason studied her face. He reckoned she was maybe a year younger than his own daughter in Hereford. Joanna would be worried about him by now, wondering if he was still alive, probably glued to the TV news or waiting by the phone for a text from him. He had always promised her that he would come home no matter what and it was a promise he intended to keep.

He took the Yemeni girl by the wrist and dragged her back around the edge of the watering hole, up the gorge and through the ravine to the cave where he had hidden his motorcycle. He pulled the bike out from its hiding place and motioned for the girl to climb on board. When she resisted for a moment, he tugged her robes to show her that he would force her to get on if needed. There was nothing to gain from frightening her any more than he had to, but he needed her to comply. She was a liability and he was taking a risk.

He kickstarted the bike and together they resumed the journey north, carefully picking a route between the ravines and crevasses that split the desert floor. They made slow but solid progress as the sun rose behind them to the east. Mason kept a close eye on their mileage, the whole time imagining their position on the map, sure to avoid any human settlement or main roads where he might encounter trouble. When they were within five miles of the Saudi border, Mason felt the girl's phone buzz in his pocket.

Mason stopped the bike and took out the old Nokia. It had made a connection with a phone mast and buzzed to indicate that it had come back into range. His first thought was to dial the camp in Hereford, but a recorded message informed him that the phone did not allow for international calls. Next he called the number for the Ops room in Sana'a which he had memorised for just such an emergency. When the number rang, he felt a wave of relief pass through his whole body.

'Hello?' He recognised the voice instantly.

'Hopkins? It's Mace.'

Peter Hopkins went silent for a moment but once it sunk in that he was not having some sort of auditory hallucination, he became giddy with excitement. He could barely contain himself. All at once, he let out a blend of relief, joy, awe and admiration. Of course Matt Mason had escaped. He was the hardest nut in the whole army. Although that was easier to say after Matt Mason had escaped. Five minutes ago, he'd been of a very different opinion, namely that Matt Mason was dead.

'Zero, this is call sign Bravo One, Matthew Mason.' Mason knew the drill and was keen to move things forward.

Peter Hopkins struggled for the words. He knew the voice on the other end of the line but Mason's tone reminded him that there was a protocol. He had to ask Mason a question that only he would know.

'Roger that Bravo One. Confirming proof of life: what's your favourite food, Mace?' he asked the question with a grin already spreading across his face.

'Fucking pizza, mate. Every time.'

'With extra pepperoni! Fuck the fucking fuck, you're alive. You beauty!' Hopkins began waving manically to everyone else in the Ops room. Pointing to the receiver, mouthing 'it's Mace' over and over. 'It's good to hear your voice, mate,' he said. 'The boys will go mad.'

'They all good, mate?'

Hopkins was surprised all over again. Mason was behind enemy lines, fatigued, hungry, exposed and God knows what else but still his first thought was for the men in his team.

'Jack, Briggsy? How's Andy doing, mate?'

'Um . . .' Hopkins realised that his hesitation was a mistake. Protocol was not to relay information that was not pertinent to the task in hand, which was simply to get Mason out from wherever he was.

'Mace, what's your location, give as much information as you have—'

'Fuck that, mate,' Mason interrupted. 'How's Andy?' Mace felt Hopkins hesitate. He knew the Rupert couldn't lie. He didn't need to because Mason already knew what he was about to say next.

'Andy didn't make it, Mace. I'm sorry.'

The line went quiet for what seemed like an eternity. On the other end of the call, Matt Mason felt a crushing weight of grief and responsibility land squarely on his shoulders as he realised that, for the first time in his career, he had lost a soldier under his command. He felt sick with guilt. The young Scouser with so much potential had served his country and given his life in the service of others. Mason quickly felt an anger replace the guilt, a fury that shot out in search of a target like an Exocet missile, and what it zeroed in on was Ruak Shahlai. The Iranian general had done this. Mason had had the chance to take him out back in Sana'a but he had missed it and now Andy was dead.

'Mace?'

He heard Hopkins' voice again on the line. Mason thought about hanging up. He thought about getting back on the bike, turning it around and not stopping again until he reached Sa'dah. He thought about finding Shahlai and putting a bullet in the bastard's head. The satisfaction of killing the man who had killed Andy would make everything feel better. It would help to control the rage and the sadness that he now felt. But Matt Mason caught himself. He had learned over the years to control such urges. Going it alone into the heart of the enemy's territory was for unbelievable movie heroes and suicidal idiots. He would get his revenge on Shahlai, but he would do it properly. He would do it with the support of his team and the Regiment. The first thing he had to do was get back to base, regroup and then, with all the tools at his command, come back and avenge Andy's death.

'Mate,' he said calmly into the phone. 'I'm four miles south of Saudi. I want extraction ASAP.'

'We can ping the phone location, Mace. Stand by.'

Mason held the phone aloft while the team in the Ops room used its signal to triangulate his location. He was suddenly aware of the young Yemeni girl watching him. Now that the extraction team had been alerted, he no longer needed to keep her there.

'I need to keep this,' he said to her, holding up the phone.

The girl studied the curious white man who had taken her captive and stood in front of her speaking in her own tongue. His body was muscular but thin, the skin burned red by the sun, his face haggard and his beard patchy. Everything about him was foreign and unfamiliar except for one thing. She saw a deep sadness in his eyes that she recognised, because she had seen that same sadness many times before.

She nodded to indicate that he could keep the phone.

'Can you ride a bike?' he asked, offering her the key.

She shook her head and simply pointed back in the direction that they had come. Her herd was five miles away, through the desert, on foot. That would be a challenge for many but not for her. She smiled gently and waved to reassure Mason that she would be okay. Then she pointed to her hat. She could not return without it.

Mason hesitated for a moment before he removed the hat and handed it over. She punched out the top to return the hat's shape before she placed it carefully on her head and, without a word, turned and left. Mason watched her walk away, following along the line of tyre tracks in the sand that led back to her herd and her life.

'Mace?' Peter Hopkins was on the line again. 'Stay where you are. The cavalry will be there in six minutes, mate. Looking forward to having you back.'

TWENTY-THREE

Hereford, England

Outside of Joanna Mason's bedroom window, the Hereford countryside glistened while the morning rain subsided and the sun finally put in an appearance. Not that she had any interest in going outside that day – her hair was a state, she had a spot on her chin and she was still dressed in her pyjamas. She lay on her bed and checked her phone for the umpteenth time, scrolling down to her father's name and studying the half-dozen messages that she had sent him. Every one had a single tick next to it. Her dad hadn't switched his phone on now for nearly six days.

Growing up in Hereford as the daughter of a special forces soldier was not particularly unusual. The barracks were located ten miles outside of town and most serving soldiers' families lived in camp and sent their kids to local schools. The town itself was also where the majority of SAS men moved to once their active service was over, so the kids you met at school were as often as not just like you; born to fathers who came and went without notice and who never talked about where they'd been or what they'd done.

Joanna had actually been born in Aldershot when Mason was still with the Parachute Regiment. They had lived on the base briefly before the family moved to Hereford when he was selected for the SAS. How different everything was back in those days when the house had been full of laughter and fun. She remembered now how the radio used to always be on and how her mum and dad had danced together in the kitchen. It was years since she'd heard the old radio now. Dad was always away and on the rare occasions when he came back, Mum would go out dancing with Aunty Sheila.

When her father had told her was leaving again, she'd begged him, as she always did, to tell her where he was being posted, but Mason had said nothing more than 'the Horn of Africa'. She'd been instantly jealous, imagining the huge superyachts that sailed on the warm crystal waters off the coast of Djibouti and Eritrea. Her dream was to one day skipper such a boat, taking wealthy clients on exclusive charters to the most beautiful places on earth, while she pocketed the generous salary on offer. Some of the older kids from the sailing club in Newport who'd gone on to work the circuit talked of tips in the thousands of dollars. What could be better than getting rich while doing the thing you loved most?

And she did love the sea. Every Saturday and Sunday since she was twelve years old, come rain or shine, Joanna made the fifty-mile trip south to the Welsh coast to sail. She had graduated from the small, single-crew Toppers, in which she'd won medals and championships all over the country, to crewing on larger racing yachts. The next step was to get a place at naval college in Devon and serve as her dad had, and then maybe one day, when she was older, to return to the private sector and cash in. Joanna Mason was a young woman who was in no doubt about what she wanted to do with her life.

She jumped when the phone lit up and started buzzing in her hand, but it was only her best friend, Tilly. Joanna guessed that she was calling to relay news from her latest rendezvous with Mark Jacobson the night before. Joanna had left them to it in the pub and gone home early. She wanted to get up first thing to study, as their exams were starting the following week.

'Walk of shame?' she asked without even saying hello.

'Bitch please,' Tilly replied before she changed her tone and continued. 'Actually, yeah.'

Joanna laughed at how predictable her mate was. And how unstoppable. She always got exactly what she wanted without ever showing it. She'd probably get straight As in her exams without doing any work.

'You heard from your dad yet?' Tilly asked.

'No. Hasn't been online since Tuesday.' Joanna twirled her long blonde hair around her finger and tucked it into her mouth, aimlessly biting down on her split ends.

'Imagine going a week without looking at your phone.'

'Six days.'

'Whatever. He's fine. He's always fine. Probably just killing terrorists, innit?'

Joanna smiled. As ridiculous as her friend sounded, the truth was that she was probably right. She knew her dad was in the SAS and she knew what the SAS did. Even though her dad never talked about his trips, she was old enough now to fill in the gaps for herself. More than once, when he'd come home, exhausted and distracted, literally the day after some huge story had been all over the news about a hostage rescue in Iraq or an assassination in Iran, she'd put two and two together and wondered if her father had been involved. She and Tilly had made up a million stories about Matt Mason's secret double life, but they would never be sure if they were closer to fact or fiction.

Just then her phone vibrated. She'd received a new message. Joanna jumped. 'I'll call you back,' she said before she scrolled to her messages.

Her father was online and he was typing. She watched the ellipsis for what felt like an eternity before his message appeared. It simply read, 'Hi love'. But she could see that he was writing something else. Thank God he was all right. She bit her bottom lip while she waited for the next text. She knew that he wouldn't be able to offer her any explanation for where he'd been or why he hadn't been able to reply until now, but at least he was back online, which meant that wherever he was, he was safe.

The phone vibrated again and Joanna read the message from her father. From the other side of the world, Matt Mason, who'd been almost killed twice, who'd been captured and tortured, who had escaped and been evacuated, was texting his eighteen-year-old daughter lying on her bed, in the house he'd bought with her mother four years before.

'Sorry. Busy couple of days at work. I love you.'

TWENTY-FOUR

Aden, Yemen

Agent Redford jolted awake as the plane touched down on the runway. Had she been asleep? How long for? It couldn't have been more than minutes in any case. She felt as though she hadn't slept in days. She'd covered over seven thousand miles in less than twenty-four hours, London was now a blur, and with Matt Mason still missing and Ruak Shahlai's plans still unknown, there was little prospect of sleep anytime soon.

She looked out the window of the jet and saw how the searing Yemeni sun was nearly melting the asphalt as they taxied into a quiet corner of Aden International Airport reserved for the US military. The airport had officially been under the control of the Southern Transitional Council, which in turn was under the supervision of the UAE, since the ousting of the Houthi forces from Aden nearly two years before. Since then, Abu Dhabi had invested heavily in Aden so that, despite continuing outbursts of violence, the city and its suburbs were operating independently of the rest of the country.

And as the plane pulled to a stop, Redford saw a Pave Hawk helicopter standing on its landing zone, rotor blades slowly idling as its huge twin-turboshaft engine turned over ready for action. She saw that her security detail was already waiting diligently next to it, just as she had requested. She wanted to waste no time in making the trip north to the British camp.

Despite the circumstances and what she was about to do, Redford felt an ease at being back in Yemen. Everywhere in the world had its own flavour of crazy but she'd grown accustomed to Yemen's particular brand. As a girl, she'd been screened somewhat from the reality of the region. International school kids were a cosseted bunch, forever on the move, so that they could be there one week and gone the next when Daddy's job (and it was always the dad) changed and the family were rostered on to his next posting. None of the kids she'd met at school knew anything about what she did in her adult life beyond that she had a 'government job' which required her to travel. Over time the few 'friends' that she'd made had grown distant and, as she had no social media accounts with which to track their progress, she'd slowly lost touch with what anyone who could be described as a 'normal' person was doing with their lives.

The last time she'd been back to the US was for Thanksgiving nearly eighteen months ago, when she'd visited her parents, now retired, in California. Her father had made the traditional dinner and invited some of the extended family over so that her mother had the audience she required. While she breathlessly regaled everyone with the minutia of her daily life for six hours, Redford's father played his supporting role dutifully, laughing in all the right places, even when nobody else did. Eventually their guests shuffled out the door again, thankful in the main that the whole experience was over for another year. Redford sometimes wondered if her father, who knew the Middle East well from his time working in the oil business, had his suspicions about what his adopted daughter did for a living but he never said anything. Of course, her mother never asked.

In contrast, when Redford was in Yemen, she felt alone but comparatively at ease. Here, she didn't have to do anything except be good at what she knew she was good at, and as far as she was concerned, that was a very lucky way to spend your life. Ever since she had committed herself to returning to the Arab world, she had been satisfied with her choices. The circle of her childhood and adult life felt complete, as though one made sense of the other. She couldn't ever imagine herself living in the United States again, couldn't imagine how she would fit in there. Instead, she would dedicate her life to making sure that those who did live there could do so safely. Somehow, knowing that made her feel better about everything that had gone before.

She came down the airplane stairs and smiled at her number two in-country, Agent Nat Shwartzman. She realised that she'd never seen Nat smile. He was more of a nod and grunt kind of guy. She shrugged off his offer to help with her luggage and tossed her duffle bag into the back of the chopper before she climbed in next to it. Nat jumped into the space opposite and handed her a pair of earphones.

'You're gonna need to go easy on those pull-ups, dude,' she said, noticing that he'd gained another couple of inches since she'd seen him last.

Most of the guys in her team filled dead-time by working out, so that the less they had to do, the larger they got. Nat flashed her a flex of his enormous bicep for good measure. The guy was a tank. He was a fellow graduate of The Farm, three years her junior, and had survived being shot twice in Baghdad before he'd requested the move to join her team. He spoke good Arabic and his dark colouring and black hair helped him fit in pretty well out in the field. But the huge muscles were starting to look anything but Yemeni.

'That's an order,' she said, only half joking.

Nat nodded to acknowledge that he'd heard her. He was the kind of guy who didn't ask questions unless he was invited to, preferring to listen and quietly form his own view. He could offer an opinion when it was asked for. He was no dummy, but he knew his place in the pecking order and that made him the perfect colleague in Redford's mind. She disliked opinionated subordinates almost as much as she disliked Ruak Shahlai.

The pilots of the Pave Hawk cranked up the rotor blades to full speed as the US Air Force gunner took his position next to Redford. He tightened his helmet while the nose of the chopper lifted off the tarmac, and then he eased himself into a more comfortable position, legs straddling the .50-calibre XM218 machine gun. The flight path to Sana'a took them over STC territory and then into loyalist-controlled areas before they crossed the frontier into potentially dangerous Houthi lands in the middle of the country. The Houthis had strengthened their anti-aircraft capabilities in the last couple of years so it wasn't worth taking any chances.

'Sitrep?' Redford asked, speaking into her mic.

'Quiet,' Nat replied.

'What's the word on Saladin?' She'd sent a team to pick up the translator as soon as she was done with Erica in London.

'Nada. He's vanished.'

'Fuck,' she said, pulling a file from her bag. 'Okay, let's just get up there ASAP.'

'Copy that.'

The helicopter flew at over 180 mph, high over the northern suburbs of Aden, quickly passing into the surrounding countryside where people lived in small villages of single-storey mud-brick houses. A single tarmacked road ran north to south, dividing the country in half, flanked on either side by what seemed like endless sprawls of flat barren desert. All the while, the gunner trained his weapon on the human figures moving below, every one oblivious to how their deaths were only a twitch of a trigger finger away.

Redford opened the file and, not for the first time, shook her head in disbelief at the photo of Matt Mason that rested on top. She still couldn't believe that the motherfucker had managed to escape. She flicked to the summary notes on the debrief interview she'd been sent from Langley and scanned them again.

After being held captive at a Houthi safe house near Al Hudaydah, Mason had escaped somewhere on the road north of Abs and mobilised to just a few miles shy of the Saudi border, where he called in emergency EVAC. According to the file, he had still to conduct his medical, but he was in-country, which suggested that he was, mentally at least, in decent shape. According to the report, he had stated his desire to return to active service immediately. She had to give the guy some credit; he was tough. And resourceful.

On her tablet, she called up a detailed satellite map of Yemen and zoomed in on the road from Al Hudaydah to Abs. Mason's report suggested that he'd escaped as the vehicle he was hostage in had made the turn east towards Sa'dah. The Houthi movement had emerged from the tribal lands around Sa'dah in the mid 1990s. It was where their leader Hussein had been betrayed and murdered by his Yemeni guards in 2004, which had provoked the uprising that led to the current civil war. As far as the Houthis were concerned now, that mistake would never be made again, and so the city had been turned into an impenetrable fortress from where Hussein's brother, Abdul Malik, safely conducted operations.

But why was Shahlai moving Mason and Eli Drake to Sa'dah? If he was just planning to execute them then he could do that from Al Hudaydah, so there had to be a reason for the move. She thought again about what Erica Atkins had said to her. Erica clearly knew something, but what had she meant when she'd said that America needed Shahlai because he was a threat to Saudi Arabia? If Shahlai was planning to attack Saudi Arabia from the north of Yemen, then where did Mason and Drake fit into that? She needed to speak to Matt Mason.

Redford reviewed her map again. The problem, as she could see all too clearly from the screen in front of her, was that the area north of Sa'dah, below the Saudi border, was huge. The whole of northern Yemen bordered Saudi territory, so if Shahlai was using the northern territories as a base, then the fact was he could strike from anywhere.

She began to compile a list of potential spots from where Shahlai could be operating, resolving to request satellite surveillance from Langley. If Erica wasn't going to play ball, then she'd have to find out the hard way. It would take a couple of days to redirect the various satellites that were passing over Yemen in the next week, but with any luck they'd turn up a needle in the haystack. Shahlai would inevitably make his move and they would be waiting, watching it from the sky.

TWENTY-FIVE

Riyadh, Saudi Arabia

It was hard for Erica Atkins to believe that less than a hundred years ago, Riyadh was nothing more than a collection of mud huts huddled around a crumbling fort in the middle of the Najd desert. Now its skyscrapers towered over one thousand feet in the air, peering down on an urban sprawl of housing developments and shopping districts that catered to the city's five million inhabitants. It was mightily impressive to the American that a country could build a city the equivalent of Chicago in just a couple of generations.

Sitting in the back of her limo as they headed down the King Fahd Road to her meeting at the Al Faisaliah Hotel, she leered at the veil that sat in her lap. For a city so advanced, she despaired of its more antiquated traditions. She'd heard both men and women in the Arab world make the case for the veil; how it 'protected women from the unwanted attention of less noble men' or that it was an 'empowering rejection of being judged by your appearance'. Both arguments made Erica laugh, as though men were entitled to act like predators, while women should take the blame, or that a woman should minimise her appearance just to be taken seriously by a man who'd otherwise get 'distracted'.

Erica Atkins was in no doubt that many of the men whom she did business with wanted to fuck her. So what? As far as she was concerned, that was their problem, not hers. To make her cover herself up seemed like a low-down dirty tactic to give the men an unfair advantage. Yet, as the car pulled into the carpark below the hotel, with a heavy sigh she lifted the black niqab and slid it carefully over her head. Whatever her feelings, she was on their patch and that meant playing by their rules. The customer might be an asshole, but he was still always right.

A short, bearded man dressed in traditional thawb and gutra welcomed Erica as she stepped out of the car with a polite bow. Her abaya caught the breeze and billowed all around her. She momentarily reached out to shake the man's hand before she remembered the convention. While Saudis were consistently welcoming and gracious, they embraced few aspects of the Western lifestyle beyond a mutual appreciation of luxury goods. Saudi men stuck to their tribal customs and the whole country maintained an adherence to a strict Islamic code that was unparalleled anywhere else in the Arab world. The strictest of those rules meant that a man would never shake hands with a woman. Indeed, a woman could not even be alone in public with a non-related male. For that reason, Erica's driver (an exception to the rule) greeted the man on her behalf and followed behind them as they stepped into the elevator to the rooftop restaurant.

The first thing Erica noticed as she walked out into the Al Faisaliah rooftop restaurant were the stunning views of the city, sixty floors below. The room was encased in a huge glass globe, designed to give diners a 360-degree perspective of Riyadh while they ate international food prepared by the country's top chefs. The second thing she noticed was that the restaurant was entirely empty and silent. She remembered that music was banned in public places in Saudi, but she had not anticipated that the place would be deserted.

The short man invited her to follow him across the restaurant floor, through the area reserved for men and past a frosted glass screen that led to the area set aside for families. She saw a solitary figure sitting at a table, dressed in traditional robes, looking down the main drag to the bottle-opener-shaped Kingdom Centre building. He stood as he noticed her approach and she instantly recognised him, even though he was not the man whom she had arranged to meet.

Prince Mohammed bin Salman, the Crown Prince of Saudi Arabia, stood before her and gestured for her to sit. He simultaneously dismissed the two other men with a wave.

'You may remove your niqab, Miss Atkins,' he said with a broad smile, extending his hand in the customary Western greeting.

Erica placed her Fendi handbag on the table and carefully removed her headscarf before she shook the hand of royalty.

'I had the restaurant closed for us this evening,' he said. 'I thought that you might be more comfortable this way.'

'Thank you, Your Highness,' she said. She took in her surroundings and glanced down at the streets below and the lines of cars backed up in both directions. Red lights on one side, white on the other. Saudis led a far more nocturnal life than their Western counterparts, so that once the evening prayer was out, it felt as though the whole city was on the street seeking out places to eat and enjoy the cooler end of the day. The crown prince followed her gaze, smiling with an almost paternal pride.

'My people are enjoying life,' he said.

'We'd sure like to help you keep it that way,' she said. 'Will Prince Fahd be joining us?'

A waiter appeared from nowhere and poured mint tea from a heavy gold teapot, all the while carefully avoiding eye contact with either of his patrons. The prince continued as though he could not see him either.

'My cousin has moved to a different position. One from where he can better serve the Kingdom,' he said.

Erica told herself to remain calm despite the obvious problem. The crown prince, known widely as MBS, was known to 'move' people when he was displeased with them. The oblique reference to his cousin suggested that something was wrong.

Since coming to power, MBS had already openly imprisoned two of his own cousins as well as his uncle. He had also brazenly held dozens of the Saudi elite, including royalty, ministers and businessmen, for several days in the Ritz Carlton Hotel until they had been 'persuaded' to collectively part with over one hundred billion dollars in contributions to his programme of reforms. He'd successfully spun it to his people and to the wider world as an 'anti-corruption' drive. He'd been less successful in explaining away the permanent silencing of dozens of his opponents and critics, not least authorising the murder of an outspoken journalist called Jamal Khashoggi in the Saudi Embassy in Istanbul.

'Southerlin are happy to work with whoever you appoint as his successor,' Erica offered. 'Because when it comes to the capability of our hardware—'

'Come, come,' he interrupted with a note of scorn in his voice, 'nobody doubts the quality of the kit, Miss Atkins.'

'But you do doubt something else?'

The prince smiled at her directness, a smile that failed to convey happiness or humour. 'I have enemies, near and far, Miss Atkins,' he said.

'We're not one of them, Your Highness.'

'I hope not, but it appears my cousin had a very different idea about how to fight those enemies,' he said.

'Okay?' She drew out the word; she didn't know where he was going with this. 'From my point of view, Prince Fahd has always been an easy person to do business with.'

'Unfortunately, you are not the only one to hold that view,' he said, waving to his guard to bring him a paper file, which he handed to Erica.

Erica opened the dossier, quickly scanning what was inside: a copy of the same paperwork that she had handed to Dominic Strous in Home House in London weeks before. It contained copies of all the same manifests authorising the release of Southerlin weapons. There were also plane logs which Erica had not seen before, detailing take-offs from Saudi airfields and drop-offs to covert locations within Yemen, all counter-signed by Prince Fahd. Erica's heart sank. The crown prince's cousin had been running a side hustle, syphoning off the last shipment of weapons that she had supplied, to sell on to someone on the other side of the border.

'I can assure you that neither I nor anyone at Southerlin Webber had any knowledge of this,' she said.

The prince took a sip of his tea. He sat stone-faced, held up a finger and pressed it against his forehead while he assessed his guest and whether or not he believed what she was saying. His cousin had already been sent on a semi-permanent vacation and would never hold a position of responsibility in the Kingdom's administration ever again.

If MBS suspected that Erica was complicit too, then the relationship with her and with her company would end there tonight. But he found nothing in her eyes by which to read her. Unlike most of his countrymen, he had learned that Western women could be formidable operators. His father had known that, but not his uncles or most of their generation. Instead, they had tragically underestimated women their whole lives and paid the price.

'Saudi Arabia's interests are Southerlin Webber's interests, Your Highness.' Erica held eye contact and used her most earnest voice, which she hardly ever did. 'It is in those interests that we do everything to make sure that, as our most important customer, nothing compromises you.'

The prince gave a half-laugh. He had to give her credit. If she was lying then she lied well. But then if she was telling the truth, she could still be a useful asset. For the time being, he needed to know more before making a judgement.

'I am suspending all orders until I have more information,' he said.

'Your Highness, we are at a critical stage of development on the Y-project. Now isn't the time to delay. If anything, this only reinforces the need for you to bolster your defences.'

'*Shway, shway*, Miss Atkins,' he said. Slowly, slowly.

'Actually, I'd hoped to get approval confirmed on this trip,' she said, now internally flustered but trying one last time to stop what was happening without sounding desperate.

'Now, I'm afraid that I must apologise. I have another engagement.' He stood and pushed his chair back to give her a clear indication that the conversation was over. 'Whatever you require, simply ask.' He called the waiter back over, and with a final deferent nod to his guest, said, 'Good evening, Miss Atkins.'

The prince left the same way that Erica had come in, flanked either side by his bodyguards. Erica sat at the table for just long enough to allow him to clear the room before she stood up and made for the exit. She took the elevator down to the lobby and stomped out of the front of the hotel, blood boiling, her Fendi handbag in one hand, her veil in the other, desperately looking up and down the street for a taxi. She didn't even notice the two old men in short white thawbs with long beards who approached her. Their official agency title was 'The Commission for the Promotion of Virtue and Prevention of Vice', but in Riyadh they were more commonly known simply as 'The Commission'. She saw them only when they were standing right next to her.

'What?' she barked.

'Cover your head,' the older of the men said, the only English phrase he knew.

Erica stared him deep in the eye until she felt she could see his soul. The anger inside of her was at boiling point and all her frustrations were spilling over the edge.

'Oh, screw you,' she said before she turned and strutted away, pulling her abaya in close as she disappeared down the street.

TWENTY-SIX

East of Sa'dah, Yemen

The lights of the convoy appeared first in the distance, the headlight beams peeking over the hills seconds before the pickup trucks came into view and kicked up a huge cloud of dust, enveloping the heavy-goods truck that followed behind them. Ruak Shahlai lifted his field binoculars and scanned each vehicle in turn, scoffing at the ostentatious display of black flags that adorned every one. The relentless efforts of Al-Qaeda to portray themselves as a legitimate army were contemptible.

But Shahlai knew better than to dismiss Al-Qaeda simply as a terror group. That would be a mistake. They were quite different to the other mob who operated in the country – ISIS. Because while ISIS sought to inspire fear in the local people, Al-Qaeda had leveraged Yemen's chaos to their own advantage and become part of the country's fabric. They infiltrated local communities and worked to support them, buying loyalties and even marrying into major families. So many deals had been made that it had become almost impossible to untangle who was Al-Qaeda and who was not.

The result was that Yemen was now such a sanctuary for Al-Qaeda and its rag-tag bunch of jihadist militants that they had taken control of the country's sparsely populated, dry, desert highlands to the east.

Like Shahlai himself, the US had launched several unsuccessful drone campaigns against Al-Qaeda. For him, it was for his ties to Iran, for them, it was in response to the group's continued attempts to strike targets within the US and abroad. But like him, Al-Qaeda had shrugged off the US attacks and steadily re-established themselves as a fighting force. They liked targeting high-profile individuals as well as conducting attacks on international soil. They had put a shooter inside a US naval base in Florida and even taken down the blasphemous French magazine, Charlie Hebdo, killing the men who had so publicly disrespected the Prophet, peace be upon him.

But as far as Shahlai was concerned, Al-Qaeda's obsession with the West was their main weakness. They wasted too much time killing a single US soldier or bombing an embassy that nobody cared about. He had settled on finding a way to turn that weakness into an opportunity for Iran, and in the process he had discovered that Al-Qaeda had one quality in particular that could be of use to him. They had forged a remarkable link with Saudi Arabia.

The convoy continued forward to where he could get a better view of what he was dealing with. To the front were two pickup trucks, each one loaded with a heavy machine gun and three armed men. Following behind were the two heavy-equipment support vehicles and bringing up the rear was another pickup truck. In all, he estimated maybe twenty men. Ten more than they had agreed. Ten less than he had brought himself.

He turned to Faisal Ahadi standing next to him and gave him the nod to prepare for the arrival. Immediately Faisal shouted the order and thirty armed men piled out of their vehicles. Like the convoy that was coming towards them, they had a collection of armed pickup trucks and two heavy-goods support vehicles. Only the difference in their number and uniforms told them apart. Where the Al-Qaeda fighters all wore black turbans, Shahlai's men wore white. The innocent observer could be forgiven for thinking that the Houthis were the good guys.

As the lead vehicle slowed, Shahlai squinted over the headlights to make out the face of the man sitting up front in the passenger seat. He saw that he wore Afghan-style garb: salwar kutar and the woollen pakol hat that looked like a flattened pancake on his head. This was indeed the man whom he had arranged to meet – Farook al-Rimi.

Shahlai had known the name for some time. Farook was a notorious Yemeni, a veteran of Afghanistan's training camps, one of the few Al-Qaeda leaders whose pedigree traced back to before the September 11 attacks. It was said he was captured by the Americans and sentenced to five years in prison for plotting to kill their ambassador but broke out and returned to Yemen. Since then, he'd risen through the ranks and now had five thousand fighters under his command. That was not a force to be sniffed at, but still not what Shahlai considered to be a serious threat. What interested him most was that Farook had a reputation for doing deals.

Farook stepped out of the lead vehicle on to the dirt. He was carrying an AK-47 emblazoned with the Al-Qaeda logo, which he slung over his shoulder as he strode confidently towards Shahlai with a huge smile and his arms flung wide. If he was feeling any trepidation about the situation then he wasn't showing it. Shahlai stood down from the vehicle and walked a little more cautiously to meet him.

In the ground between the two groups, under the watchful eye of fifty fighters, the men greeted each other with a warm hug as though they were old friends. Another time, they would have fought each other to the death, but not today. Today was about business.

'Brother,' Farook greeted his old foe. 'Today is a dark day for those who live under the tyranny of America. There is no rule except that of Allah.' He looked around, making eye contact with each and every one of Shahlai's assembled men, smiling warmly at them, even as they trained their guns back upon him. 'I stand by my mujahideen brothers in the fight against our sworn enemy.'

Shahlai would grant Al-Qaeda one thing – they hated the Saudis nearly as much as he did. Yet he also knew that they were not 'mujahideen brothers', but in fact sworn enemies. Al-Qaeda in the Arabian Peninsula were the perfect example of how complicated and counterintuitive Yemen's conflict was. The logic of 'the enemy of my enemy is my friend' simply didn't apply in Yemen.

'Our country has become an American colony,' Farook continued. 'Allowing their troops on to our holy land, trading with Israel.'

Al-Qaeda's aim was to conquer Saudi Arabia, the land of the Two Holy Mosques, the land from where Islam had first originated, and, from there, to re-establish an Islamic empire that could take on the West. They had appointed Hamza bin Laden, son of Osama, as heir to his father's throne; their new prince of jihad. And they hoped to use Yemen as a springboard from which to start a backlash that would help him to better position himself to turn people against the House of Saud.

But even though Al-Qaeda and the House of Saud were long-standing, sworn enemies, the Saudis were players of the game. As with everything, Yemen was a question of priorities. For the Saudis, that meant fighting the Houthis over everything else, even over battling Al-Qaeda. But evidently, judging from Farook's presence in the desert that night, the same was not entirely true of Al-Qaeda.

One of Hamza bin Laden's tactics to try to provoke revolt in Saudi Arabia was to make ordinary Saudis feel vulnerable under the current leadership. He routinely released videos on the internet alleging that Saudi Arabia's actions in Yemen had actually helped the Shi'ite Houthi rebels to threaten the Kingdom's own stability. He used social media to constantly suggest that by attacking Al-Qaeda in Yemen, the Saudis were hindering them in their fight against the common Houthi enemy.

And yet, here they were. Because as with everything in Yemen, the truth was a little more complex. Maybe in response to bin Laden's accusations or possibly for their own reasons, someone within Saudi Arabia had been covertly equipping Al-Qaeda fighters, using weapons to buy their loyalty and influence them to fight against the Houthis. For several months, routine night-time Saudi airdrops had been delivering American-made guns, anti-tank missiles, drones, even artillery, to Al-Qaeda's fighters in the desert.

'Come,' said Farook, guiding his old enemy and new friend to the rear of one of the large trucks that he had brought. Shahlai gestured for Faisal to follow with a group of his own men, which made Farook laugh. 'You are quite safe, my friend. A guest is like a prince when he comes.'

When they reached the truck, two of Farook's men pulled away a tarpaulin and dropped the tailgate. Each man stepped into the darkness and emerged holding one side of a large wooden crate. Another two men carried it down and laid it on the dirt. Faisal Ahadi noted the Southerlin Webber tags as Farook encouraged the men to bust it open.

'Allahu Akbar,' Shahlai said as the top of the crate came off, revealing the high-explosive anti-tank missile inside. God is great.

'Three more of these. Detonators are separate. Plus the small arms and drones as we discussed.'

As Shahlai gave his approval, Farook added, 'And your word that we will never see these weapons again.'

Shahlai smiled at Farook before he nodded to Faisal. The younger man walked back to their own truck and barked an order. The guard opened the back of the truck and with a wave of his rifle, he called inside. 'Come!'

First one man and then four more, naked, tied and blind-folded, stumbled outside into the night air. One by one, the guard removed their blindfolds so that Farook could see their faces. He did not react. He hid the pain that he felt inside his heart at the sight of his brothers in arms, so diminished by their captivity. But he knew, too, that they would become strong again and soon rejoin the jihad.

While Shahlai's men finished unloading the rest of Farook's cargo, Farook's men helped the released captives into the back of their own trucks, until finally both loads had been transferred. Arms in one direction, men in the other.

With the business completed, Shahlai and Farook offered each other a respectful nod before they climbed back into their vehicles and headed in opposite directions, each returning to the corner of the desert from which they had come.

TWENTY-SEVEN

British HQ, Sana'a, Yemen

The Regiment medic's torch made Mason's left eye twitch slightly as she shone it into what felt like the back of his head. She pressed tightly on his eyelid to hold him still. 'Nearly there,' she said with barely concealed frustration. Her professional advice to the squadron commander had been that Mason should be sent back to Hereford for a full medical. The idea of him remaining in the field after what he'd just been through was patently irresponsible. Yet somehow that recommendation had been overruled by someone right at the top of the chain of command. Not for the first time in her career, she felt as though her Hippocratic oath took a back seat to her military oath of allegiance.

'What do you reckon, Doc?' Mason asked. 'Will I live?'

'It's no joke, Mace.'

'I've had worse.'

'The shrapnel wounds in your shoulder are infected, you've got several symptoms of heat exhaustion including dehydration and low blood pressure, and I'm not entirely sure you're not lying to me about the dizziness.'

Mason stood up and looked as though he was about to topple over. Just as the doctor reached out to grab a hold of him, he stood up straight again on both feet with a bold grin. 'Ahhh . . . gotcha!'

'Staff Sergeant,' she said, with withering disdain.

The truth was that Mason's whole body hurt like he'd been on the wrong end of a bar brawl in Walsall. His limbs were weak from a lack of sustenance compounded over several days without food that he knew would take more than a few canteen feeds to put right. His skin clung tight to his bones from the deep sunburn that he'd endured running around naked in the desert. But by far the worst was the brain-splitting headache behind his eyes, which he put down to the damage the sun had done. Frankly, the doc's concerns about his low blood pressure were the tip of the iceberg.

He put his shirt back on and buttoned himself up while she fetched a handful of pills and rehydration packs for him.

'I like the blackberry one better,' he said, pulling a face.

She swapped out the banana-flavoured pack and replaced it with the blackberry flavour. As she went to pass it to him, she paused.

'I'm sorry about Andy,' she said.

Mason shrugged. He thought about making another wisecrack but it didn't come. Most of the lads fell back on humour during the dark times. It wasn't out of disrespect, it was just the way they'd found to cope. But sometimes even Mason couldn't seem to find the right gag.

'How much do you remember?' she asked.

'Not much,' he said.

It was true. The blast had knocked him clean out so that he'd been oblivious to everything that happened afterwards. Of course, the guys had told him how Andy had died. They'd explained how a cord running from the window connected to the pin of a grenade set inches below, which meant that once Andy had tilted the window open, he stood no chance of avoiding what came next. He'd taken the full force of the blow. The blast had taken one of his arms clean off and peppered his head and neck with shrapnel. The shock had hopefully kept the pain at bay until Briggs filled him full of morphine on the chopper. But despite everything they'd tried to do, including an attempt to resuscitate, he was pronounced dead before they landed back at the UN compound.

'How are you feeling now about what happened?' She didn't want to push, but it was her job.

'Is it head-shrinking time?' he said.

'We could talk about it, Mace. It might even help.'

'Yeah,' he said. He'd been expecting the chat. There was no getting away from a psych evaluation and he respected the doc. She had an important job to do. Every time a task went off, there was a debrief and part of that meant having to get your head read. The Regiment couldn't afford to send anyone back out there if his head wasn't straight.

'I felt proud of the lad, you know?' he said. 'He had a future.'

'I've seen the report,' she said. 'Everyone agrees there was nothing that could have been done.'

She was inviting him to disagree with her. Guilt was a huge part of PTSD, and while she wasn't a psychiatrist, she had been trained to look for signs that a man was mentally not fit to return to duty. She needed Mace to start by acknowledging the tragedy of the experience, and if there was a whiff that he was blaming himself for what happened, then he'd be on the next flight back to Hereford to see a specialist.

But Mason knew the game too. He knew that the doc was looking for those signs, making sure that he wasn't having a breakdown, that he was able to get back out there without cracking up. He thought about the last time he'd seen Andy alive, working in Al Hudaydah, showing good aptitude for the task. Mason felt a physical pang when he thought about how Andy's future had ended on his watch. How could he not feel guilty? The fact was that he felt nothing but guilt and shame. He also knew that nothing he or anyone else said would ever make it feel right. For the time being, he had to just pack those feelings up inside himself and bury them somewhere, because the only thing that would ever put it right was to avenge Andy's death himself. Mason knew the release would only come when he had personally ensured that the man responsible – Ruak Shahlai – was dead.

Mason couldn't possibly know when he would get that chance, but he felt that it wouldn't be long. Not that he was the sort of man who believed in fate or destiny, but still he had a sense of anticipation that the day when he would come face to face with Shahlai was not far off. And when it came, he would avenge the death of his friend.

But he couldn't say any of that out loud. If he were to do that, then he'd never get the chance. If he were to open up to the doc and let her know a fraction of what he was feeling, then she'd have no choice to but to send him back to Hereford. What good would that do anyone? He wasn't any use if he was back in England talking about his feelings. There was only one way that Andy was going to get justice and that was if Matt Mason made it his sole mission to get it for him. So he smiled back at the doctor and decided to keep his own counsel.

'It's just one of those things, Doc,' he said in his most re-assuring voice. 'We all know the risks when we get into this. Scouse was no different. It's nobody's fault.'

The doctor nodded silently, watching Mason closely, looking for non-verbal signs that what he was saying might be incongruent with what he was feeling. But he gave her nothing. He remained totally still, maintaining eye contact with her the whole time. Her intuition told her that he must be covering something up, but at the same time he was putting on quite the show. Some of the rookies that she'd seen would give themselves away in an instant, but Mason was a seasoned veteran. She had to remind herself that he'd been trained to deal with interrogation and also that he knew the risks. There was one last thing that she thought she could try.

'How about your family back home? Do you feel you should go and spend time with them?'

'No, Doc,' he said. 'I've a job to do here.'

She sighed. Expecting him to give anything away and allow her insight into what he was really thinking or feeling was a fool's errand. She saw nothing that could help her make a diagnosis either way. Frustrated that there was little more that she could do, she handed him the bag of antibiotics and rehydration salts. He took it with an appreciative nod.

'Okay, Mace. But we'll keep a close eye on you for the next twenty-four hours, all right?'

'You're the doc, Doc,' he said.

The medic watched as Mason pulled the door to the surgery behind him. She hadn't met many men as hard as Matt Mason before, but she'd met even fewer who she admired as much. He was a strong man physically, no doubt, some might say almost indestructible, but more she wondered what kind of man could go year after year experiencing the kind of things that he had seen and still be ready to pick himself up and go straight back out there to serve his country. There were no clues. He never gave anything away to reveal his actual state of mind.

Mason paused in the corridor of the medic station and took out his phone. The doc's question had reminded him just how much he missed his kids, his daughter especially. He and Joanna had an unusually close bond. He'd spoken to her on the phone when he'd first got back to base, but just like with the doc, he'd been careful not to give much away. Despite that, she always seemed to have a sixth sense for what was going on with him. Often before he knew himself. On occasions, she would point out something that didn't look right, and she had an uncanny habit of being right. When they'd spoken, she'd said he 'sounded funny' and made him promise to get checked out by the medic. He stopped outside the clinic and sent his daughter a selfie, the red cross visible in the background, a clownish smile across his face.

'Doc says I'll live forever', he wrote.

Joanna would be happy that he'd done what she said and seen the doctor. His phone pinged and he opened her reply. 'Your skin looks dry. You need to drink more water'. The message was followed by a water-drop emoji and a heart.

Typical.

He pushed open the door to the courtyard and saw Mad Jack leaning against the wall, smoking a rollie.

'They let you out?' Jack asked, handing him the tobacco.

'Yeah, just making sure that I hadn't fucking flipped. You know.'

'You flipped long before they recruited you, mate,' he said.

Mason laughed and rolled himself a cigarette. He was happy to be back, back on the base, back with his squad. There was a storm coming their way but there was nobody he'd rather meet it with than Jack and the other lads. None of them needed to say anything. They all knew what they had to do. All they needed was the command to do it.

TWENTY-EIGHT

North of Sa'dah, Yemen

The wind that blew off the Sarawat Mountains to the west of Sa'dah brought some relief from the searing heat of the desert below, but Ruak Shahlai had ordered his men to shut the doors. For the time being, he would rather have the privacy than the cooling air. Yet the rage that was burning inside him was going to come out soon and would burn hotter than the desert itself.

Over the previous year, in the suburbs north of Sa'dah, Shahlai had developed one of the world's most sophisticated underground munitions factories. The operation was housed inside the old three-storey, open-roofed market, which allowed the production line to vent the incredible heat of the smelter, capable of boiling down copper wiring, engine blocks, even whole vehicle chassis as they required. The old market buildings had been turned into a huge industrial complex, filled with work areas for tool-and-die sets, high-end saws and injection-moulding machines. Each area was operated by an army of highly skilled workers who had been trained how to make intricate parts from specifications downloaded from the dark web. By cannibalising other weapons and melting down scrap metal, his engineers had gradually developed the ability to create their own rockets and bombs. They could even adapt drones and vehicles and, at the same time, mask the identity of everything they used, so that their operation would remain untraceable.

The factory had the blessing of Tehran, whose only instruction had been clear: nothing must ever be traced back to Iran. Nearly all military munitions, from rifle cartridges to aircraft bombs, regardless of the country of origin, are engraved and marked in some defining way, enabling investigators to define the date and place of manufacture. It was Shahlai's challenge to ensure that any arms from Iran were obfuscated or substituted for parts from other countries. After the attack that he was planning, there would undoubtedly be an enquiry, from which nobody must be able to point the finger at the Islamic Republic. Rather, his idea was to turn the finger of blame back on itself by using the Americans' own weapons against them.

Allah, peace be upon him, had given him the idea while he was watching Abdul Malik al-Houthi on TV. The Houthi leader was sitting on top of his favourite armoured vehicle, a US-made MRAP, speaking to his followers in Sana'a. While the people chanted 'death to America' all around him, Shahlai asked himself: how could the Houthi leader be driving a million-dollar military vehicle? When he had asked al-Houthi, the leader himself had shown Shahlai the export label showing the vehicle had been made in Beaumont, Texas, manufactured by the largest provider of armoured vehicles for the US military. It was a sign. Al-Houthi had only be able to acquire the vehicle because the Saudis and their allies could not be trusted to keep their end-user agreements and not sell kit to unlicensed buyers.

Shahlai walked through his factory, stopping momentarily to admire the skill of one of his engineers, adapting a bomb with injection-moulded plastic, creating a stabilisation mechanism so that it could be dropped from a drone. At the next station, one of his men was manufacturing fuses: gleaming silver conical plugs adapted with ordinary safety pins. He admired the minimalist design, the simple ingenuity of the work, enabling one standard fuse to be used to trigger a whole range of rockets, mortars and bombs. The US and their allies designed specific fuses for each type of ordnance, but Shahlai's adaptations were modular, safe and untraceable to their source.

At the end of the main factory building was the most important workstation of all, where a team of men were mass producing IEDs on a scale only previously achieved by ISIS. Dozens of deconstructed warheads were laid out on workbenches awaiting modification. If the Americans could see this, Shahlai laughed to himself, it would be a gold mine of intelligence to them. But they remained oblivious.

Three weeks before, a US arms company had sold the warheads to the Saudis and the Saudis had signed an end-use certificate, a document that stated the munitions would only be used by Saudi forces and never sold on to anyone else. Only that certificate was not worth the paper it was written on. The shipment made its way to Yemen, on the lie that it was destined for Al-Qaeda to use against the common foe – the Houthis. However, Al-Qaeda could not be trusted any more than the Saudis could, and instead it was Shahlai who had taken the shipment.

Now his engineers were adapting those warheads in preparation for the greatest attack that the devils of the House of Saud had ever suffered. Shahlai could hardly contain his amusement at the irony of it all. The Saudis were so obsessed with wealth and so corrupt in their pursuit of material pleasure, that they had unwittingly armed their own enemies with the means to destroy them. Once the new features were completed, he would begin the next step in his plan to destroy their empire forever.

His scheme to strike at the heart of his sworn enemy who lived across the Sarawat Mountains was now so close to being ready. For a whole year, he had planned the attack and worked steadily to acquire the intelligence as well as the technology he needed to ensure its success. The last remaining pieces of the puzzle were all that he required. And they were meant to have been securely delivered in the boot of a Toyota Corolla when it arrived last night from Al Hudaydah. But that had not come to pass. When the car pulled in and his men had popped the boot, they found that it contained only one hostage. Ruak Shahlai had promptly lost his shit.

For the last twenty-four hours, the general had personally conducted the interrogation of the two men responsible. He had brought the full weight of his fury to bear upon them. They had been charged with the simple task of delivering two prisoners from the facility in Al Hudaydah. They had clear instructions to drive to the factory in the west of Sa'dah. They had a full tank of gas and orders not to stop along the route. There was no room for anything to go wrong. But the problem with employing these kinds of men, Shahlai realised, was that they were not reliable. They could not be trusted at the best of times, let alone when their lives were on the line. And the way Ruak Shahlai was feeling, their lives were most certainly on the line.

The men had told him the story of the British soldier's escape many times. Each time they had repeated over and over that they had shot the British man as he tried to escape. They said that he had given them no choice. They said that they had checked that he was dead and then left his body in the desert for the birds. But something about their story did not ring true for Ruak Shahlai, and so he had held the men while he sent his right-hand man, Faisal Ahadi, to Abs to investigate.

If the British soldier was truly dead, then it would be a disappointment rather than a disaster. For what the general was planning, a single hostage – the Christian man, Eli Drake – would suffice. Two men would have been better, but the plan was still viable without Sergeant Mason. However, if his men were lying to him, then the situation would be entirely different. Because firstly, General Ruak Shahlai was not a man whom you ever lied to. And secondly, Mason could become a liability. How much did he know? In all likelihood, nothing specific, but as an SAS soldier, he could be relied upon to have made an assessment of the vehicle's direction and formed a view of his current location. In short, if the British soldier had escaped, then it would mean the plan had to be brought forward.

Shahlai walked to the door of the factory and peered outside. The sun was again disappearing and the temperature would soon drop. The camp they had made a little way from the factory buildings consisted of five large white canvas tents which housed twenty men. He had personally selected every one of those fighters: Iranians, not Houthis. He had overseen their training and development using many of the same techniques used by the Islamic Revolutionary Guards, to create the finest fighting force in the Middle East. He had no doubt that they could strike their target, engage the plan and withdraw to safety at a moment's notice.

He thought about how his men were strong, and how Allah would reward their efforts, but also thought about how they deserved to know the truth about what might await them. Truth was everything, an army could not function on a diet of lies.

He stepped out into the night and walked in the direction of the camp, spotting the lights of a vehicle approaching on the desert road from the west. It turned into the small track that ran up the hill to the factory, and Shahlai knew that it could only be Faisal returning with news from Abs. He shouted for one of his men to bring the two drivers from the interrogation cell and ducked into his tent to prepare.

TWENTY-NINE

Southerlin Webber, Arlington, Virginia

It was a gloomy morning in Arlington, Virginia and the rain blowing over from Delaware smeared across the glass windows on the forty-sixth floor of the Southerlin Webber building just off the George Washington Memorial Parkway. As a metaphor for Erica Atkins' mood that morning, it couldn't have been closer to the mark.

Erica limped meekly out of the boardroom, allowing the door to close behind her, and proceeded to shuffle down the hall to the elevator. She didn't return the casual good mornings she received from either of the long-serving executive assistants she passed along the way. Instead she focused on making it back to the safety of her office, where she pulled the door behind her and immediately instructed her assistant to hold her calls.

She looked out of her office window, down at the traffic already gridlocked along the Theodore Roosevelt Bridge, commuters crawling their way slowly over the Potomac River to sit at their desks and grind the gears that turned the wheels of power at the centre of the free world. She wondered how much longer she would enjoy being part of it, how much longer she could enjoy her office, which she'd always boasted had the best view of the Lincoln Memorial in Washington.

The Southerlin board had called her back to Virginia last night for an emergency meeting specifically to discuss developments within Saudi Arabia. Since her conversation in Riyadh, the Saudis had not only put a hold on all new ballistics and artillery orders, but contributions to R&D on the Y-project too. To say that the board wanted to 'express their concern' would be like saying Trump had been 'disappointed' by the US election result. Make no bones about it, Atkins was facing an unmitigated disaster.

Graham Kaplan had barely made eye contact with her and Geoff Schiller, former chief of naval operations, the most senior position in the US Navy, who pretty much single-handedly restructured the whole military before Southerlin offered him a seven-figure salary, had given her a particularly rough time. As the one specialist in unmanned air and underwater systems on the board, she needed Geoff to back her on the Y-project more than anyone, so the fact that the asshole had torn her a new one felt like the ultimate betrayal. She sat down at her desk in total shock, feeling the pain of the knife in her back, knowing that her career was wounded, possibly fatally.

Everything that she had worked for was now on the line and she had very little time to get it back on track. Fortunately, the Saudis had, in their usual diplomatic manner, avoided confronting the issue head on. They had simply informed Southerlin that their next order was on hold, blaming falling oil prices and the crown prince's stated ambition to step down the conflict in Yemen. Erica knew that wasn't true, but she wasn't going to be the one to bring the board up to speed on what the real reason was. Namely that she had okayed a shipment of artillery to Saudi Arabia that had fallen into the hands of Al-Qaeda.

The board were concerned with getting Saudi orders back online, but more than that, they needed to ensure their investment in the Y-project was assured. They wouldn't hesitate to drop Erica like a stone if they had to.

Erica fidgeted with a tennis ball she kept on her desk and considered her position. Why was she feeling so disempowered in this process? For her whole life she had been on the winning side because she had wanted it more than anyone else. She had once broken her best friend's nose quite deliberately in a school lacrosse trial, feigning that it was accidental, in order to take her place on the team. Rules were traps, to be avoided not obeyed.

The memory of Anna Cartwright's bleeding schnozz came back to mind and her cries echoed around Erica's head like a clarion call. Erica was not someone who liked to be behind the curve or out of the loop, and yet that is exactly where she had ended up. She had allowed circumstances to get ahead of her, and that for sure was why she was feeling this way. The only way out was to speed up, get back in front of the problem. Break some noses if need be, but the bottom line was that information was power, and right now, she didn't have the information.

She took out her phone and thought about sending a message to Saladin. Her thumb scrolled down her list of contacts until it paused over his name. No. Saladin's comms were almost certainly still being monitored by Agent Redford and the CIA, so there was little point in continuing to use him as a go-between. In any case, their last correspondence had been over a week ago and she'd heard nothing from him in the meantime. He might already have fled or be in custody or just dead. She continued scrolling until she reached Faisal Ahadi's number. The protocol that they had agreed was clear: to only communicate via Saladin. But this was a crisis, which is why she had gone direct.

She looked at the messages that she had sent to Faisal Ahadi. All encrypted, all coded in everyday Arabic questions that would not arouse suspicion, just as they had agreed. The last message she had sent simply read, 'كيف حالك صديقي؟'. 'What's up bro?' It was their code for a full-on emergency.

It had been her idea for Southerlin to set up a foundation for sponsoring bright young Muslims from underprivileged backgrounds in the English-speaking world; selecting the best potential from the US and Europe and giving them a free ride to study at the top universities. She'd sold it to the board as a good piece of PR and they'd liked the old-fashioned altruism of it. Faisal was one of the first of several young British Iranians who they had identified and sponsored to complete a STEM degree. The company had given him everything that he needed to succeed, as well as the promise of a lucrative position at Southerlin when he graduated with top honours. Faisal had done well, but surprised them when he announced that he was returning to Iran to complete his military conscription. Erica hadn't flinched. She'd right away seen the opportunity and insisted that Southerlin continue to give him full support. It was a stroke of genius on her part, spotting the potential to put one of her own protégés on the inside of the region's most destabilising unit. The more that Faisal had thrived in Tehran, the longer she'd left him there, and the better the intel that he'd provided.

But why had he not replied now? She considered for a moment the possibility that he had been uncovered and that their communication could already be compromised but dismissed it as unlikely. If the Iranians had become aware that he was passing intelligence to a US arms company, then he'd be toast, and Shahlai would have seen some advantage to having a secure line to a Southerlin executive. No, if Shahlai knew about Erica, then he would have come knocking by now.

The only explanation was that she'd lost her asset. Faisal was either dead or had turned. Either way, he could no longer be trusted, and she no longer had time for him to prove her wrong. She was out of options and the boy had become expendable. In her current position, his greatest value to her now had changed. She knew then that she had found the solution. She had her way to get back out in front.

She fished a business card from inside of her jacket pocket and copied the number into her phone. It rang once before the person she was calling picked up.

'Agent Redford, it's Erica Atkins,' she said. 'We need to talk about Faisal Ahadi.'

THIRTY

North of Sa'dah, Yemen

Faisal Ahadi bounced along in the driver's seat of the SUV, steadying himself enough to glance down at his phone. The message that he had received simply read, 'What's up bro?' It was a good question and not one that he could answer with any certainty, but given what he had heard in Abs and what Ruak Shahlai was about to hear for himself, he was pretty sure the answer to the question was time. Time was up.

He thought about replying to the text before he arrived at the camp. The message was a clear sign that his boss in the US wanted information urgently and that she wasn't prepared to wait for the usual channels to get it, but what was he supposed to do? For years now he had been operating this double life, working his way up the ranks of the Iranian military, all the while ignorantly betraying them. Not so ignorantly now though. He looked again at the message, realising that this was crunch time. If he replied now, then that would be the sign that it was time to leave Yemen and return to the West.

He put down the phone, deciding that it was better to wait before he replied. He checked to make sure that the

passenger in the back seat had not seen what he was looking at, then realised he was only being paranoid and that she
was probably illiterate. He put the phone back in his bag.
The car pulled into the camp and parked directly outside
of Shahlai's tent. Faisal leapt out and opened the back door.
'Come!' he instructed the young Yemeni woman sitting
quietly in the back.

Faisal walked quickly to Shahlai's tent, closely followed
by the young Yemeni goat herder, who was having the
most remarkable few days of her life. They entered cautiously, Faisal already sensing the atmosphere inside the
tent was fraught with tension. In the middle of the space
were the two drivers of the Toyota Corolla, sitting up on
their knees, hands tied behind their backs, flanked on either side by Iranian guards. General Shahlai sat calmly on
a rug directly opposite them. His hands were laid across
his lap but in his right hand he was holding a Browning
HP pistol. He gave Faisal a curious look when he saw the
girl accompanying him. He enjoyed his protégé's ability
to surprise him sometimes and a girl was definitely not
what he was expecting to see.

'Salaam, young woman,' he said, extending a hand to her,
offering her a place to sit.

'Salaam,' she said meekly underneath her breath. She nodded politely to accept the hospitality but remained standing.
Her eyes darted around the tent, trying to take everything
in.

'She is a goat herder from a village on the plateau above
the town of Abs,' Faisal said by way of introduction.

Shahlai smiled a broad and sinister smile, quickly putting together the pieces of where the story was going, at least much faster than the two unfortunate wretches kneeling on the floor in front of him were. He waved the barrel of the pistol towards the girl, encouraging her again to sit down. This time, she did what she was told.

'He who does not beat his child will later beat his breast,' Shahlai said to nobody in particular.

Faisal, who was used to his boss talking in proverbs, simply replied, 'General.'

'Does your father beat you, child?' Shahlai asked the girl.

'Yes, sir.'

'Good. So you can be trusted to speak the truth.'

The girl dropped her eyes, not wanting to challenge the terrifying old man.

Faisal watched as Shahlai stood up slowly and walked around behind the driver of the Corolla. He leaned down until his mouth was next to the man's ear and whispered something quietly; Faisal saw the man's eyes open wide with fear. He figured that the question Shahlai had asked him was the same one he had answered many times before. What had happened in the desert? There was no way the man could change his answer now. He would have to stick to his story and trust in Allah.

'He ran to the desert, so we shot him,' the man spluttered. 'We shot many times until we hit him in the back and his body fell. We left him for the birds and we brought the other British man here, General. By almighty Allah, peace be upon him, this is the truth.'

Shahlai listened and nodded to show that he had understood the man's testimony. Then he motioned to the young girl to approach him. Faisal could almost smell the fear coming off her as she stood up and edged steadily to the centre of the tent. Shahlai was assessing her with his dark eyes, judging her courage. Faisal knew that for a young uneducated woman from the tribal lands of the desert to be in the presence of men whom she did not know would certainly earn the girl another beating from her father. Yet he could also see that she was fighting to overcome her fear and maintain her pride.

'Tell me, child,' Shahlai said with more compassion than Faisal had ever heard from him before. 'What did you see in the desert?'

The goat herder bit her bottom lip. Faisal could barely watch, seeing how her frail body was now trembling. She flashed a look to Faisal, but he could offer her no help in return now. He felt happy that he had at least been kind to her when he had found her in the village and forced her to come with him. All he could do now was to offer her a look of encouragement.

She turned back to face Shahlai, and in the strongest voice she could muster, she said, 'A man, sir, a white man.'

'She lies!' screamed the driver of the car. 'Lying whore!'

'Silence!' Shahlai slapped him hard across the side of the head with the handle of the gun, knocking him flat on the ground.

The guards helped him back on to his knees and the general strode purposefully towards the girl until he was standing right next to her. 'And what happened to the white man, child?'

The girl started to tremble harder as Shahlai crouched down, almost nose to nose, looking her dead in the eye with a death-defying stillness.

'Helicopter,' she said, her eyes incapable of breaking his gaze. She raised her hand to motion that the chopper had flown away into the sky before she added for good measure, 'He took my phone.'

'Helicopter,' Shahlai repeated with a laugh. He turned around again to face the men kneeling on the floor. 'Tell the truth too early, you are laughed at, too late and you are stoned.'

He lifted the Browning and put a 0.4-inch bullet in the forehead of each of the men. Their bodies recoiled, hitting the ground with a thump. Shahlai handed the gun to one of the guards and walked back to his seat.

'Take them away,' he said to the guards. 'Give the girl some food. And a new phone. But do not touch her. She has shown more courage, more integrity, than any man today.'

The guards stepped forward to lead the girl away, but Faisal held up his hand.

'Wait,' he said.

He looked intensely at the girl. He had never seen such a child before, never encountered such courage, such honesty, such integrity. The small, frail child who now stood before one of the most feared generals in the whole of Iran while two grown men lay dead at her feet hadn't flinched. In a country where children perished from bombs and disease every day in their thousands, where they had so much to fear, this little girl had a conviction that he envied. The general was right. The child had shown that with the truth on her side, Allah would reward her.

The girl stood still, innocently looking back at him, and Faisal felt a burden lifting. This girl he saw before him had more strength in her than he had ever felt before in his life and he realised he wanted to share in it. He wanted to feel what she felt and he had wanted to feel it for his whole life. He took out his own phone, cracked open the back and removed the SIM card, snapping it between his fingers. Never again would he use that phone. No longer would he stand with a foot in two opposing worlds. It was time to choose and his choice was clear. He handed the handset to the girl with a sigh of relief.

'Have mine. I don't need it.'

The girl hesitated for a moment, but Faisal gestured for her to accept it, until finally she took it with a bow, admiring how much swankier it was than the old one Mason had taken from her. As the guards led her away, Faisal looked down at the fragments of plastic chip in his hand, his last broken connection to Southerlin and the West. He had finally turned his back on the life of wealth and fortune that was waiting for him in America and at last made the decision to follow a different destiny. He was turning his back on the life he had always thought he wanted but now saw could never offer him satisfaction.

He threw the pieces of SIM card into the fire where the teapot sat simmering and stood to attention in front of the general. He knew not to speak, better to let his boss ruminate and communicate when he was ready. Finally Shahlai sat up again and turned to his acolyte with a burning clarity in his eyes.

'Make the preparations, you will travel by nightfall tomorrow. Do it while they sleep.'

Faisal paused while he considered the implications of what the general had said. 'General, it is too soon for—'

'Do it!' he barked. 'Now that they have the British soldier, it will not take long for them to estimate our position. They will be looking for us. We do it now.'

Faisal gave a slight bow before he left the tent to enact the general's orders. Again the British soldier, Matt Mason, had interrupted their plans, but again his general had reacted and adapted. He was right, the plan would have to be brought forward. Compromises would have to be made but they would be overcome. In less than forty-eight hours, the world would be changed forever, and the dogs of Saudi Arabia and its allies would be brought to their knees, insh'allah.

THIRTY-ONE

British HQ, Sana'a, Yemen

Agent Redford moved at what was almost a run, snaking through the corridors of the British camp that led to the main Ops room. She could hardly contain the excitement she felt, having received fresh intel that might finally help her nail the man she'd been chasing for five long years. She felt an almost giddy thrill at the prospect of sharing what she'd just heard with the rest of the team.

Thirty minutes earlier, Redford had received an unsolicited call from Arlington, Virginia. She was amazed to discover the caller was none other than Erica Atkins. However, the Atkins on the line could not have been more different to the Atkins she met in London. The new Atkins had been conciliatory, collaborative, even contrite. In London, it had been Redford who had wanted something from Erica, whereas now it was her countrywoman who was in need.

Redford had been careful to suppress her initial instinct to tell Atkins where to go. She had flown back to Yemen from London in a very dark place, deep-seated feelings of anger and hatred growing in her heart for the tall woman from California. She had vowed then to find some way to bring the woman to justice. However, she also knew that holding on to such feelings would not provide results, so when the phone rang, she had been as open and approachable as if they were speaking for the first time.

Erica's confession had contained a quite extraordinary list of admissions. First, the revelation that Southerlin were aware that a consignment of their weapons and artillery had been airdropped to Al-Qaeda in the eastern Yemeni desert four nights ago. Erica had insisted that it was done without her knowledge and in flagrant disregard for their own end-user agreements, but the source had come from the top within the Saudi administration so had to be believed. It had struck Redford how Erica seemed particularly anxious to ensure that, above all, those weapons were never used.

The second extraordinary revelation had concerned Faisal Ahadi, who Erica had previously sworn blind was not an associate. Now she offered a rather different account. In fact, she had been grooming Faisal for several years, sponsoring him through Southerlin's youth development scheme to complete his university studies. In return for the promise of a lucrative career in the US, Faisal had been relaying operational information from within the Islamic Revolutionary Guard and subsequently from within Ruak Shahlai's inner circle.

Redford had been dumbfounded by the admission. Atkins had brought Faisal Ahadi into Southerlin while he was studying in the UK and included him on a list of talented programmers and engineers, even promising to help him achieve dual nationality status in the US. The deal had been that he would stay put until the ink was dry on Southerlin's Y-project order from Saudi, at which point they would bring him back stateside. That a US Fortune 500 company would be in the practice of privately sponsoring terrorists, running their own assets like – well like the CIA – was shocking, not to say highly illegal. To bury Faisal within an enemy force was in contravention of so many statutes that a string of indictments would surely follow. But first, she wanted to see what she could do.

First Redford had to consider what to do with Atkins' offer to give Faisal up. There was nobody closer to Shahlai, and if she could add him to her own assets then it was a big step to landing Shahlai himself. If she could turn a Southerlin asset into a CIA asset, then there was a considerable upside. The problem was that Faisal had gone dark. His last communication with Atkins had been days ago. He had relayed to Erica that he was headed north with Shahlai to RV with Mason and Drake. Somehow, the two hostages were part of whatever Shahlai was planning. The question, still, was how?

The second she entered the Ops room, Redford felt the tension and the heat. A malfunction with the air-conditioning system throughout the building had sent the indoor temperature to a stifling 40°C. Captain Peter Hopkins had barely been back in Yemen twenty-four hours and he was already sweating into his uniform so hard that he looked as though he'd showered in it. He stood to welcome Agent Redford, but she motioned for him to sit. She noticed too that Mason had yet to join them.

Her colleague Agent Shwartzman was already in position, setting up the tech for her presentation. A moment later, Mason entered, and everyone stood up again to shake hands and exchange pleasantries the way the Brits always seemed to need to do. Finally, everyone sat down and Redford took the chance to steal a sideways look at Mason. She'd read the whole report on his capture and escape, but she hadn't had a chance to debrief him personally yet. She was curious as to his state of mind but wasn't going to say anything. She still remembered the cold reception she'd received the last time they'd met.

'Agent Redford.' Hopkins gestured to the screens. 'We are at your disposal.'

Redford stood and straight away called up a detailed map of the Yemeni and Saudi Arabian Peninsula. Everyone surveilled the screen as she pointed out that various Houthi strongholds had been identified in Yemen, as well as within Saudi Arabia on the other side of the border. Most of those attending knew them well; they were all refineries.

'Gentlemen, we have received intelligence from within Ruak Shahlai's network that suggests he is planning an attack. We believe it likely that will be on a target within Saudi.'

'Who from?' Hopkins asked.

'Sorry, that's classified, but I can personally vouch for it.' She shrugged before she continued. 'We believe the target will be a commercial centre within Saudi Arabia's oil industry, potentially a production facility at one of the refineries in Jeddah, Medina or Abqaiq.'

All the men in the room nodded while Redford high-lighted three locations on the Yemeni side of the border.

'Everything we've got is on surveillance in these areas.' She pointed to the Houthi bases on the map. 'Based on Sergeant Mason's intel, we believe that Ruak Shahlai is hiding out somewhere near Sa'dah.'

'Anything more specific?' Mason said. The area she was describing was twice the size of Herefordshire. Shwartzman flashed him a snarl like an attack dog, irked that the Brit was interrupting his boss. Mason shrugged, as unfazed as if he were facing a kitten.

'Negative. Langley has only identified these areas. My own personal feeling is he won't risk using Sa'dah itself as a base for an attack out of fear of retaliation, in which case we're most likely looking for an attack coming from somewhere outside of the city.'

She watched Mason scanning the map. Other than her, she reckoned he knew Yemen better than anyone in the room; she was curious what he was thinking. The marks on the map identified a small village northeast of Sa'dah called Albuqa and the border town of Baqim. She couldn't read his face or whether he thought those options seemed likely or not.

'We have local assets on the ground in Albuqa,' Redford continued, 'but we're relying solely on satellite surveillance for Baqim. Langley have redirected every satellite in the region, so we've pretty good eyes on them day and night.'

She saw Mason bow his head with a sigh and begin to scratch at the beard that had grown out on his chin since she'd seen him last. She'd been expecting him to weigh into this briefing and give them his opinion, but instead he'd kept his head down and said nothing. He'd been wrong during the Drake raid in Sana'a and she had been right, but that was all done now and his silence was becoming off-putting.

'Do you have something to contribute, Staff Sergeant?' Redford asked, hating that she sounded like a schoolteacher who'd caught one of her six-year-olds talking in class.

'Albuqa is five hundred miles from the Aramco refinery in north Jeddah,' he said.

'You don't say,' said Redford sarcastically, already regretting asking him to contribute. 'The Houthis launched a cruise missile attack on the Barakah nuclear power plant in UAE last month. It's a similar distance. We're confident they have that capability.'

'And what happened to the missile?' Mason asked.

'The Saudis shot it down over the Empty Quarter.'

'You don't say,' Mason said.

Redford glared at Mason. Mason smiled back.

'Guys.' Hopkins dived in to deflate the tension.

Mason leaned back in his chair and held his hands up. 'No offence,' he said. 'What's the thinking on Baqim?'

Redford asked herself why she'd wanted to engage with this asshole again. Matt Mason wasn't running this operation, she was, and so all she needed was for him to shut up and listen. But the deal with the Brits was that, while Langley would lead operationally, they were the ones who had boots on the ground and so anything that had to happen would happen with them. It was better to have them on board than not.

'Baqim is tribal stronghold territory, so Shahlai would have zero interruption if he launched from there,' she said. She couldn't resist adding, 'And it's fifty miles closer to Jeddah than Albuqa.'

'But it's still inland,' said Mason.

'The Saudi Navy have the whole coastline tied up, Staff Sergeant. The Houthis have no capacity to launch an attack from the water.'

About ten years before, the Saudis had started to develop refineries in the west of the country and built a fleet of tankers to serve their Red Sea ports. The logic had been that, if the Iranians were ever to block the Strait of Hormuz on the other coast, then the Saudis would need an alternative outlet for their oil. In the years that followed, they had constructed not only a pipeline across the desert, but three state-of-the-art oil refineries on the Red Sea coast, the largest of which was at Rabigh.

Since then, the Houthi leadership had constantly made thinly veiled threats about their potential to strike Saudi oil targets from the sea. An attack way up in the north of Saudi would be where they could inflict maximum damage on their neighbours while minimising the damage on their own doorstep. The cost to the Saudis of losing a refinery or a tanker would run to millions of dollars, but the larger economic fallout of a clean-up operation, not to mention the impact on shipping, fishing and wider trade through oil price shocks, would run into the billions.

But the problem the Houthis had was that the range of their missiles was insufficient to target the northern refineries directly without getting shot down. And that they had a lack of strength on the water. It's one thing to build a guerrilla land army but quite a different task to assemble a navy. As a result, Saudi domination on the water was absolute and the sea was an area where they did not need to worry. Although that did not stop the Houthis from trying. Several attempts were made to send fast boats, powered by big 200-horsepower Yamaha outboard motors, fitted with cameras, hydraulic steering, GPS antennae and navigation computers, to take out Saudi targets. Container ships and oil tankers were the prize, but each time the Houthis tried, the Saudis had sunk their boats before they even reached the high seas.

'I'm just saying don't rule it out,' said Mason.

'Shahlai's no idiot,' said Redford. 'Whatever he's planning, it's not something that they've tried before.'

'Agreed,' said Mason, 'but . . .'

'But . . .?' Redford repeated, biting her tongue, waiting for what was coming.

'The guys in the cell with me were Yemenis.'

'Except Drake,' said Hopkins.

'But the others. All fishermen.'

'Your point?' Redford asked. She was genuinely curious where he was going with this.

'From here.' Mason stood and walked to the map. He pointed to a small port right on the Saudi border.

'Midi?' Redford said, sounding unconvinced. 'The Saudis took Midi back from the Houthis last year. It's still under Saudi control.'

'But the Yemenis run boats out of Midi.'

'The Saudis have all of them vetted and checked. You can be damn sure they don't let anyone fish in Saudi waters otherwise.'

'Something weird is going on there, that's all I'm saying. What does Shahlai want with a load of fishermen?'

'I can't build a strategy around "something weird",' Redford said, wondering if Mason had actually lost it after all.

Mason traced his finger along the coastline, past Midi, north into Saudi water, all the way to Jeddah. 'You're right,' he said, 'but something was off.'

Redford evaluated him. Mason seemed different to her from the man she'd locked horns with before. He was more distant, vague, not the arrogant force that he was last time they had met. It was disconcerting but also a blessed relief.

'I'm not here to get your approval, gentlemen.' Redford turned off the display and stood confidently in the centre of the room. 'I just need you to be ready if anything goes operational before the US can get boots on the ground.'

'We're ready to go on a five-minute call, Agent Redford,' Hopkins said.

'Yeah.' Mason nodded. 'Just give the word. You're the boss.'

She smiled at his gesture. That was more like it. She was going to be the brains of the operation this time; she had no doubt that he could play the muscle role competently, and she needed him to do just that.

THIRTY-TWO

Harad–Midi highway, Yemen

An old beat-up Nissan truck turned off the highway and on to a dark, single-track road that ran west towards the sea. Faisal Ahadi sat silently in the passenger seat and noted the bullet-hole-ridden sign by the road read 'Midi 27'. Like his three co-passengers, he was dressed as a simple local fisherman.

The road was the only way in and out of Midi. Once you reached the town from the highway, the road continued west until it reached the port, one mile away. There was no way to access the latter without going through the former, which was why Midi, as the town serving Yemen's most northerly deep-water port, capable of taking the kind of large heavy-loaded ships that might contain, say, weapons, was considered of huge strategic importance to the Houthis.

To their chagrin, the Houthis had conspired to throw away control of Midi three years earlier, when they allowed forces loyal to President Hadi and his Saudi allies to take it from them in a prolonged battle. Dozens of Houthi fighters had perished in the battle, but more importantly an invaluable resource was lost that day, and with it, a vital trading route between Houthi territory and the outside world.

Subsequent attempts to retake Midi had been defeated with relentless Saudi airstrikes, until finally the Houthis had given up on the town and retreated to their stronghold in Harad, a bombed-out ghost town twenty miles away. Since then, an uneasy calm had settled over Midi as the Saudis had begun the battle for hearts and minds, and pumped redevelopment money into the town. Already they had rebuilt the school and started regenerating the local fishing industry, providing Midi's men with new boats and equipment. It was just such soft tactics that Ruak Shahlai had identified as a vulnerability for him to exploit.

Less than three miles from the highway turning, Faisal saw torchlight in the distance. He correctly assumed it was coming from a checkpoint controlled by loyalist forces. As they got closer, he saw the torch belonged to a solitary soldier, who walked into the road and waved for the truck to slow. Everybody inside the vehicle knew what they had to do. Faisal released the safety on his favoured Beretta pistol and tucked it between his feet, knowing that if everything went according to plan, he would not need to fire it.

As the Nissan truck slowed to a stop, the soldier casually discarded a cigarette and approached the window on the driver's side. Faisal noticed that a barrier was already lowered across the road, manned by another, younger soldier. He estimated that the boy was still in his teens and he noted that he nervously kept an eye on his superior officer, waiting for the order to release the rope that allowed them to pass.

Faisal returned his attention to the older fighter now standing outside the window of the vehicle. Faisal's comrade wound it down and kept his eyes lowered, partly to feign a gesture of fear and respect, partly to avoid any unnecessary social interaction.

'Papers,' the soldier said, holding out his flattened hand while looking back at the tarpaulin tied over the truck's contents behind the cab.

The driver handed over a raggedy paper document.

'All,' said the soldier, pointing his torch in through the window so that he could get a closer look at the other men sitting inside the truck.

They did as they were asked. One by one, they passed their paper identities through the window to the soldier and waited silently while he passed his torch carefully over each document.

'What's in the back?' he asked.

'Fishing equipment, sir,' the driver replied, exactly as he'd been ordered to say.

Midi's fishermen might have been benefitting from Saudi charity, but they could still not live day to day without travelling through the checkpoints to the highway which led to the markets south of Harad to sell their fish. Over the previous two weeks, Shahlai's men had apprehended half a dozen Midi men who all had one thing in common – they were fishermen who'd been lucky enough to receive brand-new Saudi fishing boats. Those men now languished in Shahlai's pressure cooker in Al Hudaydah, and now Faisal and his comrades were using their identities to pass freely into the town. Once there, they would have access to the port where the boats were moored and the seas were beyond. The new Saudi scheme allowed the Midi boats access to fishing grounds in Saudi Arabian waters, which was exactly where the general wanted his men to be.

The soldier turned the torch to the back of the vehicle and walked around to inspect its cargo. With a heavy sigh, Faisal reached across the driver and turned off the truck's headlights. He gestured to the two men sitting behind him, and at once the three men quietly unlatched their car doors. Faisal's comrades moved quickly to the rear of the vehicle to deal with the problem that was about to occur, while Faisal disappeared alone into the darkness to the front.

The young boy sitting at the barrier was stunned as the vehicle's headlights went out and cast him into darkness. He could just make out the dim glow of his corporal's torch coming from behind the truck. He felt himself shiver momentarily, and when he looked down he saw that his hand, still holding the rope that controlled the barrier, was shaking. He wondered if he should go and investigate why the lights had gone out or see if his comrade needed assistance, but he had been given an order to remain at his post. So he remained frozen to the upturned oil drum he sat on and grimaced, trying in vain to see what was happening behind the rear of the truck. As he did, he heard a loud thud just as he saw the torch go dark.

Suddenly the boy was sitting alone in total darkness, his eyes slow to adjust, his ears straining for some sense of what was happening around him. His strict instructions were to hold the rope until he was given the order to release it. His corporal had been very clear. It was simple and easy to follow.

He jolted when, seemingly from nowhere, he heard a voice whispering directly into his ear, 'Open the barrier.'

The words were spoken in a very strange accent, one which he did not recognise, but he was certain that it was not his corporal's voice, so he continued to hold on to the rope with all his worth. His mind raced through the possibilities of what was happening and finally settled on the most optimistic one – that this was some kind of test.

But again the voice came in a dark foreboding whisper, 'I said, open the barrier.'

This time the words were followed by the cold feeling of Italian-made steel forcing its way into his ear. But still the young man held the rope tight.

When the headlights of the truck came back on and its engine roared back to life, the whole scene was lit again and the young man saw Faisal's shadow on the ground in front of him. He saw too the shape of the Beretta 92 pointed directly at his head. His whole body began shaking with an uncontrollable force and it took every ounce of strength that he had to keep hold of that rope.

Faisal lowered the gun and looked back at the truck, throwing his arms wide in a sign of total disbelief. He shook his head and smiled to the driver, who was gesticulating that they had no more time to wait. Faisal looked down again to the kid sitting on the barrel and again raised the gun.

'Open the fucking barrier, kid,' he said again, only this time reverting to his native English.

The young soldier did not speak English, but he did now at least realise the reason why he was not able to place the accent before. He looked up to face the foreigner, the dark silhouetted gunman who stood before him, pointing a gun at his head. As he did, he felt the shakes fade away and his grip on the rope grew tighter than ever. Squinting slightly into the headlights, he defiantly shook his head.

Faisal was momentarily lit up by the flash from the barrel of the Beretta, not that the boy would remember seeing it. Nor did he hear the sound of the shot as it was effortlessly absorbed by the wide-open desert all around him. Faisal bent down over his body to collect the casing from the dirt and realised that one of his own men had walked over to his side. Together they lifted the boy's limp carcass and carried it around to the back of the truck.

The driver stood waiting for them, guiding them with the corporal's torch. He pointed the light for the two men as they lifted the boy's body and threw it down on to the back of the truck, next to a dead corporal, four warheads and a gagged-and-bound British priest.

Faisal pulled the tarpaulin back over everything again and secured it with the rope. The idea to enter Midi by stealth had not gone according to plan. New guards would come to relieve their post at dawn. At best they might assume the corporal and his young soldier had deserted, which was not uncommon among the loyalist forces, but it was not something on which Faisal could rely. Instead, he would have to move forward with the next phase immediately. They had to get the truck to the port and start preparing the boats before morning.

THIRTY-THREE

British HQ, Sana'a, Yemen

Matt Mason was getting bored of hanging around and so were his men. It had been days since he'd returned from the desert and the team was itching to get back to action. He knew from experience that men with a fight in their bellies weren't best left to dwell on it for too long or they started to turn in on themselves. What everybody needed was to get out in the field and do what they did best. But first they needed to turn up something solid. They'd been running shifts, day and night, to achieve just that, but so far they'd found nothing concrete.

Mason hadn't slept in days, which is to say that he had stopped sleeping. The squad were taking it in turns to run shifts in the Ops room, working around the clock, but every time it was his turn to rest, he hadn't seemed to be able to switch off. There was a point at which you just had to settle for lying down and drinking a cup of tea. He lit a cigarette, took a sip from his mug and told himself to at least do that.

A second later, Jonny Elves stuck his head around the door and said, 'Mace, they need you back in Ops, mate.'

Mason hurried to the Ops room and burst through the door. Everyone inside was running around with their heads on fire. The spooks were gathered around a screen all talking over each other, the signallers were busy relaying messages back and forth from London and Langley. Hopkins and Craig Bell were analysing everything, every intercept, every image from the satellites, running their eyes over the intel, making sure that nothing was missed. Everything in that room was moving at speed, everyone needed something and they needed it yesterday.

As soon as Craig saw Mason enter, he pointed to Redford sitting at a screen in the corner of the room. 'Over there, Mace,' he said. 'They want you on the call.'

Mason pulled up a chair just in time to see Redford, already on a group call, uploading satellite images on to the screen. Mason scanned everyone on the call, recognising a few of the faces. The biggest dick in the virtual room was the US Joint Chief of Staff, General Mitch Parry, but there were also a couple of big wigs from Langley as well as General Ronnie Blandford and the defence minister Dominic Strous. Redford began describing the image which showed a group of vehicles clustered together in the desert.

'Gentlemen,' she began, 'what you're seeing here is a meeting between General Ruak Shahlai and Al-Qaeda operatives.'

Since Redford had received the intel about Shahlai's planned attack, she had identified his likely base as being somewhere in the area surrounding Sa'dah. The eyes in the sky had been busy combing the area until they eventually established that Shahlai was using an old market north of the city. Since then, she'd had Langley run twenty-four-hour surveillance, following all the vehicles that came and went, tracking them across vast areas of desert until, nearly two days earlier, they had made an important discovery.

'We believe the man leading the Al-Qaeda convoy to be Farook al-Rimi.' She called up a US Army mugshot of Farook on the screen. 'Farook is known to us as a former commander of Al-Qaeda in Afghanistan, known associate of Osama bin Laden and until his escape in 2015, was residing at the Parwan Detention Facility outside of Bagram.'

'What is Al-Qaeda doing meeting an Iranian general?' Parry asked. 'Aren't they meant to hate each other's guts?'

Redford was quietly dismayed by the general's reply. For the last three years she had been filing report after report from Yemen alerting her superiors to the growing evidence that covert deals were being struck between opposing factions. There were an overwhelming number of anecdotal examples of US-made military equipment, legally traded with Saudi Arabia and the UAE, falling into the hands of Houthi fighters. The official response had always been that weapons caches must have been abducted or recovered following skirmishes or withdrawals from battle. Certainly there were cases of UAE fighters leaving weapons behind which were discovered by advancing Houthi divisions, but she'd long suspected that something more coordinated was at play. Now she finally had the hard evidence that vindicated everything that she'd previously said, but it was important not to ram that fact down her superiors' throats.

'We believe some sort of deal was being struck, General,' she explained.

'Excuse me, Agent Redford,' interrupted Strous, 'but do we know who's buying what?'

Redford allowed the video to play, zooming in on Shahlai's men loading several crates on to the back of their trucks. She froze the tape as the men climbed back into their vehicles to drive away.

'I'd say it's clear that Shahlai is the buyer. We can't get a close enough look at this resolution to see exactly what is in those crates, but our best estimate is that they contain small arms, possibly artillery.'

'Chinese?' Parry was again first to chime in. 'Or Russian?'

'American,' Redford replied.

'Bullshit.' Parry wasn't a man to mince his words.

'I wish it was, General.' Redford fast-forwarded the tape, following Shahlai's trucks to his munitions factory in Sa'dah. She blew up an image of the buildings. 'We now believe that Shahlai has been using this location to develop and adapt weapons for some time. We are concerned that could have long-term impact on our R&D, but our immediate fear is that he is planning to use US weapons in an attack against the Saudis.'

There was a collective draw of breath from every screen in the room. Redford didn't pause to acknowledge it, instead she drew up the next tape. She played the tape showing a solitary truck leaving the market building and then fast forwarded to show it reaching the checkpoint on the road to Midi.

'This vehicle left Shahlai's base at 17:00 today, reaching the loyalist checkpoint outside of Midi at approximately 21:00 hours.'

'Saudi-controlled territory?'

'Correct. It's what happens next that concerns us.'

She played the tape, just in from the spooks, so new that even Mason hadn't seen it. The video clearly depicted the scene that had played out at the Midi checkpoint, the flash of the gun was clear for all to see. She froze the action and zoomed in on the grainy image until they could see the shooter's face.

'We've been able to make a positive ID from the image on Faisal Ahadi, one of Shahlai's closest associates. It would seem they have accessed Midi.' She ran the tape again, describing to the room what they were watching. 'The vehicle doesn't stop in the town but continues to the port, where it disappears into this track that leads to the beach. They kill the headlights here, so after that we don't have pictures.'

The screen went dark for a moment as Redford stopped the tape and the faces appeared again.

'What's your assessment, Agent Redford?'

Redford was surprised to see that the question had come from Matt Mason sitting next to her. He'd ignored her when they'd had the chance to take Shahlai in Sana'a and Shahlai had escaped. She'd been so angry after that that she'd shut herself down to him in return. That had been a mistake. His assessment of what Shahlai was doing on the coast would now seem to have been accurate and it had been pig-headed of her to ignore him. They had lost valuable time as a result.

'I . . . we believe that Ruak Shahlai is planning to use Midi port as a base from which to use US weapons in an attack against our ally, Saudi Arabia. I personally believe that is because it appeals to his sense of irony and because it gives Iran plausible deniability when the international community inevitably point the finger. But make no bones about it, gentlemen, he intends to create an environmental holocaust in the Red Sea.'

'So, what exactly are we talking?' Parry asked.

'An oil spill five times the size of Exxon Valdez, which, due to the geography of the Red Sea, would result in losing the entire ecosystem of marine life, sea birds, fish stocks, dolphins, you name it – all gone, totally destroyed.'

'Dolphins?' The general rubbed his hand wearily over his eyes. 'Agent Redford, can I remind you of Deepwater Horizon? Our own little oil spill right here in America not so long ago, which precisely zero people give one single fuck about any more. If Americans don't give a fuck about American dolphins, Agent Redford, then you can be sure as shit they don't give a fuck about Saudi ones.'

Redford bit her tongue and zoomed in on the map of the region, highlighting the coast north of Midi. She traced a line showing that the northern refineries were clustered around the city of Rabigh, a full six hundred miles north of the border.

'Maybe they'll care more about the economic impact,' she said, highlighting all the Saudi refineries and ports along the coast. 'This attack will take out every single Saudi oil-exporting port for a minimum of six months. Given Saudi's central role in the international supply, you're looking at hitting an oil price of two, three, maybe four hundred dollars in days. And if they retaliate against Iran, which they certainly will, then you can go north of eight hundred with that estimate. Do you know what an eight-hundred-dollar oil price would do to the US economy, General? It would mean deep structural damage to supply lines and industry, unemployment lines like we haven't seen since the 1930s. In fact, you can take the Great Depression, throw in Lehman's and the coronavirus, then triple it.'

'Stop! Okay, I get it. Shit, you've got me thinking of buying a wind farm over here all of a sudden.'

'It's too late for that now, General.' She addressed him directly. 'At least, it is unless we stop this.'

'Look, this is still conjecture, and we all know what the technological capabilities of the Houthis are,' Dominic Strous finally chimed in, and not in a helpful way. 'That's way beyond their range.'

He was right, all previous attempts by the Houthis had proven that there was no way they could hit a ship in the sea from that kind of range.

'But what if Shahlai's found a way to strike in the north?' Redford replied.

'That's rather a large assumption. I think we need to proceed with extreme caution,' Strous said.

'Agreed, we cannot afford another mistake,' said one of Redford's bosses.

'How about we continue to run satellite observation for now and monitor how things progress?' said Blandford.

There was a murmur of agreement in the room. Redford, on the other hand, heard the words and slowly felt her message start to disappear in a fog of political buck-passing. Neither side wanted to be the one to sanction another sortie into Yemeni sovereign territory so soon after the last fiasco. It dawned on her that another chance to stop Shahlai might be slipping through her grip, only this time the consequences would be catastrophic.

Langley had not listened to her before. They had underestimated Shahlai time and again, assuming him to be an agitator, a petty-minded thug whose ambitions stretched only to beheading a heathen or two on YouTube. Nobody but her had expected him to actually create real damage. But now there was a very real danger that he would seriously damage the whole planet. The monster that had been allowed to grow in Yemen was going to become the rest of the world's very own nightmare unless they did something about it fast.

'We could take a small team,' Mason said finally, interrupting the politicians. 'If there's nothing there, then we pull back. If there is, then we take them out.'

'Aren't you the guy who got us into this mess?' asked Parry.

'Staff Sergeant Mason was hardly—' Redford began, but Mason cut across her.

'Yes I am, General. And I lost one of my best men, so I want to sort this out more than anyone.'

'I appreciate that, Staff Sergeant,' Parry said, 'not easy losing a guy on your watch.'

'No, sir.'

The room waited for the general to speak again. Whatever power dynamic they'd all come into the room with, it was clear who they were expecting to make the final call. The general rubbed his eyes again and let out a snort.

'Okay, well look. Here's my play,' he said. 'A small operational team. We go in under cover. Get eyes on whatever these guys are up to in the port, and if we need to, then we take him out. Otherwise we're out of there fast as we came in. Can we agree?'

Another general murmur of agreement. The British pair stayed particularly quiet, happy that the US were seen to be making the call. Redford's boss shrugged to indicate that it wouldn't have been the call that she would have made, but she could live with it.

'Okay. So we're go. Godspeed.' The general hung up the call.

Redford looked round to Mason and without anyone else in the room noticing, she mouthed, 'Thank you'.

Mason nodded back. They had finally developed some kind of an understanding. They'd both fucked up once and there couldn't be a next time. They officially had to work together, but unofficially, they knew that they had to make sure that whatever Shahlai was planning, they stopped it before it was too late. After that, they could focus on bringing him in.

THIRTY-FOUR

Midi, Yemen

The old port of Midi could be better described these days as a graveyard. What once had been the epicentre of a flourishing community of fishermen and traders was now nothing more than a bombed-out scrapyard of decommissioned ships and hollowed-out fishing boats. The sea wall that once protected the boats from storms, reinforced with local stone, was now littered with the debris of shattered hulls and rusty containers. The dockside, which had once teemed with dockers landing food and goods from boats around the world, and later served as a landing site for arms from Iran, was now just a pock-marked crater, destroyed systematically by relentless aerial bombardment from Saudi planes.

In the last year since the town had fallen to forces loyal to Hadi and the House of Saud, the Houthi forces had fled back to the safety of the desert and some hope had slowly returned. The Saudis had donated new fishing boats to several families in the town and offered them safe passage through the heavily mined waters to the north, into their own fishing grounds, where they could operate in safety under the cover of the Saudi Navy. Steadily, life had returned to Midi's shoreline.

Faisal Ahadi had made it his mission to study the area and also what had gone wrong on previous attempts by the Houthis to strike at Saudi targets in the sea. A keen student, he had been intrigued to discover that the use of suicide boats could be traced all the way back to the American Civil War, when Confederate forces used semi-submersible crafts packed with explosives against Union forces. Later, during World War Two, the Italians, Japanese and even the Germans had used suicide boats with success. Al-Qaeda had brought the technique into the twenty-first century when they had used a suicide boat to destroy the USS Cole, killing dozens of US marines. But the prospect of success for the Houthis repeating such a feat had diminished with each failure. The Saudi coalition had learned quickly and had strengthened the naval blockade around Yemen, using its huge superiority on the seas to maintain calm.

Both coasts of the Red Sea were of major commercial interest to the Saudis. On the East African coast, there were several important Emirati and Saudi naval and military bases in Eritrea and Djibouti, which played an important role in the war in Yemen, serving as logistical staging areas for Saudi operations and for the control of the sea lanes. It was Faisal's ambition that, if he could refine the suicide boats and make them more successful, then one day even those bases would become legitimate targets.

But for now, he was focused on something closer to home. He believed that the previous attempts to use the fast boats had been scuppered because they were too obvious. The strategy in the past had been only to go fast, without considering that the Saudis would always go faster. When the general had set him the task of getting past the Saudis, he had decided that sacrificing speed was worth it if, in return, the boats could remain unseen. Faisal had seen that was a much smarter way to approach the problem and so his solution was to get to the target using boats that nobody would suspect.

With the port in tatters, Midi's fishermen had instead started to pull their new fishing boats up on to the sandy beach to the south at the end of each day. The beach ran a clear mile south of the marina and the fishermen had built a collection of single-storey mud-brick shacks along its length to house their equipment and engines.

By the time Faisal Ahadi and his men had arrived at the beach, they had already acquired a detailed knowledge of every one of the boats along it from their owners, the men that Ruak Shahlai had kidnapped and tortured in Al Hudaydah over the previous two weeks. Four of the fishermen who owned the new Saudi boats had eventually been very forthcoming in sharing the details of their day-to-day lives. They had explained not only where their boats were positioned on the beach, but also their routes and in which shack their equipment was stored.

Faisal had been able to easily access one of the mud-brick shacks, and once inside, he and his comrades began carefully unpacking the contents of their truck. Once everything was unloaded, they had hidden the truck among the sand dunes, locked themselves in the shack and got to work.

The four men set themselves up in opposite corners of the building and began carefully unpacking the contents of four of five wooden crates from the truck, laying their contents out on blankets on the ground. Once all the crates were empty, they each began placing the items according to the schematic drawings that they had downloaded on their phones.

The explosives from the munitions factory in Sa'dah were arranged in paired sets of armaments, each allocated to their appropriate mechanism. They had been developed expertly, adapted by the craftsmen in Sa'dah so that each man had four charges to be matched with the stripped-out contents of four fin-stabilised M120 mortar rounds. The warheads from each mortar had been stripped from their casings and repurposed, so that they could be set with an impact fuse. Once in place, the fuse allowed the pin to come directly into contact with its target, upon which the percussion cap would create a small spark that fired down into the detonator and caused the main explosion.

It was essential to have no distance between the explosion and the boat to get the full impact. The first set of charges would be placed on the bow and set to explode on impact, while the two placed port and starboard were set with a half-second delay. Once the first bombs had done the damage and penetrated the steel outer skin on the tanker, the second pair of bombs would do the same to the inner skin.

As well as the four warheads, they had a quantity of plastic explosive to strap to each device. The warhead explosion alone would almost certainly do enough damage, but the plastic explosives were there to be doubly sure. Once the whole lot went up, there wasn't much it wouldn't take with it.

The icing on the cake came from four jerrycans full of petrol and a sack of washing powder. Faisal shared the washing powder out in smaller bags, strapping each one to each can of fuel. When the explosives went off, the petrol would go up like the American Fourth of July, and the sticky washing powder would ensure that the flames attached to the hull, turning each boat into a devastating incendiary device.

Faisal surveilled the assembled parts that lay in front of him, marvelling at how not a single piece would be traceable back to Iran. In fact, other than the jerrycans which were Yemeni, everything was labelled with US manufacturers' serial codes. The scheme devised by General Shahlai was brilliant; striking at the heart of their enemy while exposing the corruption and hypocrisy that typified their regime.

Once he had all the components set, Faisal began connecting each part together just as he had been told, following the instructions that he had memorised before leaving the munitions factory. He moved slowly and methodically first, wiring the warheads to the fuses and then packing the plastic explosives. He thought to himself how there really was nothing that they could not do now, even from a base in the northern regions of the Yemeni desert. Everything was at their fingertips. The domination of smaller powers by their larger neighbours would soon be a thing of the past. War had been democratised, even if the people had not.

When he was satisfied that he had finished, he placed the four explosive devices to one side and returned to the last remaining crate. The last thing each man had to do was to put together a radio-controlled kit. The engineers had designed four sets of servos with electric fuses and motors stripped from car windshield wipers and had adapted them to fit to the throttle and tiller inside of the boats. Using a simple remote-control joystick, an operator could remotely control the speed and direction of the boat from up to half a mile away. It would be enough to get the boat through the minefields and the Saudi blockade and into the open waters of the Red Sea. From there, they could set the boats on a specific heading for the point of impact and later adjustments could be made using GPS technology adapted from the US drones they had shot down over the desert.

He checked his watch. If they continued to work through the night, they would have the kits assembled and fitted before the other fishermen woke in their beds. After that, another couple of hours to wait until the first light of the dawn, when they would be ready to make their final prayer. If it was Allah's will, then he would help them achieve their goal. Immediately afterwards they would push four radio-controlled suicide boats out on to the waves and steer them in the direction of Saudi Arabia and the fishing grounds to the north. With His Divine Will, they would succeed where previous attempts had failed. By tomorrow morning, the House of Saud would be a billion dollars poorer, Yemen's children would be free from their endless plight, Faisal would have atoned for his previous errors of judgement and Iran would take its rightful place as the beating heart of the region's power.

THIRTY-FIVE

The pair of Puma helicopters nosed their way through the warm desert night air like a pair of lions on the hunt. Although their destination was the port of Midi almost due north, they were flying west, following a route that had been preloaded on to their navigation systems to ensure they avoided flying over any Houthi-controlled towns, villages or military positions. Staying close to the ground, a little under 200 feet, they blasted along within a few hundred feet of each other at over 100 mph towards the Red Sea. On reaching the shore, the Pumas jackknifed right and banked low along the coast.

In the back of the leading chopper, Matt Mason tried to relax his mind. While they were in the air, there was nothing he could do to affect the outcome of the task, so it was better to leave the job of getting there to the experts. He looked at the gunner, Donny Mac, a strong, wiry Welshman, hanging out of the side of the Puma, clutching his 7.62mm mini-gun, night-vision goggles on, eyes glued to the ground below, ready to tear into any unfriendlies that they might accidentally encounter. Woe betide them if they did. Donny had a deadeye and being blasted by him from above was like encountering a fire-breathing dragon.

As they hit the coast, the air cooled and Mason could smell the sea on the draught that blew in from the open hatches. The feeling of the breeze on his face afforded him a moment's relief from the tension in his gut. The memory of his last time leading a team on a task was playing on his mind. He could almost see Andy sitting right there opposite him, his gun pimped out with all the 'ally' gear, making cheeky wisecracks in his Scouse drawl. Mason felt a pang of regret for having been so harsh with the lad.

The helicopter banked hard left and right, twisting its way through the air, staying low to the sea while hugging the coastline. Mason quietly cursed the pilot, Charles Wise, a bit of a legend in the RAF because he flew faster and harder than anyone else. It was a gut-churning experience being in Charles's chopper, like being on a fairground ride, but a rollercoaster only lasts a couple of minutes for a reason – that's all most people can stomach. The journey from the LZ to Midi had already taken over an hour. Mason closed down his urge to vomit again, he'd never quite grown used to having his guts thrown around, even after all these years. He focused instead on the task, mentally going over his to-do list one last time.

Sitting opposite him he had his core team back on board. He knew that Mad Jack, Pommy, Briggs and Carl were all in the same boat as him. None of them ever needed to say it, but he understood that they all felt the same way about what had happened to Andy and that they'd all rather die than let it lie. Whatever happened next, Ruak Shahlai was going to pay for what he'd done to their mate. The most important thing that Mason had to do next was get his team into that port, because he knew he could trust them to do the rest.

A few minutes later, Mason felt the helicopter begin to slow, which meant they were getting close to the LZ. Suddenly, Charles banked again to port and the back end dropped, lowering them fast towards the ground. The force of it didn't bother Mason this time, nor any of the other guys, they were too busy preparing for what was coming next, gathering their gear, getting ready to hit the ground running.

The second Puma landed less than a hundred feet away while the five men unloaded their equipment from the lead chopper. Just like the other men, Mason had his own 5.56 Diemaco rifle, a laser and night scopes, and eight magazines of thirty armour-piercing rounds. In his leg holster he wore a 9mm pistol with three spare mags of fifteen rounds. Lastly, he had half a dozen L2 fragmentation grenades in a quick access pouch.

He helped Mad Jack lug the massive M72 LAW, a portable one-shot 66mm unguided anti-tank gun, up off the ground and then watched as he slung it over his broad shoulders like it was a scarf. The man was an ox. Once they had eyes on exactly where Faisal was launching from, the LAW warhead could be dispatched to take him out along with everything else within a thirty-metre radius.

Pommy and Briggs discarded their Diemacos, preferring instead to use the Belgian FN Minimi 5.56-calibre light machine gun. Each man packed his sack with eight hundred rounds in link. As far as Mason was concerned, the Minimi was the absolute best weapon in the world for reliability and firepower. And in the hands of Pom and Briggsy, it turned them into a two-man infantry division.

Waiting for them all, Craig Bell stood patiently, ready to move. Despite the darkness, he had already assembled his bolt-action sniper rifle in seconds, equipping it with a 25x scope and suppressor, giving him the ability to take out a target from over half a mile away without making a sound.

Mason nodded to all of his men, satisfied that they were ready to move out. He turned and watched Hopkins and his team unloading the equipment from the second bird. The captain and four men would bring up the rear, operating an 81mm mortar. If things got hairy, their orders were to lay the whole fucking port flatter than a Shrove Tuesday pancake.

The last man out of the chopper was Agent Redford.

'Sure you got enough kit for nine guys?' she said sarcastically, releasing the safety on her Glock and cocking it to put a bullet in the chamber.

'If we hadn't brought you, we'd have had ten,' Mason said.

'Yeah, but if you hadn't brought me, you'd have fucked up again.'

The laughter coming from behind him stopped Mason in his tracks, but he decided to let it slide. It was probably for the best to keep quiet. She had a point.

'Let's just hope you don't need to use that,' he said.

Mason looked again at the gun in her hand and then scanned the enormous arsenal of weapons laid out before them. If she had to use a Glock, he thought, then they really were in trouble. He saw Redford glance up to the mountains above. The sun was not yet up but its light was already peeking over the ridge. The port was still three miles from the LZ, at a point deliberately selected to ensure that Faisal would not see nor hear the birds landing. If they moved fast and unhindered, they should be there in an hour.

'You'd better get going,' said Redford.

The plan was for the American to accompany Hopkins and the fire support team, while Mason led the asssault team directly on to the primary target. But as Redford turned away from him to walk back towards Hopkins and the others, he reached out to stop her.

'Hang on,' he said, picking up Briggsy's discarded Diemaco. He threw the rifle to her, and she caught it in one hand.

'You know how to use that?' he asked.

'Yes, Sergeant,' she said.

'Well you better fucking had,' he said. Then with a wave of his arm, he gestured for his team to move.

One by one the men filed out, Jack, Briggs, Pommy and Craig set off, moving quietly and quickly over the rough ground. Mason motioned for Redford to follow behind them and she fell in with Mason bringing up the rear.

An hour from now they would be in the port of Midi, where a man from Coventry and a team of Iranian jihadists were diligently preparing to create the largest man-made disaster that the world had ever seen.

THIRTY-SIX

The sky to the east of Midi was still dark, but the tips of the mountain peaks along the highest ridge were gradually appearing as dim silhouettes. The dawn light had begun to bleed into the blackness, turning everything a shade of inky blue. The day was coming and there was nothing anyone could do now to stop it.

On the beach below, four men lined up along the sand. They were already deep in their third devotion of the day, the ṣalāt al-Fajr, or morning prayer. Faisal Ahadi led his comrades, quietly recanting the two rakats of the Fajr, kneeling on the sand with only their palms, knees, toes, foreheads and noses touching the ground. 'Glory be to God, the highest,' they repeated three times before they rose into a more comfortable seated pose, feet tucked in underneath, eyes closed, hands on laps, taking a moment to reflect on their own prayer.

Faisal recited aloud his favourite verses from the Koran, 'We have awoken, and all of creation has awoken, for Allah, Lord of all the Worlds. Allah, I ask You for the best the day has to offer, victory, support, light, blessings and guidance; and I seek refuge in You from the evil in it, and the evil to come after it.'

The men either side of him silently nodded their approval before they raised their right index fingers to the sky and privately asked Allah for His forgiveness and mercy. Then the men stood and turned first to their right, then to their left, offering their neighbour the greeting of peace. 'Peace be upon you, and the mercy and blessings of Allah.'

With their souls cleansed, it was time to get on with the important business of completing the last stages of their work. The men returned to the hut to collect the last pieces of the gear while Faisal walked along the line of boats, making final checks to the automated rigs and the explosives they had modified on board. He looked out to sea and felt relieved to see that the waters were as calm as a Coventry canal. The last thing he needed to contend with today were choppy seas.

On the road to the far end of the beach he heard the high-pitched buzz of a cheap Chinese scooter and saw the dim beam from its headlights cast across the sand. The first of the local fishermen had arrived. Pretty soon the whole beach would come alive with men from the town, preparing for the day's work. Faisal and the others had deliberately set themselves up at the southern end of the beach, some distance away from the other boats, so as not to draw attention to themselves. But in the event that any nosey parkers had questions to ask, then zero tolerance would be the policy of the day.

The sight of the bike focused his mind. He was in no doubt about the path he had chosen. Indeed, he felt that his life finally made sense now that he better understood his role in it. He had been bestowed with a great honour and as long as he performed as he knew he was capable, then he would get his reward. He felt a flush of pride in his heart, and for the first time in a long time, a longing for his parents. He wished that his father could see how what he was doing would bring honour to their family. Maybe even what he was going to achieve here in Midi would enable his family to return to Iran one day as celebrated patriots. He imagined the joy that his father would feel, walking again through the streets of Tehran. How proud he would be of his son; the soldier, the fighter, the hero.

When the last pieces of kit had been loaded on to the boat and he had satisfied himself that they were ready to launch, Faisal whistled to the hut where they had spent the night preparing. With a tilt of his head, he signalled to the men inside that everything was ready for the launch. There was only one more detail he had to attend to.

The door to the hut opened and the largest of his comrades emerged, pushing the hapless, blindfolded Eli Drake down the beach. Eli's hands were tied behind his back and he stumbled as he tried to find his footing. Faisal realised that the priest was mumbling to himself and he recognised the words as familiar. Of course, it was the Christian Lord's Prayer. He had heard it recited every morning in his British school. His teacher had insisted that, even though Faisal was not of their faith, he learn it along with the rest of his class. How fitting that the priest should be choosing it now as his final words.

When Eli reached the water, Faisal tore off his blindfold, causing the Christian to recoil from the light. It was still only ten minutes since the dawn, but Eli had been blindfolded and kept in darkness for several days. When he could finally make out where he was, he seemed disorientated and unsure of himself.

'Do you know how to drive a boat, Mr Drake?' Faisal asked.

Eli shook his head, surprised to hear the question asked in English. By the sound of the accent, he'd say that the speaker came from somewhere in the Midlands.

'I'm afraid not,' he replied.

Faisal laughed and translated their exchange into Arabic for the other men, upon which they all laughed too.

'Well, don't worry. We've thought of everything, so you don't miss out.'

Eli looked baffled, but before he could say another word, the strongman was pushing him again, this time into the water. He didn't even try to resist, just did as he was told as he splashed into the shallows.

The two men yanked him up on board the boat and guided him on to the seat at the rear, near to the tiller. One man held him down, while the other strapped his legs to the seat with a length of rope. His legs were bound tightly so that he couldn't move forwards or backwards, and his hands remained tied behind his back, so that all he could do was slump helplessly against the side of the boat.

When the men had finished, Faisal climbed on and assessed their work.

'Not bad,' he said. 'Just one thing missing.'

He took off his own turban and placed it down hard on Eli's head.

'Now,' said Faisal with a smile, 'that is perfect.'

The three men left Eli and returned to the hut for the final part of their plan – to collect the corpses of the two soldiers they had killed at the checkpoint the previous night. Faisal had seen an opportunity the second their bodies had hit the dirt. They lifted them inside the two remaining boats and tied them in place just as they had done with Eli.

Faisal was happy with the effect. A change of clothes, some careful manipulation and a well-placed turban meant that, at a casual glance, they looked like ordinary fishermen driving their boats. A manned vessel would be a lot less suspicious to a passing Saudi naval ship than an unmanned one. Now he had three registered Saudi fishing boats loaded with enough explosives to take out a tanker, each equipped with a driver.

By now the beach was bustling with activity. Many more fishermen had arrived on the shore and had begun preparing their equipment for the day. They performed their routines, carrying nets and lines from the huts, lugging them up on to their boats. One or two may have glanced quickly towards the other end of the beach where Faisal and the others were pushing their boats into the water, but they said nothing. Interfering got you nowhere good in Yemen. Better to keep your business to yourself.

If they had looked more closely, they would have seen that the four men pushing the boats into the water were not fishermen, they would have seen that not one of them boarded the boats themselves once they were beyond the breakwater. They might even have noticed that instead, the men retreated to their hut and closed the door, while the boats continued on without them, slowly making their way out to deeper water, before turning along the shore, past the old bombed-out harbour, to the open sea.

THIRTY-SEVEN

The road from Midi to the port ran west for half a kilometre and then turned due north, parallel with the shoreline of the Red Sea for another kilometre, before it stopped abruptly at the old harbour. Mason checked his watch. 4.30 a.m. Early for most people in the UK but not for the people of Yemen. Thirty minutes back along the track, just after they'd left Hopkins and the fire support team, he'd heard the muezzin in Midi calling the Fajr. After morning prayers were over, the town's men had appeared, driving their scooters along the road to the beach to collect their boats and head out to sea. Fishing was the lifeblood of most Yemeni towns along this stretch of coast, but the men of Midi were the fortunate ones who had been given access to the rich fishing waters to the north. The reward for cooperating with the Saudis was that they would have more fish to sell in the markets than their countrymen to the south.

Checking that there were no late stragglers coming from the south, Mason lifted himself up and ran fast across the track. He threw himself down again on the beach's soft sand and seconds later felt the thud of Mad Jack, Redford and the others landing either side of him. Five men and one woman lifted their heads slowly to take a look at the beach below.

To his north, Mason could see the remains of the destroyed harbour, and then, running south along the beach, a line of seven single-storey mud-brick buildings. There were men milling around, some were dragging nets and equipment to a line of fishing boats pulled up on the water's edge, others were already heaving their boats off the sand and into the breakwater. Mason could see a few boats in the distance, already on the sea, heading north. Taking care to keep his head low, he fetched his binoculars from his pocket and passed them to Redford.

'Can you see him?' he asked.

Redford took the field glasses and scanned along the beach. In total she estimated that she could see around thirty fishermen. The two buildings to the north, nearest to the harbour, seemed quiet except for a group of older men sat around smoking cigarettes. Next, she carefully scrutinised the huts to the south. Every one had men working around it except for the last hut on the beach, the hut right at the end, which seemed to be unoccupied. She shook her head and passed the glasses back to Mason. She couldn't see Faisal Ahadi.

Mason rubbed his beard while he thought. The fire support team led by Hopkins was waiting for him to give an order to launch a mortar attack on the beach. With one call, in five minutes' time, the scene that he was looking at could be reduced to a crater of sand and bones. But there was no way he could give that order given the number of friendlies down there. Never mind that he hadn't confirmed the presence of Ahadi. No. They had no choice but to go down and take a closer look.

When he gave the command, the team filed along the track, double-timing it to the harbour at the north end of the beach. Following after Mason, they dropped in behind the harbour wall, and then, still unnoticed by the few fishermen working at the water's edge, slid in behind the first hut. Jack stuck his head through the small window at the rear of the building.

'Clear,' Jack said quietly under his breath.

They wasted no time moving on to the second hut, finding it similarly unoccupied. When they reached the third, Mason could hear sounds coming from inside. With a wave of his hand, he instructed Briggs and Pommy to stay at the rear while he led the others to the front. When everyone was set, Mason burst in through the open door.

The inside of the hut was a mess of fishing nets, broken buoys and engine parts. The space was dark save for a dim solitary battery-powered light that balanced precariously on the window ledge. The whole place stank of fish and oil. Looking directly down the barrel of his rifle, Mason swept the room, stopping when he saw the terrified face of an old Yemeni man looking back at him. The man dropped a box of fish hooks from his hand and closed his eyes.

'Down,' Mason said in Arabic.

Keeping his eyes firmly shut, the man kneeled on the floor and fell prostrate at Mason's feet. While Jack, Craig and Redford covered the door, Mason crouched down and spoke calmly to him.

'We're looking for a man who is not from this place. Do you understand?'

The old man nodded and without lifting his head, slowly stretched out his left hand and pointed his long spindly finger south, along the beach.

Mason could see the old geezer was shaking with fear; a good sign that he was telling the truth. He patted him on the shoulder and left him lying where he was, figuring it was probably the safest place for him.

They left the hut and continued south. Mason knew their cover was blown as they could clearly be seen now by the fishermen on the beach. But nobody spoke to them. The fishermen just continued their work, preparing their boats, careful not to make eye contact with the foreign soldiers, just as they had with the men they'd seen pushing boats into the water a few minutes earlier.

At the second-to-last hut, Mason and his five colleagues dropped to the ground, sitting with their backs against its northern wall. If the old man was right, then Faisal and his team were in the last hut less than fifty yards away. The distance from Faisal's hut to their current position made calling in a mortar strike from Hopkins and the fire support team impossible. Mason had seen mortars in action too many times to rely on their accuracy. Seen too many good men killed by their own rounds. No, the only way now was to advance on to the hut and hope that they had the element of surprise.

Mason turned his head around the wall to get a better look at Faisal's position, but as soon as he did, he saw the flash of the rifle. The bullet bit into the corner of the wall inches above Mason's head. He spun on his heel, diving back for cover as the shooter unleashed a volley of bullets, peppering the walls, showering the team in fragments of dried mud and sand.

'So much for the element of fucking surprise.'

THIRTY-EIGHT

The four huge rotor blades of the Puma HC2 helicopter idled slowly round and round, barely disturbing the dust below. Inside the cockpit, Flight Lieutenant Jim Sparke sat, eyes glued to his inflight radar screen. He could see that four minutes earlier Mason's assault team had stopped on Midi beach and that their position had not moved since. The six small blue dots on the screen were lined up so close to each other that he figured they were likely now in an emergency response situation. It looked like the guys had run into some action. He checked his watch. It was eight minutes since Mason had last initiated a voice check, three minutes longer than protocol but still seven minutes before he had to put contingency plans in place.

'Lifter One. This is Ground Call Sign Charlie One.' It was the voice of Captain Hopkins coming over his comms. 'Five-minute check. All quiet. Over.'

Jim spoke into his mic, 'Charlie One. This is Lifter One. Roger that.'

He cut the comms and stared out to the Red Sea, forty kilometres away on the horizon. Without even realising that he was saying it, he whispered, 'Come on, Mace.'

Fifty yards to his left, the other Puma was also idling, waiting for the call to go. Both helicopters were ready to scramble in seconds and were capable of reaching Midi beach in under three minutes. Jim knew the two men on board the other helicopter well, Flight Captain Charles Wise had flown with him in Afghanistan. He wasn't much to look at, in fact they often joked they were the only two bald pilots in the whole RAF, but what Charles lacked in hair, he made up for in balls. After Afghanistan, he'd been awarded the Distinguished Flying Cross for flying eight missions in two days right into the heart of a hot zone to save twenty-five British servicemen under a hail of Taliban bullets. The man had nerves of steel. The gunner he had on board was cut from the same cloth. Although Jim had never met a gunner who wasn't just a little bit crazy. It went with the job, and Donny Mac was as mad as he was lethal. They were good men and Jim couldn't have asked to be on a better team.

'What do you reckon, Charles?' he said over their private channel.

Charles turned to look over to him. 'Sit tight, mate. Probably just having a nice swim down the beach.'

Jim forced out a chuckle before he checked his watch again; ten minutes since they'd heard from the assault team. What were they playing at?

Suddenly Mason's voice came over the comms. 'Lifter One this is Bravo One. Over.'

'This is Lifter One. Over.' Jim could hear rapid and heavy gunfire in the background.

'Winchester, mate. Winchester.'

Both pilots instantly recognised the coded call. Jim opened the throttle on his engine and fired up the twin turboshafts to full speed, pushing the rotors to 265 rpm. He went through his take-off protocol, something he could do in his sleep because the bird was by now an extension of himself. He had been trained for moments like this and the course of adrenaline that he could now feel was nothing but energy for his body. He turned to Charles and seeing that Lifter Two was in good shape, he gave his buddy the thumbs up, and both Pumas lifted into the air, sucking up a tornado of dust and sand below them.

'Low level, high speed, Jimbo. Be prepared for QBOs,' said Charles.

Quick Battle Orders were almost inevitable given Mason's position. The contingency plan had been clearly laid out before the task had begun. In the event of a quick-reaction force response, Jim would fly directly east to extract Hopkins' fire support team before continuing on for Mason and his squad. At the same time, Charles in the other helicopter would bank around to the north of Midi town and provide cover for Mason from the air. As the Puma with the guns, Charles and Donny Mac's bird was the one that could give Mason's team the firepower they needed on the beach.

The Pumas flew low over the desert, barely 100 feet above the ground at a speed of over 100 mph. Ninety seconds later they were just ten kilometres out from the shoreline and Jim got eyes on Hopkins' team. As he began his approach, Charles's Puma banked south, following the agreed path, skirting just north of the town towards the beach. Again, Mason's voice came over the comms.

'Lifter One. This is Bravo One. Be aware we are pinned down at target location. Do not go north of us. Stay south of our location. Repeat do not approach from the north.'

'Roger that, Bravo One.' Jim heard Charles confirming Mason's directions. 'T-minus ninety seconds. Hang in there, Mace.'

Inside Charles's Puma, Donny Mac hoisted the big twin 7.62mm belt-chain general purpose machine gun over to the starboard side and began preparing for an attack from the south. The huge twin guns would make mincemeat of whomever they were about to encounter, and Donny reckoned that meant someone had just over a minute to say their final prayers. With the gun in position, he strapped himself in tight and readied himself for his work.

In the other helicopter, three hundred metres out from Hopkins' position, Jim pulled hard on the cyclic, angling the pitch lever, sending the nose of the bird up hard and fast, effectively slamming on the helicopter's brakes. Using his feet to operate the pedals below, he turned the Puma as he lowered it to the ground, swinging the nose round to the south, giving the men below the fastest way on board. Twenty feet from the ground, he looked up. He was facing due south and he could see Charles's helicopter tearing along the sky between him and Midi town. But a split second later he saw something that would haunt him for the rest of his life.

A Toyota Hilux was not an unusual sight in Yemen. It was considered the most desirable vehicle in the country, given the mixture of potholed highways and rough desert tracks that answered for roads in the country. The other advantage of the Hilux was its reinforced suspension that supported a generously proportioned flat rear bed. The back was easily big enough to support a month's supply of water or half a dozen goats or a single jihadi carrying an M72 LAW rocket-propelled grenade, which emits a very prominent flash when it's dispatched.

From his position, Jim couldn't see the jihadist, nor indeed the Hilux or the Iranian general Ruak Shahlai sitting in the passenger seat. What Jim did see was the flash, followed by the distinct hot red trail of the eight-pound grenade speeding at 145m/s towards Charles's helicopter. In the 1.2 seconds that filled the time between the flash and its impact, Jim could not formulate a coherent thought. All his brain was capable of processing was that he was about to witness the worst thing he had ever seen.

The explosion that followed was absolute. And for 5,813 microseconds, it was entirely silent. In that fraction of an instant, Jim saw the flames engulf the fuselage, breaking it apart before it vanished into smoke. He saw the rotors scatter in different directions, one firing straight up into the air like a rocket, the others spinning east and west. He felt the certainty of death and the tragedy of its significance just before he felt the blast and the sound that accompanied it.

His helicopter lurched backwards with the force of the shockwave so hard that he had to fight with the stick for a moment to keep control. As Jim regained command of his own chopper, he watched Charles's bird plummeting to the ground in a ball of flame and twisted metal.

He was jolted out of his trance by the sound of Mason's voice. 'Lifter One. This is Bravo One. Sitrep. Repeat sitrep. What the fuck was that, Jimmy?'

Some instinct kicked in within Jim Sparke and he began to speak slowly into the comms. 'All call signs, Lifter Two is down. Lifter Two is down.'

'Fuck,' Mason came back on the comms.

'Diverting to support Lifter Two,' Jim said, pulling hard on the stick, firing the Puma upwards, drowning Hopkins and his team in a dust cloud below.

'Negative, Lifter One,' Mason barked into the comms. 'Continue with task. Do you understand?'

Jim looked across the rocky scrubland stretched out in front of him. Less than two miles away, his friends had no-sedived into the desert. He swallowed hard, fighting to concentrate, holding off some conflict that was telling him to go and also to stay.

'Lifter One?' Mason's voice was again in his ear but this time it seemed distant to him. 'They're gone, mate. We need you here now.'

Jim Sparke could hear his own breath, it sounded louder than he remembered, the stick in his hand felt bigger than it had before, and the Puma felt heavy and unmanageable. He looked down at the men below, staring up at him, waiting to see what he was going to do, and again he heard Mason's voice.

'Lifter One, proceed north of target location for immediate extraction. Over.'

Jim nodded. He felt a clarity wash over him. His friends were dead but the living needed him. He thought about Charles Wise, the bravest fucker he'd ever known, and about Donny, the mad gunner. He thought about what they would have done. Charles wouldn't have hesitated. He'd have flown into the hot zone and pulled Mason and his team out to safety. Now it was Jim's turn to do the same. For Charles, for Donny and for the living. He pushed the pedal and turned the Puma east. He opened the throttle and pushed the nose towards Mason and the Midi harbour.

THIRTY-NINE

The last volley of bullets coming from Faisal's hut had been an almost continuous blast, lasting for over thirty seconds. The mud walls that Mason, Jack, Redford, Briggs, Pom and Craig were taking cover behind were rapidly coming apart, but when the shooting stopped, Jack gave Mason a thumbs up. They were happy to let Faisal and his mates blast off full magazines. Eventually, they both knew he'd run out of ammunition.

Mace gave Pommy a nod and the hairy giant from Portsmouth hopped to his feet and lifted the seven-kilogram Minimi off the ground. He spun around the corner and returned fire, careful to let off only three or four rounds from the big gun, enough to do some serious damage to Faisal's hut, but controlled enough to retain the ammo for when he really needed it. When he pulled back again, the shooting resumed from the other side, another continuous blast of a whole belt.

While both sides had ammunition, Mason could see the situation was going to remain a stand-off. But what didn't make sense to him was that, if Faisal's aim was to launch an attack from the water, why wasn't he making any attempt to move? What was he doing sitting inside a hut on the beach?

'Something's not right,' he said.

Redford was having similar thoughts. 'You mean, he seems too happy to just shoot it out?'

'Yeah, unless . . .'

'Unless he's already launched.' Redford looked back out to sea. The boats that they'd seen on the water before were now already far out of view. If Faisal had already launched his attack, then they were wasting their time engaging him in a shootout.

Mason pointed to Jack's bag of phosphorus grenades. 'Give me that,' he said. 'And keep 'em here until I get back, all right?'

'They ain't going nowhere, mate,' Jack said.

'Right, you're with me,' Mason said, grabbing hold of Redford. 'Let's go.'

The team didn't need any more instructions. Pommy and Briggs unleashed another blast from their Minimis, peppering Faisal's hut, giving Mason and Redford cover as they crawled away to the north. Until Mace got back, their job was simply to hold the position and keep Faisal pinned down.

Flight Lieutenant Jim Sparke was waiting in his helicopter beyond the harbour wall. The second Mason and Redford climbed on board, Mason screamed at him to get them back airborne and after the boats. Jim lifted them up and guided the Puma out to sea, banking right, flying north along the shoreline towards Saudi Arabia.

Mason passed Redford her headphones. 'Call HQ,' he said. 'Warn the Saudis, cos the last thing we need is heat from one of their gunboats.'

Redford immediately got on the radio, opening the channel to HQ, clearing their path through the Saudi blockade. 'This is Charlie Four on board Lifter One,' she explained. 'We are in pursuit of target vessels. Inform all relevant agents we are in progress to Saudi waters. We are friendly forces. Repeat friendly forces. Do not engage. Over.'

'How long until we have eyes-on, Jim?' Mason asked the pilot. He was already adjusting the scope to his rifle. If Faisal had sent his 'martyrs' on a suicide mission to blow up a tanker, then he could take them out from the air before they reached the target. When his rifle was ready, he swung his legs out of the starboard side of the Puma and lifted his gun, getting ready to take the shot as soon as he had it.

Jim could already see that three boats had broken away from where all the other fishing boats were working. 'Multiple vessels on the move, Mace. We're coming in low. On top of the first in T-minus thirty.'

Mason looked down the scope, waiting for the first boat to come into view as Jim Sparke kept the helicopter steady, flying less than 30 feet above the waves, moving at nearly 150 mph. Twenty seconds later, they were two hundred metres from the boat and Mason got a clear view of the driver, sat at the tiller to the rear. He aimed his rifle, adjusting until he had the back of the man's head in the centre of his sight.

He needed a clean head shot. He steadied himself, picked his spot and pulled the trigger. Bullseye. He saw the bullet make a clean contact, taking out half of the man's head. But other than a slight shake, the driver didn't move. Mason lowered his rifle.

'Fuck,' he said.

Redford looked confused, trying to see what was going on as the Puma pulled alongside the boat.

'Decoys,' said Mason. 'Faisal must be controlling them remotely.'

The Puma overtook the boat and Redford could see what Mason was talking about. The exit wound had removed most of the driver's face, but the boat carried on regardless.

'So what now?' she said.

'I hope you can throw,' said Mace. 'Jim, bring us back around, close as you can.'

Mason passed Jack's bag to Redford. She looked inside and saw that it contained a half-dozen grenades.

'Phosphorus,' Mason explained. 'If the explosion doesn't take it out, then the fire will.'

'And how—'

'We're gonna drop them in.' He answered her question before she finished it.

The helicopter swooped down hard, tucking into the same heading that the boat was on. Jim lined them up, aiming to pass along its port side less than ten feet away. Redford took two grenades out of the bag and handed one to Mason, shuffling alongside him so they were now both hanging out of the side of a helicopter, 20 feet above the sea, flying at 150 mph with one shot each to throw a grenade into a moving boat.

'T-minus ten, Mace,' Jim came over the comms. Mace nodded to Redford.

The seconds slowed as they pulled alongside, when suddenly time flipped the other way into fast forward. Mason threw his grenade, but it landed at an angle, catching the side of the boat and bouncing off into the sea. 'Fuck . . .' He had barely got the word out when he realised that Redford had launched her own grenade. He willed it on, watching as it dipped into the boat and landed squarely inside the bowels. She'd done it. She'd hit the target.

'Bank, bank, bank!' he roared into his comms.

Jim pulled hard on the stick, wrenching the Puma up and left, taking it as far from the path of the boat below as he could. The grenade had already done its job and the blast lifted the hull clean up and out of the water while the fire caught on the plastic explosives packed inside. Suddenly the whole thing went up. The blast created a shockwave that tore through the air, racing fast after the chopper. They were less than one hundred metres away when it caught up with them and lifted the whole 3.5 tonnes of metal another forty feet like a breeze catching a child's kite. Jim wrestled with the stick while Mason and Redford were hurled into the air. Mason felt for a moment that he might be thrown completely clear, but when he hit the deck again he reached out and grabbed hold of the frame of Jim's seat. Redford landed more awkwardly, the bag of grenades flying from her grasp, shooting across the floor and out of the far door into the sea below. She began to slide after it, inches from going the same way, before Mason grabbed hold of her ankle. Neither of them dared move. They lay still, hanging by a thread until Jim righted the bird again.

'Everyone okay back there?' he asked.

Mason pulled Redford back inside the helicopter and she looked forlornly down into the water where the grenades had long since disappeared.

'Sorry,' she said.

'Fuck 'em, they're gone,' Mason replied.

'What was Plan B?'

Mason was already unclipping a new magazine from his belt. 'Tracer rounds.'

'Coming along now, Mace.' Jim held the Puma in position to give Mason a clean shot.

He lifted his rifle again. With a decent shot and a bit of luck he reckoned that he could use the tracers to set off the plastic explosives. As soon as they were level, he unleashed a whole magazine of armour-piercing tracer rounds into the second boat, aiming for the area where the explosives were packed inside the hull. The bullets burned red through the air as they tore into their target. Every shot made contact until the magazine was empty. But there was no explosion.

'Fuck!' Mason screamed. 'That's it. We're out of ammo.'

Redford began scrambling around the helicopter, desperately looking for anything they might have missed. 'What else have we got?' she said. 'We have to stop that boat!'

Mason looked around and could see there was nothing else in the chopper, but as he did so, he also realised that there was one other option open to them. 'Jim!' he shouted. 'You're up, mate.'

Jim Sparke turned around to face Matt Mason and saw no doubt on Mason's face. He was looking straight back at the pilot with a certainty that left no room for hesitation. 'Bring her round, mate. Come in from behind. We're gonna push it under.'

The manoeuvre that Mason was suggesting was not un-heard of, and Jim knew of pilots who had done it before. Be he was not one of them. He wondered if Charles had ever done it. And if not, what would Charles do now? He would do what he had to do, that's what.

'Okay, Mace. Let's do this.'

Jim banked the Puma around again and fell in behind the second boat. Redford grimaced, feeling a sharp pain in her side from the fall. Her whole body was clammy with layers of days-old sweat, her red hair had clumped into a series of dreadlocks and she couldn't remember the last time she'd eaten. She looked at Mason, wondering how his body must be feeling. His uniform was covered in red mud and there was blood smeared across his cheek, leaking again from the freshly opened gash on his forehead. She was impressed with the job he did of not letting it show. She sucked up her own pain and decided to put it out of her mind. There'd be plenty of time to compare war wounds later.

Mason leaned over until his whole body was hanging out of the side of the chopper. He licked his lips, tasting the spray of the sea as they dropped again, flying at exactly the same speed as the second boat, less than twenty feet behind, fifteen feet above the water. His eyes were looking along the undercarriage, judging the distance below. 'Nice and easy mate,' he told Jim over the comms, 'bring it in over the top.'

Mason knew he had to try to keep his voice level, to sound calm even though the truth was he was shitting it. Like Jim, he'd only heard of this manoeuvre before, never seen it with his own eyes, although he could see enough now to know that one wrong move would mean they were all dead. He felt a drop of blood run into his eye and wiped it away with his free hand. For years he'd lived by the motto that as long as your head was in the game, then your body would just follow, but the last few weeks had really put that idea to the test.

'You got it, mate,' Mason said, guiding the pilot. 'Now ease her down.'

Jim nudged the stick forward again, just a fraction of an inch. Inside his helmet, his face was sweating, his eyes stinging and his mouth was as dry as a bone. He lowered the Puma another ten feet until the skids actually clipped the head of the dead guy strapped into the back of the boat. He glanced at the dials, they were doing over 30 knots and he was less than 3 feet above sea level.

Jim took a deep breath. This was it. Get it even slightly wrong and he could cause the boat to flip over and ignite the explosives inside or he could catch a skid and send the chopper head first into the sea. Either way, they'd all be dead. He nudged the stick again, the slightest fraction he could manage, until he felt the skids make contact with the surface of the boat. Mason was saying something, but Jim couldn't hear him any more. It was all instinct from now on.

Mason's teeth were clenched tight as he watched the helicopter touch down on to the boat. Redford didn't realise it, but she was now holding Mason's sleeve tight, not knowing whether to look or not. Jim applied the weight of the Puma, slowly pushing down on the stern, forcing it lower and lower into the water.

The boat's engine whined as it began taking in water and the skids themselves were only inches from the surface of the sea. Mason saw that the boat was going down.

'Up!' he screamed into the comms.

Jim pulled back and the helicopter violently lurched into the air again. Meanwhile the boat headed in the opposite direction. The stern sunk first, heavy with the weight of seawater flooding into it, while the bow rose high up into the air until the whole vessel was vertical and the weight of the engine dragged it, arse first, to a watery grave.

Mason whooped and Redford gave him a high five. 'Fucking A!' she shouted.

'Class work, Jim,' Mason said punching the air.

Jim Sparke gave them both a thumbs up. He felt a need to be violently sick, but he fought it off. He could see the last remaining suicide boat three hundred metres away and, beyond that, around three miles in front of them, the enormous bulk of a Saudi oil tanker. The small boat was set on a perfect collision-course with the port side of the ship and at the speed it was heading now, he estimated they had less than four minutes to impact.

FORTY

Where there had been three blue dots steadily making their way up his laptop screen, Faisal Ahadi could now only see one. He realised that things were looking decidedly worse than they had done an hour before. Not only was one of his men dead, and the remaining two seriously wounded, but they were running desperately low on ammunition. Added to that, their cover had been almost destroyed. The one thing in his favour was that he'd had the good foresight to launch three bomb-boats, any one of which had more than enough firepower to take down the tanker on its own. Everything now rested on the last boat.

He checked its course again on the screen, calculating from the GPS coordinates that it was heading in the right direction and moving at the correct speed for impact. Satisfied that no further adjustments were necessary, he locked its course and set the laptop down on the floor. Faisal stood up and used the butt of his rifle to smash the computer to pieces. His part in the mission was now complete, and with all communication links to the boat severed, nobody on this beach could stop it.

The inside of the fisherman's hut was now bright with sunlight. So much of the northern wall had been destroyed by the enemy's bullets that there were holes large enough to fit a man through. The floor was thick with debris, fragments of mud brick, spent shells and glass from the truck's windows. Flies had already started to gather on the corpse of his dead comrade.

Faisal thought about his mother and father. His father was an early bird; it was 5 a.m. in the UK and soon he would be waking up and faithfully doing his morning prayers. Faisal remembered the time when he had been nine or ten, when his father had first taken him to pray at the mosque. He had been nervous because his father had been so strict, so many rules of what to do and not to do, probably fearful that his young son might embarrass him. But Faisal had done exactly as he was told. He had enjoyed being among the older men, being treated like a grown-up for the first time in his life. Faisal smiled now remembering how happy he had felt that day, especially when his father had praised him for his good behaviour.

He wished that he could hear his mother's voice again. He took the phone from his pocket and considered dialling the house phone in Coventry, the only number that he knew by heart. But something stopped him. It would be selfish to make her a part of what was going to happen next. He knew that. She would hear about it soon enough. His photo would be on every front page, every news programme in the world. His actions would fatally wound their enemy and change the world forever. He hoped that his mother would see it and understand, that she would feel a pride in her son and what he had achieved.

Another volley of bullets tore through the wall, forcing Faisal to dive for cover. Above his head the gunfire showered the air with splinters of brick. He saw the pieces landing all around him but felt no fear. Maybe because his body and mind were too tired now to feel anything, perhaps because he knew that whatever the outcome, he had played his part as well as he could. Either way, Faisal kept low and buried his face in the dirt until the shooting stopped. After a few moments, he crawled over towards the dead man and prised the rifle from his still-warm grip. He checked the magazine, counting that there were eight rounds left inside. He lifted his head gingerly and peered through a hole in the wall. He could see no sign of life around the hut to the north, but he knew that the enemy were there, anticipating his surrender, waiting for their chance to capture him and take him to one of their rendition centres. If that happened, then he would quickly vanish into the system and be tortured for information. The British and Americans would use everything they could to get intelligence, maybe even use his mother and father to weaken his will. Faisal knew that he couldn't let that happen.

He looked over to where his surviving comrades lay on the ground, both slowly bleeding out from their wounds, neither of any more use to him in this fight. Faisal was alone. He lowered his head and closed his eyes, taking a moment to say a silent prayer, asking Allah to give him courage and guide his hand with skill and strength. Then he shuffled forward on his belly, crawling through the hole in the wall towards the hut to the north, towards the enemy that waited behind it.

Faisal moved fast and kept low. Seconds later he had reached the southern wall of the enemy hut. His own men's bullets had done a good job of destroying much of it, but when he looked through the holes, he could see that the northern wall was still almost intact. He would have to round it from the side and engage the enemy directly. On his side was the element of surprise. They surely would not be expecting him to counterattack, assuming instead that he would remain hidden until the tanker had been destroyed and then make a run for it. But if he did that, he knew they would simply pick him off. It wasn't an option he liked. He checked his watch; he had another three and a half minutes before impact, just enough time to strike hard and, with God's grace, give himself a real chance to escape.

With no more time to waste, he stood up and chose the eastern wall, the side which would best suit his right-handedness. He moved carefully to the edge of the hut until he was standing at the corner. His whole body felt tense and he could hear the blood pulsing in his ears. What happened in the next few seconds would determine the rest of his life. He took one final breath, readied his rifle, and spun on his left heel around the southeastern corner of the hut, moving as fast as his body would allow him to move.

It's hard to say exactly what Faisal saw next, as everything happened at such speed. For sure he saw Pommy's enormous size-twelve boots and without a doubt there was an instant when he looked right into Mad Jack's wild blue eyes. But which of those things exactly was the last thing that Faisal Ahadi ever saw is difficult to pinpoint, because before his right heel had even landed on the ground, Pommy and Jack unleashed more than thirty rounds into his head and torso. Pommy's Minimi 5.56-calibre rounds tore through Faisal's midriff, separating his legs from the rest of his body, while Jack's rifle filled his face with so many holes that nobody would ever recognise what was left of it.

Faisal Ahadi never uttered any last words. He never got the chance. The young man from Coventry died on the shore of a foreign land, believing that, even though his own life had been cut short, his work would be remembered forever.

Mad Jack stood over what remained of the dismembered body and shouted back to Craig Bell.

'Get on the radio, Craigy,' he said. 'Tell Mace our position's secured.'

FORTY-ONE

Mason put down the radio. Faisal was dead, so there was no way of him controlling the last remaining boat remotely. The problem was that the boat was already on an impact trajectory, so their only hope was to sink it the same way that they had the last – with the weight of the Puma. They were pushing their luck trying such a risky manoeuvre again. But what other choice did they have? With less than three minutes to impact, this was their only chance to avert a disaster that would kill every last living animal in the Red Sea and spark a global economic disaster.

'Mace.' Jim Sparke's voice came over the radio. 'I have eyes on the last vessel, mate.'

'Okay. Same again, Jimmy,' Mason replied. He turned to Redford. 'You good?'

She nodded but grabbed hold of the handrail to be safe.

The chopper caught up easily with the last boat and Jim lowered the nose, dropping in behind it just as he had done before. Only this time, his actions felt more confident, more assured that he could do it all again. Mason hung out of the side of the helicopter, lowering himself down so that he could help the pilot to judge the distance below. But looking along the bottom of the chopper, his heart sank. The situation this time was different. This time he recognised the long grey hair beneath the driver's turban and realised it was not another dead decoy.

'Stop, stop, stop,' he screamed. 'It's Echo One on board. Repeat Echo One. It's our hostage. It's fucking Eli.'

Jim lifted the nose again and held his position, maintaining the same speed as the boat, hovering thirty feet above and twenty feet back.

'What do you want to do, Mace?' Jim was on the comms. 'Because we haven't got long.'

He was right. Mason could see the tanker approaching. He had to think fast. He cursed the stubborn priest for not getting out of the car boot with him when they'd had the chance, but even so, there was no way they could take the boat out now with Eli on board. And with him strapped in, there was no way to lift him to safety either. There was only one way out of this that Mason could think of. He had to get on to the boat. He'd have to take it down himself and get Eli to safety.

'Give me that,' he shouted to Redford, pointing at the fast rope bag next to the door. 'Jim, I need you to get directly over the boat.'

Redford began to unfurl the fast rope from the bag as Mason checked the strut. There was no time to harness himself in, no time for gloves. As Jim brought the chopper directly over the vessel, Redford dropped forty feet of rope directly inside the hull. Mason took a hold of it, and without hesitation threw himself out of the aircraft.

He shot down the rope, the skin on his hands burning from the friction, and hit the boat at speed. He looked down at his hands, seeing that they'd been ripped open, blistered and bleeding, but he had no time to think about that now. Instead, working to keep his balance, he moved to the stern and past Eli screaming into his gag, struggling against his binds. Mason didn't have time to help the priest, he had to focus on stopping the outboard engine. He reached down and ripped out the fuel line, wincing in pain as the petrol poured into his wounds.

But still the boat carried on. Mason kicked himself, realising that there must still be enough fuel in the line to power the engine for another thirty seconds at least. He checked behind himself again. They were less than two hundred metres from the tanker. In thirty seconds, they'd be dead. The control system was a bust too, there was nothing to be gained from ripping it out as the boat was already locked on its course. He had no choice but to disarm whatever detonator Faisal had rigged it with.

He charged to the front of the boat, lurching from side to side as it crashed through the waves towards the tanker. He tried not to think about the huge ship looming large, now less than one hundred and fifty metres away, its enormous hull now casting a shadow over them as they moved ever closer to it. When he reached the bow, he dived on to his front and pushed his swollen, sore fingers in between the plastic explosives and the body of the boat, ignoring the pain, digging away until he saw a collection of wires.

He cleared his head and tried to think about his training. He was no bombs guy. He knew how to make them but disarming them was a whole other job. He gently pushed the wires to one side until he could see what he was looking for, the warhead buried underneath. There it was, the bomb that could blow them into a million pieces and send the world on a bleak downward spiral.

He stared into the hole that he'd created and knew that he had to make a decision. It looked clean but he couldn't be sure. What if there was a secondary device? Another detonator even? They were now less than a hundred metres from the tanker and the boat was still moving at speed. There was nothing else he could do. He didn't have a choice. When it's life or death you just have to do something. His hands were burning like they were on fire, but he pushed the pain from his mind and shoved them back into the hole, wrapping his fingers around the rocket. Finally, bracing himself for what might be the last decision he ever made, he tugged gently at the explosive until it came loose.

There was no bang. The wiring had been set for detonation on impact, Faisal never expecting anyone to be where Mason was right then. As long as he didn't trigger the impact detonator, Mason could remove it safely. Lifting it out slowly and steadily, he held his breath until he had the warhead clear of the boat. Allowing himself a breath, he leaned over the port side and lowered it down, releasing it softly into the water as though he was putting back a fish.

Mason looked at Eli. Even though the pastor had no clue about warheads or bombs, he could see in the man's face that he knew how close they'd both just come to death. Eli blinked back, his face ashen white, his body limp. He and Matt Mason had been through more than their fair share of scrapes together. But there was still one more danger to overcome. Mason had to get them off the boat before they were smashed into the side of a tanker.

Mason ran back along the hull as the boat bumped and jumped on the waves below. He pulled his knife from its sheath and, almost falling into Eli's lap, cut away his straps. When Eli was free, with all his strength, Mason lifted the priest into the air and launched him off the back of the boat. Finally, he took one last step and dived in after him.

Mason swam hard under the warm waters of the Red Sea, searching left and right for any sign of Eli Drake. He'd had no time to untie him, simply thrown him into the water still gagged and bound. He dived deeper, his ears screaming from the pressure, his hands burning from the salt water. Still he kicked and pulled as hard as he could until, five metres away, he saw a dark figure. It was sinking fast and drowning faster. Mason kicked hard and reached out a hand, clutching hold of the rope that was tied around Eli's body. He looked back up to the light and kicked again with everything he had.

In the seconds that followed, Mason thought about the boat heading for the tanker above his head. He hoped he'd got it right, that there'd been no secondary detonator or another explosive he'd missed, because if not, then all his efforts to save Eli were a waste of time. Any second now there could be an almighty bang that would kill them both. Mason burst through the surface of the water and dragged

Eli up next to him, ripping off his gag so that the pastor could breathe. Both men immediately sucked in the air, Eli coughing and spluttering while Mason held him above the water.

Looking over at the tanker, Mason saw that the fishing boat had smashed harmlessly against its side. What remained of its splintered hull was now bobbing weakly on the waves. There had been no explosion. There was no damage to the tanker. There would be no environmental holocaust or economic Armageddon.

Over his head he heard the helicopter bank and saw it dip down towards them. Sitting in the starboard door, Redford was pointing at him, guiding Jim towards the water. When she was close enough for him to see her clearly, he noticed that she was smiling, holding her two hands aloft with both of her thumbs fully extended.

FORTY-TWO

Mason held the radio in one hand while Redford did her best to apply a dressing to the other. Sitting next to them, Eli Drake shivered with the cold and shock. For the first time in months, his life was not in imminent danger. But the job wasn't finished yet and the helicopter was already racing back to Yemeni waters, because whoever had taken down the second Puma was still in Midi.

Hopkins and the fire support team had successfully used their mortars to destroy the road between the town and the highway. Mason had instructed the Rupert to ensure nobody could leave. He needed to give the team a chance to regroup and himself more time to formulate a plan for how to finally take out the fucker who'd been responsible.

'Bravo Two. This is Bravo One. Over,' Mason said into the radio.

Mad Jack responded immediately. 'This is Bravo Two. You still fucking around up there?'

'Target secure, mate. Sitrep?'

'Good work, bud. Our position is secure. Awaiting QBOs.'

'Hold your position. Bag the evidence and stand by for re-tasking. I'm coming in to pick you up, mate.'

'Roger that.'

Mason dropped the radio in his lap and offered Redford his other hand.

'You really need to take better care of these,' she said.

'Yeah, maybe I'll start moisturising,' he replied, trying but failing to stop a cheeky smirk creeping across his face.

Redford caught his eye and laughed. She was already re-evaluating Matt Mason in light of recent events. She'd initially thought the guy was an asshole, but when shit got real, they'd pulled together and got the job done. That's all that counted in her book. She tied off the second bandage and Mason held his hands up, admiring her handiwork and nodding his appreciation. The strapping reminded him of getting ready before boxing matches when he'd been a boy and he playfully performed a quick left–right jab combination.

'You box?' she asked.

'Used to,' he replied.

'Maybe we should spar sometime,' Redford said without irony. Again Mason found himself feeling surprised by the American as she took the radio from him and called in Hopkins. 'Charlie One. This is Charlie Four. Send sitrep. Over.'

'This is Charlie One. We are in position. Holding firm at Grid 4QFJ16334281. Got them pinned down but very quiet. Suggest you approach from the west while we continue to suppress from our position.'

Mason took the radio back. 'Charlie One, this is Bravo One. Over.'

'Loud and clear, Bravo One.'

'Understood, mate. Sounds good. Approaching you from the west, de-bird there and then continue on to target.'

'Roger that, Bravo One.'

Jim Sparke took the chopper down a hundred metres south of where Faisal Ahadi's body lay dead in the sand. Mad Jack and the rest of the assault team bundled themselves inside and Jim watched as the men high-fived each other, sharing slaps on the back and private jokes. He felt proud to have played his part, but sad, too, that he'd not get to share that with his own buddy, Charles. That was the cruel irony of war; you only got to feel that special camaraderie by putting your lives on the line together, but it came at a price, because losing a comrade hurt so much more.

Jim pulled back the stick and turned the Puma east. Behind him, he heard Mason talking fast.

'Right you lot, prepare to re-task. Agent Redford, I want you to regroup with fire support team, make sure they keep Midi pinned down and wait until you see our signal. The rest of you, with me. Jim, we'll come in from the north, fire and manoeuvre on to position. You keep Echo One and pull back to a safe position until you get further orders. Eli, you stay here, Jim's gonna keep you safe.'

Eli nodded, while Jim gave Mace a thumbs up and Jack began preparing the equipment. Craig got on to the radio, relaying Mace's instructions to the fire support team, while

Briggs and Pommy sat unmoved, rifles ready. Despite the events of the last two days, both looked as fresh as daisies.

Hopkins was waiting at the landing zone as the chopper grounded and Redford climbed down. Mace screamed last-minute instructions over the roar of the helicopter blades.

'Keep them pinned. When you see a flare, switch your fire to the east. That'll confuse them and give us safe entry.'

'Roger that, Mace,' Hopkins shouted back.

Mace gave Jim the signal and the Puma was instantly airborne again, circling the town, and sixty seconds later, laying them down on the northwestern edge of Midi. The five men on board were all thinking the same thing, the last time they'd been together like this, Andy Roberts had been with them.

Mace led them into the deserted streets of Midi. When the British helicopter had been downed, every man, woman and child had disappeared behind closed doors. Now, on the streets, the smoke from the chopper's wreckage still hung in the air, covering everything with a gloomy mist.

They moved steadily, sweeping from west to east, moving towards the area where Hopkins had last reported gunfire. Mace gave the signal for the men to fan out and take up positions of cover where they had a 360-degree view.

The shooter had tried to escape after the helicopter was downed but Hopkins' team had done a good job of pinning him back. Now he could be hiding anywhere in the town, waiting for his chance to counter. Mace crept along the wall of a single-storey house, his rifle armed and ready. Suddenly, fifty feet to his right, he heard a shutter swing open. He spun around, pointing his rifle, but a split second before he pulled the trigger, he saw the face of an old woman in the window. He lowered his gun with a heavy sigh. A fraction of a second later and she would have had a bullet in her brain.

Mason furrowed his brow partly in frustration, partly in confusion as to what she was doing. He waved at her to get back inside but the old woman stood still, looking straight at him. She seemed to be weighing him up, judging him somehow. Mason lifted his hand again to shoo her away, but instead the old lady reached out and pointed along the street to a large building on the corner. Mason realised what she was trying to tell him, the man he was looking for was in there. Mason nodded to acknowledge that he had understood, and she disappeared inside again, pulling the shutter closed.

He took a flare gun from his pack and fired a single flare into the air. Seconds later a huge mortar explosion went off to the east. That was their signal to move. He motioned to his team and they advanced on to the building on the corner.

When they were fifty metres away, two shutters flew open and Mason dived for cover just as he saw the first flash of gunfire and heard bullets zip around his head. Immediately all four of his men unleashed their firepower in return. Jack fired a 66mm round, blowing the doors of the building to pieces, tearing the wood and brick away from the walls. Pommy and Briggs ran towards the carnage, disappearing into the cloud of dust and smoke, letting rip with the Minimis as they burst into the building faster than Usain Bolt and Justin Gatlin. Mason and Craig brought up the rear but by the time Mace was inside, the firefight was over. Mace took stock of the room. Two men lay dead, another wounded face-down on the concrete and bleeding out fast. One lone survivor sat cowering in the corner.

Mason ran over to the bleeding man and kicked his weapon away. 'Call in fire support team, Craigy,' he said.

Craig got on the radio while Mason covered the cowering man with his rifle. The man raised his hands in surrender and bowed his head. 'Shahlai, Shahlai,' he said, pointing to the man lying at Mason's feet. 'It is Shahlai.'

Mason couldn't believe what he'd heard. Ruak Shahlai? He looked down at the bleeding man and flipped him over with his boot, studying the face that was looking back at him, filled with fear and struggling for breath. A round had taken out half of his neck and blood was pouring freely from the wound, pooling around Mason's boots.

General Ruak Shahlai was all Mason had thought about for days, ever since Hopkins had told him about Andy Roberts. He'd imagined this moment so many times, how he would feel, the relief he would experience when he knew that the bastard was dead. And now here it was. The moment had arrived. Yet something didn't quite feel right about it. Mason shook his head as it slowly dawned on him why not.

'No,' he said and turned back to the survivor, his face full of accusation, 'this ain't Shahlai.'

'Yes. Shahlai. It is Shahlai,' the man said, pointing again at the dying man.

'No,' Mason said, stepping over the rubble towards him. 'He's not Shahlai. You're fucking Shahlai.'

Mason knew who Ruak Shahlai was, it was the man sitting in front of him, alive and well, making a vain attempt to avoid identification. Mason had studied his face for a long time and, looking more closely now, he saw that the end of the man's left thumb was missing, confirming what he suspected. 'You're Shahlai,' he repeated, 'trying to take the coward's way out.'

The cowering man's whole demeanour changed in an instant. He lowered his hands and raised his face. He realised too who the British soldier was that was standing over him. 'Yes, I am General Ruak Shahlai of the Islamic Revolutionary Guard,' he said in clear English. 'And you can't touch me, Staff Sergeant Mason.'

Shahlai eyeballed every man in the room. He was a general and he was going to act like one in a room full of rank-and-file soldiers. He was going to take command of the situation. He steadied himself and made to stand up.

'Sit down, General,' Mason said, lifting his boot and crashing it down hard on Shahlai's shoulder, knocking him back to the floor. He resisted the urge to give him a slap too for good measure. 'You've been captured by the infidels. And once this guy finishes bleeding out, there's gonna be nobody to tell your side of it. This is your failure, mate, and your people are gonna wonder how all these died and you lived.'

'My people know that I would give my life for them,' he said.

'Yeah?'

Mason was suddenly aware of the heat. It felt like an oven inside the room and there was sweat pouring down his back. His own breathing felt shallow and fast, his pulse too, from all the adrenaline coursing through his veins. He had a choice to make. 'Kill or capture' had been his orders. But now the question was which?

'Out, lads.' He gave the order to the other men in the room.

'Ah, Mace . . . No,' Jack said.

'Take the lads out, Jack.' Mace gave his oldest mate a look that they both understood. This wasn't open for negotiation. 'That's an order, Corporal.'

Jack rubbed his hand over his thick moustache and sighed heavily through his fingers. He knew there was no changing Matt Mason's mind once it was made up. He nodded to the other lads and one by one they filed silently out of the building, leaving Mason and Shahlai alone.

The two soldiers, one Iranian, one British, eyeballed each other as Mason lifted his rifle and slid his bandaged finger over the trigger. He took aim at the centre of Shahlai's forehead and tried to force his body to relax. The general sitting at his feet didn't flinch, he simply stared back, his eyes burning with defiance and hatred.

All Mason had to do was pull the trigger. There'd be no witnesses. He could report that all enemy combatants had been killed in battle and his men would back up his story.

But something felt wrong. He'd never in his whole career killed a man who wasn't ready to kill him.

Mason lowered the rifle and laid it down on the stone floor. He kicked it to Shahlai with the end of his boot.

'Go on then,' Mason said.

Shahlai looked at the rifle and laughed. 'You hate me, Sergeant?'

'You're a coward.'

'And what does that make you?'

'I'm a soldier. I fight my enemy face to face. Not with sneaky bombs and dirty tactics.'

'And when I pick up this gun?'

Mason stood still as a rock. 'Let's see.'

Shahlai held Mason's eye. He knew there was no way out for him any more, but the rifle in front of him did at least allow him a chance to kill the man who had stood between him and a great victory. The British soldier was giving him a chance that he would surely regret not taking. He lurched forward and reached for the rifle, grabbing it and dragging it to himself as fast as he could. But Mason was already on him, the full weight of his body landing on his legs, his arms shooting upwards, fighting for control. Shahlai was nearly sixty years old but he was still a strong man and he wasn't going to give up the gun easily, but Mason was younger, stronger and faster. They battled for the weapon, but Mason began to gain an edge, forcing the barrel up under Shahlai's chin. With his left hand holding it steady, his right began to prise Shahlai's fingers from over the trigger and for the first time he saw fear in the old man's eyes.

As Mason took full control of the weapon, he wanted to make sure Shahlai knew exactly why he was about to die. 'This is for Andy Roberts,' he said, 'twice the soldier you ever were.'

'Mace.' He heard his name ring out behind him, the voice of Redford, standing in the doorway with her hands up. 'Don't, Mace.'

She walked across the room, towards the two men lying on the ground.

'Leave it, Redford.' Mason's voice was cold and detached.

'If you kill him, he gets what he wants,' she said.

'I don't give a fuck,' said Mason. 'I made a promise.'

'To who? To Andy? He's dead, Mace.'

'Yeah, because of this fucker.'

'And you kill him and then what? They'll carry his coffin through the streets of Tehran and make a martyr of him.'

'Well they're as evil as he is then.'

'And then they'll retaliate. Full-out regional war, exactly what we've been fighting to avoid.'

Shahlai let go of the rifle altogether and smiled at Mason. The American woman was right. This was the martyr's way to die. The British might have stopped his attack on the Saudi oil tanker, but now, as he saw Mason's finger hover over the trigger, he realised that the consequences would be the same. Iran would avenge his death and Saudi Arabia would suffer.

'This is not what we do, Mace,' Redford said.

Mason felt the general's body relax. The general wasn't fighting back any more, he was asking Mason to shoot him.

Redford was right, this was what the bastard wanted. He pulled the gun away, fighting hard to control the rage. He thought about Andy, how he would have called Shahlai an ''orrible gobshite' and told Mace that he wasn't worth the bullet. He'd have been right on both counts.

He stood up and looked down at the man lying at his feet. Fuck him. The spooks could have him. He'd be on a one-way flight to a rendition centre in a place that didn't officially exist before his feet touched the ground and they'd do things to him there that were worse than death. They'd crack him until he gave them everything he knew. He nodded to Redford; she was right. Killing Shahlai wasn't going to bring Andy back and it wasn't going to help them either.

'Take him away,' Mason said. 'He's all yours.'

FORTY-THREE

Hereford, England

Matt Mason pulled awkwardly at his shirt collar and tried to loosen his tie a little without his wife noticing. He hated wearing civvies almost as much as he hated hanging around with them. He clenched his teeth, looking left and right, unable to make peace with his current situation. He felt like a different species to all the proud mums and dads clapping enthusiastically as the headmistress invited the next little angel to climb to the stage to collect her A-level certificate. What was that one? Fredericks? They were still only up to the Fs? How much longer until they reached the Ms? And then how long? The problem with a surname like Mason was that even after his daughter's turn, they'd still only be halfway to the end.

He'd never liked school. From the age of fourteen, he'd only gone because it was the best place to get into a scrap. You could always count on one of the kids from the gypsy camp or the lads from the Beechdale Estate being up for a fight round the back of the toilet block. He'd had some right old ding-dongs back then before he left for good at fifteen with no qualifications. He didn't need them though, because he'd already decided he was going to join the army. Even when the army had made him wait until his seventeenth birthday, he'd just got a job down at the local metals factory. He earned good money, gave every penny to his mum and spent his evenings at the boxing club or having fights outside the dances at the British Legion.

Everything was different these days though. He knew that. You had to work hard at school now if you wanted to get on in life. His daughter was a real worker, smart like her mum but with a fight in her belly that came from his side. Kerry wanted her to go to university and study for a degree, which her grades were good enough for without a doubt, but he'd been proud as punch when she'd chosen instead to take a place at the naval college in Dartmouth. Who'd have thought that his own daughter was going to be a shaky. There'd always been a healthy rivalry between the army and the navy, but at the end of the day, they were on the same side. Putting aside his mortal fear that Jo would ever see real combat, he actually liked the idea that in a year or two, there'd be two Masons serving Queen and country. On land and sea. Not bad for a family of shit-kickers from the West Midlands, he thought.

'Joanna Mason,' the head announced. The crowd clapped again and Jo made her way up on to the stage. Kerry stood and whooped like she was at a Tom Jones gig. Mace put his fingers in his mouth and whistled while the head continued. 'With three A-levels in geography, English and sociology, Joanna will be joining the officer training course at the Brittania Naval College in Dartmouth this autumn.'

Mason clapped again and remained standing, watching his little girl, not so little now, in fact, tall and confident just like her mum, a woman about to begin her journey out in the real world. He was so in awe of everything she had achieved. He turned to Kerry and smiled. They still had their problems and they both knew it was something that they would have to address soon, but for now, for today, they'd done something good that they could enjoy together. Kerry took Mason's hand and gave it a squeeze before they both whooped again, watching their daughter come back down the stairs, holding her certificate aloft, a huge, cheesy smile plastered to her face.

Four days before, Mason had seen a very different face on a young woman. He'd stood alongside Andy Roberts' sister Sue at the graveside as they'd lowered Andy's coffin into the ground. Mason had felt stone cold when Sue looked at him, as though she'd seen straight through him like glass, and he hadn't known what to say. The hairs on his neck had stood on end when the piper played and a C-130, flanked by two Chinooks, flew low overhead as though carrying Andy's spirit to a higher place. He'd felt some relief then, that at least he'd got some justice for Andy. Faisal was dead and Shahlai was in custody, never likely to see the light of day again.

'Alexis Mulraine.' The head announced the next name, snapping Mason back to reality as he sat back down again.

Over the applause, Mason heard his phone ring, and as he fumbled for it he could already feel Kerry's eyes rolling. He looked at the screen, his face contorting into a look of concern because he recognised the number – it was a call he had to take. He looked to Kerry and mouthed 'Sorry', while she in turn, with embarrassed disbelief, mouthed 'No'. He ignored her, stood up in the middle of the row and answered the call.

'Hello?' he said, putting his finger in his other ear, trying to drown out the sound of applause for Alexis Mulraine, while he edged along the long line of parents clapping enthusiastically.

'Staff Sergeant Mason?' The voice on the other end sounded official.

'Yes,' said Mace.

'The next voice you will hear, Staff Sergeant, will be the voice of the prime minister.' The caller paused for moment. 'Perhaps you can find somewhere a little quieter?'

Mason marched as fast as he could to the back of the room as he heard a click on the line.

'Staff Sergeant Mason?' He instantly recognised the voice.

'Prime Minister,' he replied.

'Or do you prefer Matthew?'

'Most people call me Mace, sir.'

'Of course. Well Mace, I just wanted to call you personally to convey, on behalf of Her Majesty's Government, our appreciation of all your recent efforts in the Yemen.'

'Thank you, sir,' Mason said. He could see Joanna making her way towards him. She was waving her certificate, grinning from ear to ear and doing a funny little dance.

'I'm sure Her Majesty will have something she wants to pin to your chest in due course, Mace. You know how the

Palace likes to make a fuss.' The PM laughed at his own joke. 'But I wanted to say it personally. In these extraordinary times, this country needs extraordinary actions from extraordinary people. And you have proved to be just that, Sergeant.'

Joanna was now standing right in front of him. She'd stopped doing her dance and was pulling an exaggerated bored face, yawning and mocking him for being on the phone. She motioned for him to hang up at once.

'Thank you, sir. That's kind of you to say, sir.' He rolled his eyes playfully to her.

'Right, well I'll let you go and enjoy your leave then, Mace.'

'Sir.' Mason hung up.

'Bloody hell, Dad,' Joanna said. 'Who are you talking to? It's my graduation.'

'Sorry darling,' he said, making a show of turning the phone off. 'Just a work thing. Nothing important. Come here.'

He grabbed a hold of her and pulled her in tight. 'I'm so proud of you.'

FORTY-FOUR

The city of Birgu, the oldest of the three cities that surround Malta's Grand Harbour, was founded in ancient times by the Phoenicians and reconstructed by the crusading Knights of the Order of St John. Today, it was possibly the Mediterranean's most exclusive place to be seen. Birgu's port was at the centre of it all, a waterfront arcade of superyachts, and chic bars and restaurants, set among the breath-taking backdrop of ancient sandstone palaces and churches.

Erica Atkins skipped along the harbour in her new Christian Louboutin kitten heels, which perfectly matched the short tweed crepe dress she'd picked up at Gucci, a little present to herself for all her hard work. As was the chunky monkey on the end of her arm, who she'd had flown out from London specially for the weekend. She hated turning up to these kinds of social functions alone. And Steve? Chris? Whatever his name was, he had been a lot of fun back in London, so she knew what she was getting. They'd spent the whole morning in bed, while she alternated between emails and energetic sessions of roughhousing.

Erica was a satisfied woman, physically, emotionally and professionally. She gave his pert little backside a playful pat, cuddling into him as though he was her actual boyfriend. Heaven forbid.

At the far end of the harbour, past the bays of colourful blue, yellow and red fishing boats, were the berths reserved for superyachts over a hundred metres. In the middle berth stood the largest boat in the bay, one hundred and forty metres long, five storeys high, with three swimming pools, two helipads and an onboard cinema. It was reported to have cost Crown Prince Mohammed bin Salman over half a billion euros when he purchased it from a Russian oligarch on a whim. The way Erica was feeling, it seemed like the most appropriate place in the world for her to celebrate her success.

On receiving the news of the averted oil tanker disaster, Erica had wasted no time in positioning herself at the centre of the narrative. She had presented the timeline to the Southerlin board and they had in turn shared certain 'sensitive details' with the House of Saud. The chairman, Graham Kaplan, had called the prince personally to explain how it was their new vice president for development, and soon-to-be-confirmed latest addition to the Southerlin board, Erica Atkins, who had provided the crucial intelligence to the CIA. It was entirely her own vigilance that had led to the identification and capture of those rogue elements within the Houthi alliance who sought to do untold damage to the Saudi economy. While Kaplan retained some operational details in order to protect their sources, he said it was incontrovertible that without Erica's diligent surveillance on behalf of their client, the fallout would have been severe. After verifying what they could through their own intelligence, the Saudis had replied to officially express their sincere appreciation.

Once the promotion to the board was official, Erica would have everything that she'd worked so hard for. She would finally sit at the big table with the real decision-makers, be one of the establishment, get the credit that she had long deserved in the industry. She wouldn't be answerable to any man. She wouldn't allow anyone to piggy-back on her hard work and take the credit (and the cash) for it. Non-executive seats on other boards would doubtlessly follow, as would invitations to consult on various select committees. She would finally be a face around Arlington and soon Washington too. Who knows? Once her profile began to grow, political office was not unthinkable.

She hadn't been surprised when tonight's invitation had arrived on her desk. A gold-embossed privately signed request from the crown prince himself asking that Erica join him on his boat in Malta for a 'start of season' party. And now that was where she was, crossing a red-carpeted gangplank on to the world's most expensive gin palace to rub shoulders with royalty and heads of state. Not one to ever miss an opportunity, her plan was to push the prince to increase his four-billion-dollar investment in the Y-project.

Once on board, Erica helped herself to a glass of champagne and encouraged Chris or Steve to mingle with the other beautiful people, mainly escorts, who had come on the arms of their rich Saudi benefactors. She decided to explore a little, curious as to what half a billion euros could buy you these days, and found herself standing in front of a painting she recognised. It was Da Vinci's *Salvator Mundi*, sold at Christie's in New York for close to another half-billion a few years before. It had made all the headlines not only for the price tag but also because many had questioned its authenticity. Either way, Erica could hardly believe that she was now standing there looking at it only inches away.

'You like Da Vinci, Miss Atkins?' She recognised the voice and spun around to see the crown prince standing behind her, admiring the painting over her shoulder. He looked very different to when they had met in Riyadh weeks before. No longer dressed in his Saudi thawbs, the prince was now smartly dressed in chinos and a loose white cotton shirt. He looked very handsome as he smiled and gave a polite bow. 'I understand my country owes you a debt of gratitude.'

'All part of the service, Your Highness,' she said, returning the bow.

'You know while Da Vinci was painting this masterpiece, the place where we are in now, Malta and the Fort of St Angelo out there, was where the whole world changed forever.'

'I did not know that.'

'Malta belonged to the Crusaders in the fifteenth century, so Suleiman the Magnificent, maybe the greatest general of them all, sailed here from Turkey with two hundred and fifty ships and forty thousand men to take it from them.'

'I'm guessing it didn't work out?' Erica smiled.

'No,' he chuckled. He enjoyed her sense of humour. 'The Ottomans laid siege to the fort for four months, but two thousand Christian knights held out against the largest fleet since antiquity.'

'Must have been a long trip back,' she said.

'It destroyed the veneer of Ottoman invincibility, Miss Atkins. Gave the Christians hope that they could overcome, changed the course of history. Resolve and resourcefulness, you see, are everything.'

'I agree, which is why I think you should increase your order for the Y-project.'

The prince laughed. 'I admire your . . .' he reached for the right word.

'Chutzpah?' she offered.

'That's not a word we use,' he said. After a pause, he continued. 'Our own investigations into recent events have thrown up a name. Perhaps you have heard it. Faisal Ahadi?'

Erica's face froze for just long enough to confirm to the prince that she did know Faisal. Unfortunately for Erica, the prince knew all about Faisal too. After receiving a tip-off from a source within the CIA, the Saudi Secret Service had become very interested in Erica's long-standing relationship with Faisal Ahadi. More digging revealed that Erica's version of the narrative with herself as hero and saviour of the Saudi nation wasn't exactly the entire story. The Saudis had discovered how Erica used Faisal as an asset within Shahlai's network to help her win arms contracts until she lost control of him. The prince almost admired the 'chutzpah' of it, had it not nearly lead to the destruction of his whole kingdom.

Before Erica could even begin to cover herself, the prince continued.

'I'm glad we have that in the open,' he said. 'The question is what do we do with it?'

Erica was flustered. Was he threatening to expose her? Was he angling for a deal? 'I'm sure we could find a way to be even more competitive on price,' she suggested.

'I'm sure that will be useful knowledge when you come to negotiate with Southerlin,' he said.

'I'm sorry?' Her face looked quizzical.

'You will be the one doing the deal with Southerlin.'

'I don't follow.'

'I think you should come and work for me, Miss Atkins,' he said. 'Use your considerable "resourcefulness" for the good of the Kingdom.'

'That's kind but . . .'

'You'll be responsible for the world's largest arms budget.'

'I'm flattered but that really isn't poss—'

'Of course, as a foreigner, and a woman, your work must remain "unofficial". I will appoint my cousin as the new defence minister next week, but he will have clear instructions to operate under your direction. Albeit under my close supervision.'

'And if I say no?' Erica asked. She wanted to say no. Zero part of her wanted to move to Saudi Arabia, to wear a veil every day, to live without booze or sex, and be the puppet master to some rich playboy sheikh. She couldn't think of anything worse.

'A call to Southerlin with the intelligence that I have?' He paused to leave the idea hanging. 'It would make our continued relationship impossible and that would be to nobody's advantage, Miss Atkins. Least of all yours, I assure you.'

Erica could see that she was over a barrel. A call from the prince would undo everything she'd done to convince the Southerlin board that she had been in full control of the situation. If the prince exposed how she had in fact lost control of Faisal, then it would mean her position with Southerlin was over. Indeed, her whole reputation in the industry would be mud. But accepting his offer to move to Saudi Arabia would also mean losing everything she loved, not to mention living without all the things she enjoyed most about life: sex, fashion, freedom.

'I'm sure you will learn to love our country, Miss Atkins,' the prince said, glancing down at her new shoes. 'We have excellent shopping opportunities.'

With a bow, the prince excused himself and left Erica standing alone. She looked again at the fake Da Vinci on the wall in front of her and then buried her face in her hands. A handsome, muscular figure appeared at her side and offered her a glass of champagne.

'Not now, sweetie,' she said. 'Not now.'

FORTY-FIVE

Waves on the Pacific Coast sounded different to waves anywhere else in the world. They seemed to have more power, more bang for their buck somehow. Redford lay in bed, wide awake, jacked up on jet lag, and vaguely remembered something about diurnal tides from high school. How most places had two high tides a day, but California only got one. Half as often but twice the size. Maybe that was the explanation. She wasn't sure. Science was never her strong suit.

Her mom had kept a lot of her things from high school. When her parents finally left the Middle East and moved to their retirement house, long after Redford had graduated and gone to Harvard, her mom had decorated Redford's new room with them. Like she'd always lived there. It was weird now to lie in a bed that she'd never lain in as a school kid and see walls covered in photos of long-forgotten friends and posters of bands she hadn't listened to for years. But then that was her mom for you. She was weird.

She got out of bed and pulled open the curtains. She had to hand it to her parents, they'd bought a house with the best view she'd ever seen. From her window, she looked across a pool-table-flat lawn, or the croquet lawn as her mother called it, to an immaculate border of flowers that ran along the boundary between their property and the beach. On this stretch of coast, all the properties enjoyed what realtors called 'uninterrupted' views of the ocean. She pulled on a robe and slippers, thoughtfully left there for her, and went downstairs, giving herself a mental pep-talk, reminding herself to try to seem engaged, before she shuffled into the kitchen with her best painted-on smile. If, before she'd even made it through the door, she'd been asked to describe the scene, she'd have got it exactly right.

Her father stood at the oven, already busy making breakfast. He was a tall, statuesque man with a beautifully groomed head of white hair and he greeted her with a warm smile. Her mother, in housecoat and pearls, sat at the table, clutching a letter opener, steadily working her way through a pile of envelopes. Who still gets letters any more? Redford wondered.

After the customary good mornings and air kisses for them both, she accepted a mug of coffee from her dad and sat at the opposite end of the table to her mother, with her back to the ocean, watching them attend to their daily 'chores'. She wondered what it must be like to live with another person for your whole life. To grow old with someone until the routines of daily life became unspoken. Just routines. She couldn't understand how anyone could bear it.

'Mary-Beth Schulmann has some nerve,' her mother began, reading the latest missal from her pile of correspondence.

'Eggs, honey?' her father asked.

'She expects me to magically make everything happen, while she takes the credit.'

'Thanks, Dad,' Redford said.

'And it's not that I can't do it, but it'd sure be nice to get some appreciation once in a while.'

Her father carried the frying pan to the table and Redford noticed that he was wearing an apron over his freshly pressed clothes. It was made from thick canvas and had a leather waistband. Very alpha, she thought. He piled a generous helping of perfectly cooked scrambled eggs on to her plate; a little runny, just how she liked them. Then he paused, holding the tongs over a couple of bacon rashers.

'You still eating the swine, honey?' He laughed. 'Haven't gone native?'

'Not yet,' she smiled. In fact, she couldn't remember the last time she'd even seen pork, but he seemed a little too pleased with himself for her to turn it down.

'. . . But I guess I'll just have to say yes again.' Redford realised that her mother was still speaking, continuing the narrative with a roll of her eyes. 'Because I am not going to be the one to turn this into something it is not.'

Having resolved whatever the issue was with Mary-Beth Schulmann, her mother put down the letter and opened the next. Redford had been home now for nearly twenty-four hours, the first time she'd been back in nearly two years, and her mom still hadn't asked her a single question. Not one. Not a 'how are you?' or a 'what have you been up to?' Her mother was reliable like that. Even though most people might find that lack of engagement unsettling, Redford was actually grateful for it. After everything that she'd been through in the last month, her dad's eggs and her mother's social calendar would do just fine.

The Agency had asked her to return to the States to receive a commendation for her work in Yemen. Five years of graft had resulted in the apprehension of Ruak Shahlai, one of the world's deadliest terrorists. Shahlai would never appear in a US court, he was already lost in the 'dark' system reserved for the most deadly enemies of the state. From what Redford had been told, he was being interrogated in a 'facility somewhere in the jungle' along the Burmese–Thai border.

Her boss had asked that, while she was 'in town', she come in to 'discuss her options', which usually meant a promotion was on the cards. It was likely that he would offer her a chance to come back to Langley, maybe to take up a senior management role. She'd rather join her mother's golf club than do that, but there was another option. If she elected to stay in the field, then she'd get her pick of assignments, a chance to move on from Yemen even. More resources would undoubtedly be part of the package. Although her skillset favoured another posting within the Arab world, she thought if she pushed a little, then they would allow her to go further afield. Russia? Latin

America? China maybe? Whatever her decision, she felt that now was the time when she had to seriously consider where her future might lie. It would determine how the next chapter of her life played out.

She helped herself to more coffee, seeing that her father was already doing the washing-up while her mother launched into another monologue about how inappropriate it was for the local Rotarians to choose 'pandemic' as a theme for their annual costume party fundraiser.

'Don't they see all those masks would be real buzzkill?' she asked nobody in particular.

'Dad, do you mind if I . . .?' Redford asked her father, pointing to the copy of the *New York Times* on the counter. She knew he liked to sit in his chair after breakfast and read the national paper of record from cover to cover, but she wanted an excuse to avoid the Rotary Club party debate.

'Sure, honey,' he said, 'just so long as you don't touch the crossword.'

'Promise,' she said.

Redford sat back at the table and took another mouthful of coffee. She unfolded the newspaper and laid it out flat in front of her. It was a rare luxury to see how the folks back home saw the world. She was used to getting her news through Agency briefings, and she never had time to pick up a paper, let alone a book or a magazine.

She wondered for a minute what the front page would have looked like if Shahlai had completed his plan to take out the Saudi tanker. The storms of the last few days out in the Red Sea would have frustrated clean-up attempts and dispersed the oil spill over thousands of miles of shoreline. The world's press would still be covered in pictures of dead sea birds, dolphins and whales. No doubt the *Times* would have begun to calculate the economic impact, somewhere north of twenty billion dollars initially, but the truly horrific impact on the global economy as a result of the spike in oil prices would only be slowly beginning to hit home. When it did, it would have dominated the news for months.

Instead, the *Times'* headline was a piece about the Fed considering interest rate rises and the rest of the front page covered the latest game from the World Series, a story about the Pope sanctioning gay marriage, and the recent changes to the Supreme Court. It all seemed so sleepy and parochial to her. She turned to the inside pages and scanned for the section on the Middle East, finding it buried on page fourteen. The headline grabbed her attention right away. It screamed out, 'CIA Torture in Yemen'.

Redford sat up, put down her coffee and scanned the text for details. It was half a page long, a first-hand eye-witness account of how British SAS, with the full cooperation of the CIA, had engaged in acts of torture as part of a prisoner's interrogation. It described the British HQ in Sana'a in perfect detail, and although it stopped short of mentioning Ibrahim Manar or Matt Mason by name, it was clear to her who it was describing.

'Fuck,' she said. The piece was a disaster, not only for the Agency but also for Mace. She looked again at the paper, searching now for the accompanying byline. Who could possibly have written this? Her heart fell when she saw the writer's name printed in small font, directly below the headline, a name she recognised well.

By Scooter Williams.

FORTY-SIX

Only a handful of the population of London know that there is another city that exists below the streets they can see. While tourists snap selfies outside 10 Downing Street, deep below them, in the bowels of Whitehall, there is a labyrinth of secure corridors and offices where the highest-level decisions affecting the country are made. If a bomb were to drop on central London, the apparatus that ran the country would carry on unimpeded. Much of it is under the control of the most powerful department in the British government, the Ministry of Defence.

Mason stood feet apart, hands behind his back, checking his reflection in the mirror as he took the lift down into the bowels of Whitehall. He looked and felt like a new man, having finally shaved off his beard and got some much-needed rest. It was amazing how fast the human body responded to sleep and a few home-cooked meals. The gash in his forehead had healed nicely into a hairline scar and his shoulder felt as good as new.

He had been called in at short notice by the top brass, which he assumed was to go over recent revelations in the press about the interrogation of captives in Yemen. While he hadn't seen the newspaper articles personally, he had been briefed as to their contents, so he wasn't particularly worried. It wasn't the first time that the UK had been shopped for using strong-arm tactics. It was maybe the first time that they'd been stabbed in the back by the same bloke that they'd just saved from having his head cut off by terrorists, but Mason didn't hold any bad blood for Scooter Williams. He was just doing his job, same as Mason, same as everyone. The Yank should never have been allowed access to areas where he could see what was going on.

Nor did Mason regret his own actions in the interrogation of Ibrahim Manar. Torture, as the press liked to label it, was an unavoidable means to an end in modern warfare. Without it, he would never have secured access to Shahlai, and as a result, his plan to take out the Saudi tanker would have been a success. The same media would then have been up in arms about why the security forces hadn't intercepted the disaster and the world would have been facing the very real possibility of an all-out war. Mason had done exactly what he'd had to do to stop both of those things happening and he had no sympathy for people who screamed human rights without knowing the facts. Men like Ibrahim Manar, who chose to be terrorists, didn't have any human rights as far as Mace was concerned.

The lift doors opened and Mason stepped out into the corridor. He checked his watch; it was not quite 8 a.m. Assuming this was all just a routine debrief, he could still make it back to Hereford that evening. Tomorrow he was leaving early from Brize Norton on his new detail. Fighting in Azerbaijan had kicked off over disputed land and Mason had been tasked with securing the British Embassy and guarding the ambassador while he got both sides around the table for talks. He was looking forward to getting out into the field again. Too much time in the UK wasn't good for his mental health.

That was doubly true now that Joanna had gone away to college. Mason had driven her to Devon with Kerry a week before. He wanted to make sure that she got settled in all right. He'd felt sad to see his daughter leaving home but also happy for her sake that she was starting a new chapter in her life. In the car on the way home, he and Kerry had finally had 'the talk'. It had been very grown-up, amicable even, and they agreed that it was time for them to separate. Mace would move back into barracks for now, and when he got back from Baku, he could start looking for a place of his own. There would be cost implications of course, so for the first time in his life, Mace found himself thinking about money and how he could make more of it. One of the old Regiment guys had started running a good sideline in security gigs, paying some of the special forces lads more for a day's work than Mace was making in a fortnight. He'd already called Mace to say there was work there for him as soon as he was ready to come out.

There was a time when every soldier had to hold his hands up and admit that his race was run, but nobody wanted that day to come any sooner than it had to. Mason was no different. He was still an addict for the work and he couldn't imagine himself living without the thrill of it. The challenges that life threw at him as an SAS sergeant couldn't be matched in civilian life. Where else do you make life-and-death decisions every day, choices that would affect the policy of nations, your actions determining the security of your country? Nowhere. Life in the Regiment was the pinnacle of any soldier's career, and for Matt Mason, the most rewarding life a man could ever live.

He paused at the door to straighten his uniform before he knocked and entered, noting how the conversation inside immediately fell silent. General Ronnie Blandford stood up and crossed the floor, putting a hand around Mason's shoulder.

'Come in Mace,' he said. 'You know Captain Hopkins and Dom Strous from the MoD.'

Mason nodded to the Rupert and then to the minister, and thought to himself how the old boy network must have been working overtime. Mason was sure that the men on the inside would have already formulated their plan long before he was invited to join. Not that any of that stuff bothered him. Mason was used to it. While the Ruperts dreamed up plans and schemes and imagined how things might go, men like Mace brought them back down to earth and reminded them how the real world worked.

'How's the shoulder healing, Sergeant Mason?' Strous opened.

'Good, sir,' Mason replied to the minister.

'Glad to hear it.' Strous turned to Blandford and nodded for him to continue.

'Right, well we called you in today, Mace,' Blandford said, 'because we need to go over again what you remember from the Ibrahim Manar interrogation. Okay?'

Mason sucked on his teeth while he assessed the room. Ronnie Blandford had been a good soldier once upon a time, but he'd gone the same way as the rest of them. Now he was just keeping his nose clean until retirement. The man pulling his strings was clearly Strous and he stank of that smarmy, slippery, two-faced bullshit that all politicians did. Still, he addressed his reply to his DSF.

'Manar was the only survivor apprehended at the site of the original Drake hostage rescue in Sana'a, sir.'

'But Drake wasn't there, was he?' said Strous with a note of smug satisfaction.

'No, sir,' Mason said, turning his reply to the minister. He reminded himself to remain professionally detached and stick to the facts. 'We discovered that Drake had been moved to another location. We found an American hostage but not Eli Drake.'

'Yes, we know rather too well about the American journalist,' Strous said sarcastically. Mason could sense he was annoyed. What Mason didn't know was that since the story had broken, the PM had been taking constant flak from both the opposition and the media. Now the heat had worked its way down the chain until it landed on Strous, and it had fallen on the junior minister to come up with a solution that would put the issue to bed.

'Manar was subjected to shock-of-capture questioning by Private Briggs at the location,' Mace continued.

'And what did that reveal?'

'Basic stuff, sir. Name, rank, personal details about his family.'

'Yes. His mother and sister,' Strous was now reading from a file he'd picked up off the desk.

'Yes, sir. Manar lived with them.'

'So, you brought them in too?'

'No, sir. We only gave Manar that impression,' Mason said.

'Was that before or after you set the dogs on him?' Strous's tone was now more accusatory.

'Now hang on a sec, Dom.' Blandford stood up and motioned for Mason to sit. 'Let's take a little of the heat out of this shall we? Nobody's on trial here.'

'It's fine, sir.' Mason remained standing and continued to address Strous. 'The squad was tasked with rescuing Eli Drake, sir. In the circumstances we believed that his life was in imminent danger and Manar was the only witness we had.'

'And that's how we justify torturing him, is it?' Strous slapped the file down and leaned back with his arms folded across his chest.

'Eli Drake's still alive, sir. That's how I justify it.' Mason's blood was rising but he kept it under control. He didn't appreciate taking criticism from a man who'd run from a real fight. The end proved the means. The world wasn't facing a global disaster, thanks to his team, and if the top brass didn't like how they'd done it, then they could lump it.

'Unfortunately, that's not going to work for the PM. He can't just shirk this responsibility off as easily as you seem able to, Sergeant.'

'Responsibility?' Mason laughed. 'I'll tell you what responsibility is, sir. It's putting your life on the line for your country, not sitting around in offices pretending all the good ideas were yours and the bad ones were someone else's.'

'And was torturing a man in front of a journalist a good idea, would you say, Staff Sergeant?' Strous sneered.

'You know what?' Mason took off his beret. 'Fuck this.'

'Staff Sergeant Mason,' Blandford said with an air of caution. 'Remember where you are.'

'No, it's all right Ronnie. I get where this is going.'

Mason took a moment to gather himself. The cold reality of what was happening hit him like a bucket of water in the face. They'd brought him there to stitch him up and pin the blame on him. They'd already made up their minds and he was going to be the fall guy no matter what he said, so he might as well say what he meant and be done with it.

'You want to make all this go away. And it can't be the Regiment that takes the blame. I get it. Soldiers always get it. Men like you call the shots and men like Andy Roberts go out there and give their lives. And if it fucks up, it's our fault because it can't be yours. I get it.'

'It's not quite like that, Mace.' Blandford sounded like he was trying to convince himself more than anyone else in the room.

'No, he's right, Ronnie,' Strous said. 'The PM needs a solution to this.'

'I joined the army at seventeen. I didn't know much back then, just that I wanted to serve. Five years in the Paras, another twelve in the Regiment.'

'That's quite a record,' Strous said.

'I love my country and I'd give my life for it.' Mason knew what he had to do. 'So make me the scapegoat. One bad apple operating outside of orders or whatever story you make up. The Regiment has taken appropriate measures, blah blah. Say whatever you need to say.'

'No way,' Hopkins blurted. 'This is bullshit.'

'Captain Hopkins!' barked Blandford, his ruddy cheeks now positively crimson.

'It's fine, Pete.' Mason had never called the Rupert by his first name before. Hopkins actually looked shocked.

'No, it's not. The Regiment didn't protect you when you were captured. They left you to die in the desert.' Hopkins pointed an accusatory finger at Strous and Blandford.

Strous forced out a weak smile. 'We had to make contingencies for every eventuality.'

Mason returned a wry smile. He wasn't surprised to hear that Strous had been behind the order to stand down the boys when he'd been captured, nor that the snake had seen an opportunity to cover his tracks. Typical politician. Mason was more interested in Peter Hopkins. He'd misjudged him. For a Rupert, the bloke had shown some balls.

'This isn't about me and you, Pete. Not about generals and ministers neither,' Mason said. 'It's about protecting the Regiment, so it can go on protecting the people of this country. The Regiment comes before all of us fuckers, mate.'

'Well, I should be the one to go then. I was the officer responsible,' Hopkins said, with his chin held high and proud.

'No, mate.' Mason sounded calm and assured. 'It was my call, I take the hit.'

'Very noble of you, Staff Sergeant. For what it's worth, I agree,' said Strous. 'We can avoid any unpleasant talk of investigations and keep your identity out of the press. The PM will say that the individual responsible has been brought to book, but it's classified beyond that. You'll have to go with a dishonourable discharge though, I'm afraid.'

Mason shrugged. His seventeen years of service was about to end 'dishonourably'. Hopkins was right, it was bullshit, a proper kick in the face, but he wasn't lying when he said that the Regiment was more important than his personal feelings. Matt Mason was a cog in a very important machine and keeping the wheels on was all that counted.

Strous gave Blandford a satisfied nod. They'd got the result that they'd wanted and it had probably come with less grief than he'd anticipated.

Mason could see that there was nothing more to be said. 'Will that be all, sir?' he addressed the general.

'I'm sorry it had to go this way, Mace.' The general shook Mason's hand.

'Sir.'

Mason saluted his superior officer for the last time. He spun on his heel and left the room, stepping back into the lift and striding out through the corridors of Whitehall on to London's streets. He felt a hollowness in his belly as he realised that he was walking into the world as an ex-special forces soldier. His career was over and with it the status that it conferred. He'd spent his entire adult life as a member of

Her Majesty's Forces, but for the first time, he wasn't a cog in a machine, nor a part of something larger than himself. He had given his best years to his country, served it with pride and now he was just another civilian on the streets.

But Mason bore the Regiment no ill. It owed him nothing. Fuck the politicians and the Ruperts like Blandford who used it to feather their own nests. They didn't matter. All that mattered was honour and service, and Mason began to feel the emptiness in his belly fill with something else. He thought about the things that he had achieved over the past seventeen years. It had been a privilege to serve and to offer his life to protect the country he loved. He'd have done it all again, exactly the same way, in a heartbeat.

This had not been his plan, certainly not the way that he had dreamed that his career would end. But then, he'd never been able to imagine that happening anyway. He'd been following a path that had been laid out for him by others ever since he was a boy, so it was kind of fitting, too, that it would come to an end at someone else's request. Yet, as he walked away, he began to feel a sense of relief that it was all over. His marriage was done, his career was finished, he'd lost friends, almost lost his own life, but what he was experiencing were overwhelming feelings of optimism, freedom and excitement because he knew that a new life was about to begin.

Mason had lived inside the secret world where ops were deniable and tasks done without scrutiny for too long. It was always going to be a matter of time before that came undone, so from now on, everything he did would be visible.

The new life that he had been handed was going to happen out in the light where everyone could see. There would be no more hiding behind ranks and code names and call signs. He would never be called Staff Sergeant or Bravo One ever again. From now on, he was a sole agent, he was a lone wolf. From now on, he was simply Matt Mason.

Glossary of Terms

3 PARA - The 3rd Battalion, Parachute Regiment
C-130 - Lockheed C-130 Hercules
CO - Commanding Officer
DC-10 - McDonnell Douglas DC-10
DPM - Disruptive Pattern Material (camouflage)
GPS - Global Positioning System
HALO - High Altitude Low Opening
LZ - Landing Zone
M72 LAW - Light Anti-Tank Weapon
MBS - Mohammed bin Salman
MIA - Missing in Action
MRAP - Mine-Resistant Ambush Protected
NSA - National Security Agency
QBOs - Quick Battle Orders
RPG - Rocket-Propelled Grenade
RV - Rendezvous
SAS - Special Air Service aka 'the Regiment'
SCO - Senior Commanding Officer
SSOV - Safety Shut Off Valve
VAJA - Ministry of Intelligence of the Islamic Republic of Iran

Acknowledgements

Our thanks to Eve Hall, Sorcha Rose, Alice Morley, Steven Cooper, Lewis Csizmazia, Gordon Wise, Niall Harman, Miriam Woodman, Donald McIntyre, Andy McIntyre, Tim Sparke, Katherine Colombino, Ruth Martin and Jules Colombino for all your help and support.

We'll never forget those we've lost.